GRACE

UNDER SIEGE

René Voland

S / B
Solomon's Books Press
Georgia

This is a work of fiction. All the characters, locations, organizations and events portrayed in this novel are either products of the author's imagination or are used fictitiously.

 Printed in the United States of American. For information, address Solomon's Books Press, P.O. Box 216, Lovejoy, GA 30250-0216.

www.solomonsbooks.org

ISBN 978-0-9838687-7-4 (softcover)
ISBN 978-0-9838687-8-1 (e-book)

This book may be purchased for promotional, educational or business use. Please email us at ReneVoland@gmail.com

First Edition: April 2021

DEDICATION

To Edward, my muse,
And to men and woman everywhere
who thought they were the only ones.

"Normal partners do not respond to the loss of romantic interest by psychologically, emotionally or physically brutalizing the person they claim to have loved."
Dr. R. Freeman

ONE

It was the first day of winter. I will never forget that day. I was singing and getting ready for work, I pulled on my denim leggings and used the step stool in the closet to get my Lucchese western boots. At the same time, I reached for the boots, the box with my wedding shoes fell from the shelf. The heel of one shoe landed on top of my head.

"Ouch," I said as I thought about my wedding. I reached down to put the shoe back in the box. That's when I noticed something strange. The leather of my beautiful, beaded shoe had a deep, jagged cut across the top. It had been sliced through to the inside with a sharp knife.

"What!"

I gasped and fell as I stumbled backwards out of the closet, landing on my bottom. I was shocked. Then the telephone rang. Papa called to tell me Mama had a stroke. I was even more heartbroken when he hung up. I dropped the shoe and sat on the edge of the bed with my face buried in my lap and cried.

Mama's at the hospital, and I am married to Samuel Little the serial killer. Get up and wash your face. I told myself.

But, why had he cut my shoe? I knew I hadn't done it. Only the two of us lived in the house and we'd had no sleepovers since we got married.

I finished getting ready for work. The air had gone out of me. All day at work, I walked around like a zombie thinking about the shoe. I thought as I tried to finish the sales report and the new merchandise display. How could any damage that severe happen without my knowing I'd done it? If I didn't do it, what could be gained from such an act of defacement by anyone?

You didn't do it, I assured myself.

I was worried about Mama, too. The shoe had to wait. After I left work, I stopped by the hospital to get an update on her condition. I took the long, bleach-scented, slow walk to the ICU. I could hear the pump on the ventilator as I entered her room. What I learned from the charge nurse didn't make me feel any better. I drove away worried about her and the pressing issue at home.

When Narcissus came home later, I greeted him with a smile, a hug, and the shoe. I pushed it toward him. He was such a tall, handsome man. He was dark complexioned with green eyes. He was irresistible when he was nice.

"Hey, Sweetheart!" I said timidly, giving him a big hug first.

"Papa called about Mama but look at this first." I watched for his body language.

"Yeah, leather cracks," he said calmly glancing at the shoe and scratching the top of his head.

"Or maybe you hit it on something sharp. Don't make a mountain out of a mole hill, Grace. It happens. Just take it downtown to Shoe Cobbler and get it repaired. You probably don't remember doing it. Matter of fact, I've noticed you haven't been yourself lately," he said.

He walked toward the kitchen as he looked through the mail. I took a deep breath and tried again.

"I felt today was perfect weather to wear the boots you bought me last Christmas. I just love them. They always make me feel like kicking butt." I laughed alone and stalked him into the bedroom.

"Then, the cut-up wedding shoe fell out of the closet, hitting me on the head," I said as I rubbed the bump rising on my head slapped by the heel.

"Just curious why you think this kind of cut hasn't happened to any of your leather shoes," I said, pressing him for an answer.

"Well, you wear your shoes more than I do. And I think you're more forgetful than you'll admit," he said. His voice rose and became staccato.

I know now this is called gaslighting, making me doubt my own reliable memory. But back then I was confused and angry big time. I loved those shoes.

"I wore the shoes once. Then, I carefully packed them away," I nervously insisted. "I'm. Not. Crazy!"

I walked closer to Narcissus and tried to stay focused and not fall for another irrational conversation with him. It didn't work.

"There you go. You're doing it again," he shouted, turning red as he shot his fist through the wall. It was over-reactive rage I'd seen a few times since the wedding.

"Doing what, Narcissus? I don't know what you're talking about," I cried, shrinking back behind a chair to protect myself.

"In my face with foolishness and acting like my mother. Thinking you're better and smarter than everyone else and treating me like a child," he snarled in a savage voice.

Several thoughts ran through my mind. I didn't know if I should try to fight or flee. Fighting a six-foot-three Mandingo-looking man wasn't really an option for a five-foot-four female. I watched his anger escalate even further, and I'll admit I became more frightened and wanted to flee. He acted as though he could kill something. His face became beet red as he seemed to spin out of control. Then he launched into another rant. It sounded like a threat, but I knew what he meant.

"You know I walked in and caught my dad hurting my sister. I was seven years old," Narcissus shouted, looking directly at me.

"You promised to keep my secret. You know I could go to jail. It wasn't my fault he kept the pistol in the nightstand. I'd played with it all the time." He paused then continued as his fists clenched tighter.

"It had rained, and the attic was stinky and musty. There were broken pieces of our toys scattered across the dusty floor. The rotted curtains were hanging in strands at the window. I hated being up there. The tears ran down my face faster than the raindrops on the windowpanes. Then I remembered why I was in the attic. I had been bad," he said, looking wild as he drifted back in time.

"I f-forgot my chores because I was p-p-playing with my friends, and I cried, hoping my stepfather would have mercy on me," he said sounding like a frightened little boy.

My heart raced.

"Narcissus, I've never told anyone. Just calm down, honey. Everything's all right," I tried to reassure him.

He continued to pace around the room like a caged lion, his large hands rolled into human wrecking balls.

"Work on yourself, fix your anxieties, fix your insecurities. Why can't you be more supportive of me?" Narcissus then said as he paced and looked at his bleeding hand.

I didn't move, however. I knew he was having flashbacks and projecting. I tried to stay calm while I searched for the right words.

"Okay, Narcissus. I will. You're the man of the house. You're a good provider and everybody loves you. You're a great son. You're the best and you're handsome. You're right, I'll work on myself. It is okay. You're okay. Just calm down. Take some deep breaths," I coaxed.

It didn't surprise me when Narcissus sat on the side of the bed and did as I said. I watched the scary look melt from his face, and he started to breathe normally again. I knew he needed to be reassured and praised. However, I did not quite understand the reason at the time. I had learned also whenever he felt attacked, it would set him ablaze.

"One thing I can say about you, Grace. You're not afraid of anything and you know how to calm me down. I don't know why I get so angry," he said soothingly a few minutes later. "Oh, I am afraid of some things," I said, my heart still pounding.

Like you just scared the bejesus out of me.

Within thirty seconds, his emotional temperature dropped.

"Papa called with bad news about Mama." My voice cracked as I ventured out hoping the timing was right.

"Mama's in the hospital; she had a stroke. She's on a ventilator. It doesn't look good. I stopped by the hospital earlier. I'm going back to stay with her tonight. I don't want Mama to die alone if it's her time," I said without looking at him.

And you, Narcissus Bentley Little, are acting like a raging animal and I'm not sure I want to be anywhere near you.

I was relieved and surprised when Narcissus walked over to me and gently put his hand on my shoulder as I leaned against the wall through which he had just pushed his fist. His touch startled me.

"She's going to need someone to take care of her," he said as he looked empathetically at me. I exhaled, relieved I had his support.

"But it won't be you. I need you here with me," he said in a commanding voice. My relief immediately evaporated.

"Well then, what do you think about Mama coming to live with us rather than a nursing home, if she makes it out of the hospital? Papa's too old to take care of her," I said as I walked away from him nervously twisting my hands together.

"Plus, I hear elderly people don't last long at those places. Even the workers call them the elephant's graveyard," my voice squeaked.

"What's an elephant's graveyard, Grace?" Narcissus asked, seeming annoyed but smirking with interest.

"I'm not sure if it's a real place, but it's where elephants went to die in the Tarzan movies," I said, flashing him a serious glance.

He laughed hysterically and cruelly as he bent over to catch his breath.

"In Tarzan movies? He paused. "You're serious, aren't you?" he asked with the same smirky grin.

"Yes," I said, and my eyes began to mist over.

"You know your mother and I don't get along well. I don't think her living with us is a good idea," he said, still pushing back laughter.

"And besides, you won't be able to live in this house if she dies here, will you? he asked. "Why do you have to be the one to take care of her anyway? You're not an only child." Narcissus continued, sounding as though he was talking about me washing his new car rather than caring for my beloved Mama.

"Unfortunately, she'll go to the elephant's graveyard. I know you, Grace. You won't be able to handle her dying at the house. So, no," he said, devoid of empathy and immediately walked out of the bedroom and down to the kitchen.

I knew different. He was the one who would not be able to handle Mama dying in the house. His personality type caused him to behave like a six-year-old kid at times. I now know what he was doing is called projecting. I also now see he lacked empathy.

"When is dinner ready? I've got a computer job," he said as he cut a dance move. "I'll be back in a couple of hours."

You mean in the morning, I thought.

Narcissus put on his sexy, confident smile he wore for the rest of the world. Stared admiringly at himself in the hall mirror and swaggered out the door as if nothing ever happened between us.

I sighed and walked into the kitchen to prepare his dinner. Afterward, I packed a bag and drove back to the hospital. I felt emotionally drained and sad. I was too afraid of him to tell him he was cruel and needed help. He would have become even more angry, and he would have never admitted it. Later, I would discover the secret he hid from everyone.

Narcissus sent one of his buddies to the house to repair the wall I had damaged. Over the ensuing months, I'd learn more from my experience with Narcissus than I ever picked up in my psychology textbook.

There were two things I knew for sure: All those conversations as a child lying in a field had anointed me to handle anything life threw my way. I hid in the tall, yellow, comforting grasses behind our house with a large rock as my pillow. Sucking my Jolly Ranchers candies, I'd talk with God about every little thing that concerned me. The second thing was Mama had told me, "You're strong like the mythological Phoenix. You will always rise from the ashes."

And she was right. However, at the time, the only thing on me resembling a bird and ashes were my skinny brown legs.

TWO

Six Years Later

I awakened this morning with a pep in my step and a new idea for my next TV show, Still, I Rise.

Just call me Dr. Grace and believe that is who I am. I am dainty, dazzling, will cry at the drop of a hat and have just enough knowledge to make me dangerous. My Ph.D. is in hard knocks. I empower abused men and women from my own experience with cruelty. I set the captives free with the truth. There is significance and purpose when you face any type of loss. You have experienced this pain to heal, strengthen, and spare other people what you have been through.

I now know people like Narcissus live abnormal lives because they never learned as children to participate in mutually respectful and satisfying relationships. They are simply unable to do so. Their childhood didn't allow it.

Folks who date or marry people like my ex-husband, Narcissus, are shocked the day the reality of malignant narcissism slaps them across the face. They won't know what hit them. It takes a long moment to grasp. They usually deny it was real—at least for a while. I'm still reeling myself, and it's been a few years.

Narcissus once told me he didn't think like other people. He wasn't lying. However, I had no idea he was trying to tell me something important. Six years later, I've got emotional scars as proof he thinks differently. It saddens me somewhat he could not communicate his difference well, and neither was I able to listen with my heart.

It's Saturday morning. Lately, I've been feeling more social. However, while I put on a bright smile for my studio audience, I am still recovering from PTSS (Post Traumatic Stress Syndrome).

My friend Emma called last night and asked whether she could stop by today to check on me. I had self-isolated and grieved my marriage for months before taking my new job. Now, I share my journey as a talk show host on TV networks all over the world.

I pinch myself from time to time to make sure I'm not dreaming. I made it out of a dangerous situation. I know others are not so lucky. But my healing is still ongoing.

Getting this position was indeed a miracle, I tell you—quite a modern-day Joseph story straight out of the Bible. Joseph was sold into slavery by his evil brothers, and the next thing he knew, he became a high-ranked official in Egypt. Likewise, one day I was in the retail industry and the next I became host of my own television talk show.

Move over, Kelly Clarkson!

It was indeed a gift from God. He never ceases to amaze me.

Today I must mentally prepare myself for my friend Emma, who is on her way to my condo. She's a handful. She's my college girlfriend. She is overweight, high yellow and has a surgically repaired cleft palate scar. I pray she is feeling more positive than at our last get together. She hasn't seen my new digs since I became the host for Greenville's first talk show.

Emma walked through the door, gave my cheek an air kiss and then sat in my favorite chair as I stepped over to the sofa. I allowed it. After all, she was my guest.

"Well, it's been one year since your divorce became final. Are you looking forward to your new life with husband number three?" she asked with a sassy smile. "You do seem to be happier and less dramatic. Although, to be honest, I thought you would have waited a while longer before tying the knot again," she said.

"Doing fine, Emma. How are you? Wait a while for what?"

"You know . . . take the time to heal emotionally and gain a new perspective on life. I think you need to get to know Octavius a little better. Enjoy your job. Live single for a while." Emma's voice hit a higher pitch as she spoke her words.

"I'm happy. Peaceful. And I'm a grown woman. I see no reason to wait. I know well enough what I'm doing. Plus, I'm enjoying my new job," I said.

"I'm just grateful you're more aware of men who are self-absorbed, wounded and predatory. Of course, you believe your precious Octavius doesn't fall into this category. Don't listen to me. I just care about you, that's all."

"I know Octavius isn't one of those predatory types. I don't like what you're trying to insinuate. So, this the reason you refused to help with the wedding plans?" I pointedly asked.

For a moment, I had a tiny feeling I was acting like Narcissus, blaming her when she appeared to be trying to help me.

"I just don't think you are ready to marry again, and I don't want to see you hurt. Emotionally injured people just don't realize what they put their friends through. I don't want it to happen again for you or me. Just be sure. That's all I'm asking," she exclaimed. "And I told you I no longer plan weddings," she said, pursing her lips at the corners.

"I am woke, Emma, and I'm sure about Octavius! I am not talking about the way Millennials express themselves about finding out about racism and such. I woke about that stuff at age seven when I heard a white boy call my daddy a boy. I am sure about Octavius. However, I am not so sure about you right now," I shouted, rising from the sofa and stomping my feet on the floor.

"I hate it when you intentionally insult me," I said, staring into Emma's eyes as I stormed out of the room.

I left Emma staring out the large picture window of my condominium with its view of downtown Greenville. Every day I would stand in the same place and watch people flowing to and from the downtown area. It was an amazing view.

She knew I needed a moment to think about what she'd said and recover before we could continue our conversation, so she moved from my chair, plopped onto the sofa, crossed her legs and pulled out her cell phone. She also needed a moment to hide her green-eyed monster. I moved into my master bathroom and spoke to myself in the mirror.

Who did she think I was? Who did she think she was talking to Grace Smith this way? Emma was always trying to control my life when her own life was in shambles like mine used to be. At least I got out. Just maybe, Theresa was right about the friendship. Emma might not want to see me happy with Octavius or anybody else because she was not happy herself.

A few minutes later, I walked back into the living room and curled my legs underneath me on the love seat across from Emma, looking over at her.

She wasn't so bad. She got on my nerves, but she had always been there. We've shared a lot about our family and work issues. She buys clothes like mine. She bought a house like mine. She admired me. She made sure I got counseling when I needed it. If I tossed her out now, I'd have to cut her. She knows way too much about me.

Emma carefully continued.

"Well, Grace, we've both seen these arrogant, manipulative character traits on TV, in books and acted out by coworkers, politicians and family members. We even admired some of them because they were rich or charismatic," Emma ventured out and said.

"That's true. I promise you I'm not getting hurt again. Just trust me. After all, I've been through a lot and I've learned from it. Emma, do you remember the famous dictator we saw on trial last year who appeared confident and kind of sexy behind prison bars on TV?" I said lightly to change the subject away from Octavius.

"Yeah, but he was a hot-tempered, cold-blooded killer who thought he was God. Kind of like some people we know," Emma said.

"But to us, his persona was still appealing. Don't act like you didn't think he was sexy, too. How crazy were we?" I asked as I looked away.

"We should have known better. We'd both studied psychology. Counselors warned us about people like that man in the magazines and journal articles. They appear confident but have an abnormal view of themselves, an exaggerated sense of self-importance and a preoccupation with receiving attention. But when they crossed our paths, we didn't believe them and didn't think they were too dangerous. You didn't anyway," Emma said.

"No, we didn't. Girl let me repeat it. I am now more woke. I know better. Very few people know about folks like this. I didn't until I met Narcissus, who falls well into the malignant category. What about you?" I asked.

"I first learned about personality disorders in my psychology class after having to analyze the character Gregory Anton in the 1944 movie Gaslight. I think he was the malignant type," Emma said.

"I remember Gregory, too, and our assignment. The handsome, charming husband who did things to make his wife feel as if she was losing her mind. When he married her, he had connived to institutionalize her and steal her wealth. He had already murdered her rich aunt. He was something else—definitely the bad kind of narcissist," I said.

"Exactly. I never thought I would meet, date, or marry anyone like Gregory Anton. Was Narcissus anything like King Henry VIII? I watched a series about him recently. He was dashing and intelligent. He was also easily bored, angry all the time and hard to please. He beheaded two of his wives, you know. I'm so glad Octavius is different." Emma smirked trying to sound smart.

I ignored Emma's sarcasm. "There it is again. Thank you," I said. "This behavior I couldn't see before—a man who worships and then spurns and scraps the women in his life."

"You've used the word woke twice. What's up? Do you now feel more awakened about men like Narcissus?"

"I believe so. In 2018, I heard Hollywood celebrities use the word, and some of my recent friends also use the term. I had little idea of its new meaning. If my son had not schooled me, the Millennials would have called me straight-up dumb. I'm proud I can now say I am woke. Not like them, of course. However, thanks to my experience, I am aware. And I'm chomping at the bit to do some type of tell-all on my show or a book," I said.

I looked across town and noticed the steeple of the new city church glistening in the morning sunlight.

"I still haven't heard the church speak of being woke. I know a Bible verse or two. One of them warns believers to stay awake, for the devil is like a roaring lion looking for prey. The second is about those who only love themselves. It's quite a feat to wake up one day and discover the person you loved was incapable of loving you in return." I crossed my arms.

"These two passages could very well explain narcissism. Think about it. A roaring lion in love with himself," said Emma.

"Right! Well, I'm older, and I see people through matured wisdom. Life snatched the veil off my eyes. I know the lion now. He's always on the prowl for victims. Yeah, I am woke but wounded," I said.

"Did you know in Africa the native people say they can hear a lion's roar five miles away? Those dumb gazelles should know he's on the way before he attacks. It sounds like us, seeing signs and red flags and yet walk right into the devil's lair to be ripped to shreds."

"Yeah, some of us imperfects ones do." I averted my eyes. "However, recently I've started reading a blog called The Silent Pain. There are accounts of broken lives of men and women who had abandoned or been abandoned by people like Narcissus. They spoke of real-life events to which I too can now relate," I said.

"I don't think any of our professors or our textbooks revealed how this behavior would present," Emma said.

I stood up and went back to staring out the window. Even after six years, I was still glancing nervously over my shoulder since divorcing Narcissus, half expecting to see him.

"No. they didn't, other than vague general descriptions. Looking back, it appears they knew very little about malignant narcissism. They even left it out of the DSM.

"I noted, however, like me, most of the bloggers were still reeling from bad treatment. They told their stories hoping someone might open their eyes and heed their advice. Several of the writers seemed to be trapped and didn't know how to get out. Others were angry and wanted revenge.

"A few wanted to help their companions. Others vowed no contact and promised never to allow another person like that into their lives. Many were hopelessly stuck because of trauma bonding. Several bloggers admitted their abuser was one or both parents, siblings, bosses, or colleagues. The most dangerous abusers were spouses," I said.

"I remember studying trauma bonding. I just didn't know you'd gone through all of this. You definitely should have paid more attention," Emma said.

"I did pay attention, but it was hard to see it coming. These people are so stealthy. Here's my manuscript." I said as I handed it to her and continued.

"It will take some time for me to get over my experience, especially since so few people around me believed me. It tells my story; all I went through and what malignant narcissism looks like in action. The story is private and it is just for your eyes. When you read it, you may say, 'I've seen this before'—because you have seen it and may have experienced it. The behaviors and the speech patterns seem to follow a similar blueprint in both males and females who suffer from this psychological condition. It's just so unbelievable," I said.

"Remember, I studied psychology, too. I thought these abnormalities in human behavior were textbook cases we'd never actually see firsthand. Are you sure about what you experienced? Sometimes you're quite the drama queen," Emma said.

"You're sounding like all the others. I didn't imagine what I went through. The bloggers on the Silent Pain couldn't even exactly explain what had happened to them. Nobody believed their stories either. I, however, knew they were telling the truth.

"Poor thing. It's good you found out you haven't suffered alone," said Emma a little sarcastically as she text-messaged.

"More people than I originally realized have been victims. It's more common than we all know," I said.

Emma sighed, and I ignored her. She could be such an unempathetic know-it-all at times.

"They are everywhere," I continued. Some of them are our closest friends. Psychologists and movie producers have even made attempts to bring awareness to this, but there are still very few people who've ever heard about malignant narcissism and its effect on others. It sometimes reaches beyond the understanding of the average mind. People rarely speak of this malevolent type of personality. I can't believe it was omitted from the DSM," I said.

"Well, I don't know what is going on with my husband. He's gone all the time, and I'm glad. He is rude and critical. Nothing I do pleases him. He's always hiding things. I am tired of his crazy-making behavior. I don't understand him at all. What word do you feel describes these people?" asked Emma.

"Well, Ms. Drama Queen yourself. My counselor said one word is abandonment. Their caregivers abandoned or abused them in early childhood, so they continue this blueprint throughout their lives. They eventually leave or push away people who love them. I didn't know or understand either until I met Narcissus," I said, thinking Emma's husband showed traits, as well.

"I'll admit I can be dramatic sometimes. How is counseling going?" Emma asked as she popped a peppermint into her mouth.

"I have a few more sessions before the wedding. I wanted to take my time. Dr. Sherry said I have a lot to face."

"That's good. You never used to talk much about Narcissus' behavior. I always thought he was perfect. When you finally said something, it was difficult to believe," Emma said.

"One day I woke up and I no longer recognized Narcissus. He had even started to smoke and drink like a gangster in a movie. In the beginning, he had confessed his undying love and devotion to me. He said I was the best thing he'd ever had. He appeared to have a kind, generous nature. Because of his deception, he gave me no real opportunity to make the best choice for my life. It did not take long for his façade to drop after he said, 'I do'. I'd describe his exasperating deception as a type of con man."

"Con man, Grace! But he couldn't help it, right? Emma asked.

"I don't think so," I said.

"Well, you have a wedding approaching," Emma smiled as she stood and picked up her purse.

"If you're ready, then I'm ready. If you hear the lion's roar, don't ignore it," she said and laughed.

I looked at Emma and smiled. I walked her to the door and gave it a nice slam as she walked through it. Her kind of strength is best communicated with silence.

"Whatever! I still love you," muttered Emma as she walked along the hallway. I hear her clicking high heels and could imagine her big smile. I didn't even know why I continued to befriend her.

"Break a leg on your next show," she shouted.

"You break a leg, too, Emma," I said out loud.

Boy! do I have cold feet about getting married again. I miss Theresa. She'd be so much more supportive of my new job and my fiancé. Her death was so senseless. The police still don't know you probably did it. Be nice Grace.

I walked to the parking garage. I pulled my legs into my Benz, put on my sunshades and careened out of the circular parking lot.

THREE

I pushed through my workday feeling anxious. I remember my first appointment with the counselor, Dr. Sherry. I reached the address and almost turned around to go back home. I had studied to become a counselor not a counselee.

It was difficult, but I encouraged myself to set aside pride and walk in the door. The counselor looked familiar. She was tall and beautiful and her warm, friendly countenance made me feel like telling it all. She invited me to lie down on the paisley chaise lounge. I obliged because I was so tired.

"Why are you here?" she asked as I kicked off my shoes and pulled my feet up under me.

I explained what I'd been through. Then I exhaled, waiting for Dr. Sherry to say I was crazy. She surprised me.

"I don't like analyzing people without meeting them. However, based on your description, your ex-husband sounds like someone with a personality disorder. I'll admit I am concerned about your safety. He sounds like the malignant type."

"Doctor, I am familiar with narcissism, but I didn't think I would ever meet someone with the disorder. I studied it in school," I said in tears.

"Then let's bypass all the psychobabble and get right to the core of it. People with this disorder lack empathy, need lots of praise and attention and can be extremely hurtful and dangerous, especially the malignant type, who become hostile and spiteful when they lose their supply."

"Okay. Remind me. What is supply? That's what I was, right?"

"More than likely. Narcissistic supply was anything you did that fed his ego with praise and adoration and made him feel fulfilled. It may have been taking care of him, cleaning the house, being his arm candy, letting him take advantage of you, believing his lies, paying all the bills, or any of the other beautiful things healthy human beings do for one another. A narcissist's most used supply is his or her co-dependent, self-sacrificial partner.

"The pushback and torture occur when you take supply away. Then all hell breaks loose, and you unleash Dr. or Ms. Jekyll.

"Remember, too—everything a narcissist accuses you of doing or being is incorrect. He or she is projecting onto you what they think about themselves or what they are currently doing. They are very much like psychopathic six-year-olds, " she said and laughed.

"He criticized your physical appearance because he was unhappy about his own," she continued. "He told you nobody liked you because he felt nobody liked him. He probably no longer wanted you when he started talking like this and may have accused you of infidelity . . . well, it was because he was possibly being or had been unfaithful himself."

" I see. I'm in shock. I was definitely his supply," I said looking away.

"Psychologists don't know for certain what causes this condition. However, in the counseling community, we suspect a person suffering from the disorder was spoiled or abused or neglected by a parent or caregiver. It most likely occurred between birth to about seven years old—the critical developmental years."

"Can he get help? I feel so much guilt I didn't help him while we were together."

"Well, don't. First, the person you met at the beginning is not the man you now know. Furthermore, most people with this disorder are so arrogant they can't be told anything and will likely never seek help. He probably wouldn't have accepted it from you even if you'd offered. Most narcissists are so self-absorbed and superior-minded they are unable to self-analyze. And they can sometimes be a counselor's nightmare.

"Since they don't develop properly during critical years due to abuse, they are hard-wired and cannot easily change. However, some psychotherapists specialize in this type of counseling. They say help is available. However, it may take five-to-ten years to see progress."

"Dr. Sherry, I feel so disjointed and depressed. Sometimes, I don't want to live another day like this. Will I ever be happy again?" I asked.

"Yes, Grace. You will. The fact you are seeking the truth of your situation is the first step to your healing and freedom. The more you know about it, the quicker you will recover."

"This may sound shocking to you. However, Narcissus abused you, Grace. Take this chart. It'll help you understand the reason you're considered a victim of domestic violence."

I wept a little.

"Abuse? Domestic violence? Narcissus never hit me, Dr. Sherry."

"Most women think domestic violence boils down to someone hitting you. It's far more than being struck."

Dr. Sherry handed me a leaflet and I quickly glanced over it.

"Mmm," I said, as I read the list:

-Controlling or stealing money

-Putting you down in front of friends and family

-Turning the children against the other spouse

-Isolating a spouse from friends and family

-Triangulating (bringing others into a group to belittle a victim)
-Calling a person out of their name
-Raping a spouse
-Destroying personal items
-Gang-stalking (using flying monkeys to do their evil)
-Being forced to be involved in orgies, threesomes, etc.

"Wow, didn't know," I said as I looked at Dr. Sherry.

"From here, in many instances, ends in physical domestic violence. Do you get the picture? Being treated this way can lower your self-esteem and cause startle reactions, like someone who has PTSS resulting from being in an explosion or something catastrophic such as an earthquake or tsunami," she said.

"Should I even encourage him to get help?" I asked.

"Probably wouldn't do any good. As I said earlier, these individuals are highly egocentric and wouldn't believe you. And it would be rare for them to seek help on their own.

"He also probably blames you for everything. His outcome happened because of the way his early caregivers treated him. Unfortunately, Narcissus may spend his life going from relationship to relationship. He'll continue to look for something better. Prettier. Richer. Younger. Men like him are never satisfied and get bored quickly," Dr. Sherry said.

"Like King Henry VIII?" I asked.

"Good example. When you can no longer provide the supply they crave, you become a victim of their abuse. Furthermore, if you allow a malignant narcissist to know you're aware of their little secret, they'll probably do worse things to hurt you. You're probably the last person he would listen to. He most likely feels hatred towards you because you caused a narcissistic injury when you left him."

"Wow! That was a lot to take in, Dr. Sherry. In school, I learned these types of personalities cluster together. Do you think there are more people like this around me?"

"Probably. And more around him helping him, as well," she said.

"Thank you. You have opened my eyes."

"Okay, our session has come to an end. By the way, I think I recall you and Narcissus coming to me before you got married. I remember him well. I am sorry the marriage didn't work out. Let's schedule another session for next week."

"The same time and same day works for me. I need to learn more. My girlfriend Emma keeps mentioning I'm about to make the same mistake with my fiancé Octavius as I did with Narcissus. I just don't see it. I also might understand better why I keep her around," I chuckled.

"These sessions will provide some useful insight to consider for the future," assured Dr. Sherry.

I put on my dark shades and walked in slow motion to my car.

Why me, God? Why me? In six months, I'll marry Octavius. He must be different. I can't go through this again.

Today, I decided to purchase a handgun. The counselor said she was concerned about my safety. Now I am, too.

FOUR

A week later, I rose from my bed of sorrow, washed my face, and sought a deeper understanding of the person I'd married. I went back to the counselor for my next session armed with new questions.

"You said, based on what I describe is happening to me, you would diagnose my ex-husband a narcissist and we'd talk more about it. I'm ready."

"Now, Grace, you of all people know I can't make a diagnosis without seeing someone. It appears he fits the profile based on how you described his treatment of you in the marriage and the way he's acted since the separation and divorce. Tell me how the relationship progressed and ended. I'll add to his actions what we know about malignant narcissism from clinical observations."

I took a deep breath and slowly released it before starting. "I remember something Narcissus said when we first met. When he was a little boy, he had an evil temperament, and his mother took him to a psychiatrist because he drowned the neighbor's puppy. He also mentioned his stepfather would lock him in the attic for days without food. He was treated horribly by his parents. His dad also shot his dog because he whined. He was diagnosed with something, but he said he couldn't remember what the doctor said it was. He was confident he'd outgrown it."

"Interesting," Dr. Sherry said.

"Getting back to how the relationship progressed—I saw three things happen to me. First, at the beginning of the relationship, I was smothered with love and gifts and treated royally. I could do no wrong. Funny though—if he got angry with me, he'd take his gifts back, though I didn't pay any attention at the time. I guess I thought he was joking. Now I know he wasn't. He took my wedding rings, too.

"Then after being married for a short while, things started to sour and I couldn't do anything right, and he began to complain. He was always angry, too. Friends and family members stopped communicating with me. When I voiced my concerns, he said they were jealous because of the great life I had with him."

I curled a stray lock of hair behind my ear. "During our separation, while no one outright told me this, I believe everyone blamed me for neglecting the family by leaving an influential husband and his money. It appeared my fractured family had abandoned me in support of him.

"I started hearing rumors we were getting a divorce. He started telling me to move out anytime I voiced any concern I felt we needed to hash out. I later discovered he'd told the family everything going on between us, yet none of them even told me. I think they knew how vicious he could be and feared him. You know, Narcissus began talking about getting a divorce the first week after the honeymoon. I am so dumb." I said.

"He did to you what he had seen," the doctor observed. "Also, you brought something to the table he didn't have. In our last session, we discussed narcissistic supply. His narcissistic supply came from you. He was letting you know the relationship was not going to last."

"And all your friends and families who became his flying monkeys gave him supply for favors or money. Narcissus was probably able to convince them to join in criminal activity."

"He did many things," I said. "I was the person he had claimed to love. I received hang-up calls, prank calls and sexual offers from the internet, all intended to harass me."

"Right! Narcissus placed you on a pedestal against a standard you could not humanly reach. Then when you no longer appeared perfect or in any way less than he'd seen when you two met, he started devaluing you and was planning to discard you or push you away. Thus, the rumor you were getting a divorce," Dr. Sherry said.

The doctor leaned back in her chair and folded her hands on her lap. "At the beginning of the relationship, you were in the love-bombing or adoration stage. His family loved you. He thought he loved you. He was happier than a pig in the sunshine."

"Ha-ha. Right. Well, at least until he felt his family loved me more than they loved him. I should have known I was in trouble then."

Dr. Sherry smiled and continued. "You were perfect, though, in his eyes. You are an attractive and intelligent woman, so you must have been great arm candy! You were the girl of his dreams. I think you heard him say those words, right?"

I nodded in agreement.

"Now, I must help you understand how narcissists develop a false-self due to the mental, emotional or physical abuse they experienced in childhood. The false self, which he invented, made him feel protected and omnipotent. It was a shield protecting him from indifference, smothering, sadism, or whatever abuse was inflicted on him by his primary caregivers. His true self was shredded and repressed.

"He also has an uncanny gift to psychologically penetrate others. When he met you, he sized you up. He knew you had morals and you were a good person, so you'd probably go along with whatever he wanted. Unfortunately, he would later use the things he learned about you to manipulate you and annihilate you. A predator of sorts. That sly fox."

"Why did he start smearing my name in the family and the community with lies?" I asked somewhat embarrassed to even talk about it.

"He knew you would eventually expose him, so he had to discard you. He tried to get in front of it by making you look like the one who was evil so no one would believe you when he pushed you out of his life and you healed and started talking."

"He did a good job. It worked," I murmured.

"You changed, as normal humans do. How dare you are not what his false self—his bottomless pit of unrealistic expectations—needed you to be to keep him happy?" she said.

"So, the adoration stage is the fantasy stage. It was a fairy tale tailormade for me. Narcissus knew precisely how to hook me. And when I stopped trying to please him, he devalued me. When my value went from $5 million to $5, I had to go," I said, laughing.

He realized you weren't perfect and then suddenly saw your imperfections. The pain of it was too great. This is what I believe happened at each stage, Grace."

I was quiet.

"No one truly understands the hatefulness, deceitfulness and spitefulness I tolerated. I'd ask myself if these things were really happening Where was the love he'd said was mine all mine until the end of time? Was it just a lie?"

"Malignant narcissists are evil and hostile. A regular narcissist will simply follow the blueprint and reject you, but a malignant one will try to destroy you. He is the most wounded. The blueprint you saw was idealization/fantasy, then devalue/abuse, and ultimately avoid/discard with intent to destroy."

I became emotional and wept. Dr. Sherry passed me the box of tissue and scheduled an appointment for the following week. I walked out the door covering my red eyes with my sunglasses.

So . . . He knew from the beginning the relationship would not last. Unbelievable!

FIVE

The doorbell interrupted my thoughts. The wedding was just a few weeks away, and I was still an emotional mess after my last counseling session. The caterer Sakina and I had planned to go over my long checklist for my nuptials one last time. Always on time, she arrived for our 11am appointment with a few minutes to spare. The doorbell rang again.

"I'm coming," I yelled, practicing my smile while pulling my sweater over my head before I opened the door.

"Hi, Sakina. Come right in. I've been waiting for you."

"Everything is in place, Sakina said as she pulled out the armchair and flopped down at my long cherry dining room table. I'd laid out everything for the meeting.

"It will be a beautiful wedding, Grace. You'll love the menu mixed with both American and Egyptian cuisine. I've included kebobs and koftas and besarah for the vegetarians. The staff will serve all entrees on gold, black and pink dishes perfectly matched to your décor. It's a feast fit for the Queen of Egypt," said Sakina with a chuckle.

"When people treat you like an indigent, you learn to treat yourself like a queen," I said as I held back tears.

"Trust me—I understand. I'm in a situation I may soon need to leave. I work hard to keep my mind positive. So, let's go over all the details for the reception to make sure I have all the items you want."

The meeting lasted 30 minutes. "Everything looks wonderful, Sakina. Let's talk again soon if you have any questions. You have my private number. Call me anytime."

"Sure thing," Sakina said as she left.

I was still in minor pain from my early morning massage, the wedding gift the station crew had given me. I prepared for my morning soak, pouring cucumber Epsom salt and lavender baby oil into my garden tub. Water streamed into the bathtub as sweet fragrance filled my bathroom. I asked Siri to play some relaxing Chinese music and slipped into the warm water. I thought of my life with Narcissus and exhaled. I pulled the neck rest underneath my neck and closed my eyes.

Two years later, and I still got emotional when I thought about everything. I remembered being so thin I could see and feel the bones in my derriere. I'd constantly had raccoon circles around my eyes. I was broke . . . not a penny to my name. I'm an avid reader and had missed my book collection most of all. While Narcissus was not a reader, he had taken all my books, too. He had taken everything from me. He loved the shock and awe tactic, a force he'd used to destroy my will to fight back.

It had worked. I still don't know how he got my friends and family to abandon me. He was stealthy.

It's a mystery. And yet even after all that I went through, I still regretted I couldn't fix our marriage. I tried everything. Trauma had bonded me to him, and I hadn't wanted to break free. Then the ice cracked.

Dr. Sherry's sessions made a difference. I learned so much about how close I'd come to losing my sanity. That's what Narcissus wanted. He did terrible things and projected them on me. He threw so much evil at me I didn't know which way to turn. I was, however, determined to one day see the light at the end of my dark long winding tunnel. The one thing he could not take away from me was my faith in God. I am stronger, older, wiser, and more secure than ever. The pain was dissolving, and my actual life, like a pretty tulip, had started to sprout again, just like Dr. Sherry said it would.

I lay soaking in my exquisite tub for two, confident no one would ever hurt me again.

I had learned something deep and dark about human beings and would share my story at the appointed time. Right now, my new life was turning the bend. I stared at the window and took another sip of sweet Moscato.

It was a week later, and my anxiety level was high, and I was feeling overwhelmed with all the plans for my upcoming nuptials. I laid on the counselor's couch, feeling fatigued and out of breath. Dr. Sherry walked into the room.

"How are you today, Grace?"

"I am okay. Just still reeling a bit from everything I have learned about Narcissus and hyperventilating a little."

"Here. Breathe slowly into this paper bag. You will settle down in a moment." Dr. Sherry left the counseling room and returned. "Better?" she asked.

"Yes, much better," I said.

"What else is going on, Grace?"

"Well, I found a little church last Sunday to attend. I had stopped going. I have always been a church girl. I had stopped going to church after the breakup. I was ashamed my marriage had ended. Last Sunday, the minister spoke about love. He held my attention. He said things about love I had never heard before.

"The pastor reminded us love isn't a feeling. Love is an action. Lust is a feeling. He said the world has lied to us. If you fall into love, you could easily fall out of love. Now he had my attention. He said love is patient and kind. It doesn't hold grudges. It isn't arrogant. It doesn't delight in evil. It's not easily angered. It isn't rude. It is not proud or boastful. It isn't jealous."

I took a deep breath and sighed. "Lust brings two people together, but love binds them to each other. Then he left us with a quote from Billy Graham. If love is spoken and never shown, I don't care how much someone says they love you. It isn't true.

"I left the church building before the benediction. Thankfully, I didn't run into anyone I knew. I couldn't stop thinking about the message. I knew by the pain I felt in my heart I hadn't known authentic, unconditional love, neither in familial nor relational situations. There seemed to be a lot of fantasy and deception in the world. Do people even know how to love?

I now believed Narcissus was incapable of love. He based his love on everything except allowing people to just be themselves. Perhaps he didn't know how because he had not known unconditional love himself.

"What did you learn from this discovery, and how does it make you feel?" the counselor asked.

"I learned my marriage was a fantasy. I think a lot of people are living a fantasy about their relationships. I'd created my own I Love Freda Show. I, too, enjoyed the make-believe set, the lights, and the attention we got. I now know if a couple is not fighting, it doesn't necessarily mean there is no conflict. When we were in front of everyone, we were the perfect couple—for a while, anyway. Like Freda, I loved being married on TV with all its pretense of affection, fun, peace, and happiness. It was, however, nothing more than a stupid fantasy. When the camera lights switched off, Fred and Freda faced a Bobbie Brown and Whitney Houston reality show at home. Our I Love Grace show was crazy, too."

"How do you feel right now about you and Octavius? Any similarities to Narcissus?"

"Hell-to-the-No! as Whitney Houston would say." I laughed, sensing my real-life beginning. I am woke from a dream. I now know when two people are getting along swimmingly and there are no disagreements, someone is lying. They are engaged in a fantasy. I believe Octavius and I have a good foundation."

"Okay. Now you have a better understanding of narcissism, for the next session, I want to talk about the reason you attracted Narcissus into your life."

"Here's a prescription to help you sleep. Insomnia can often occur when you are facing the reality of having been abused by someone you thought loved you. And, as you wrestle through accepting the truth," she said as she handed me the prescription.

That night, I took a sleeping pill and quickly fell asleep. I began to dream. I saw myself riding a bicycle in the rain, peddling uphill with one hand on the handlebars and the other holding an umbrella. It was painful. Narcissus was walking beside me, dressed in a German police uniform. He looked like Gestapo. He paid little attention to my suffering as I tried to accomplish this task. His dead father was walking beside him, talking to him. I could see him, yet he didn't care. He whispered into Narcissus' ear, and Narcissus in turn intently listened to his father's instructions. Then I was run over by a car. Yikes!

My eyes popped wide open, and my brain engaged.
Narcissus hears voices. I knew it. What else could the dream mean? Is he schizophrenic, too? Am I headed for a crash and burn?

It was morning before I knew it. I felt more refreshed than I had in weeks.

The next morning, I got a strange call. It appeared Narcissus phoned me and forgot to hang up the line. What I'm about to write next will give you a peek inside his head.

"Hello?"

I could hear Narcissus' voice. It was like a scene in an old Vincent Price movie.

"Stop torturing me," I said. "Why are you doing this to me?" Then I realized he couldn't hear me. He was so full of himself he'd muted the line. I couldn't hang it up, so I just listened. I didn't really want to hang up. I had to admit I missed him.

"I am a king seated on my throne. You think you left me, but I pushed you away. I drove you out of my life. I know I was a monster at times, but I am extremely smart.

"I am never going to tolerate being disrespected," he said in a resounding voice.

"What most people don't know is my relationships end long before I ever walk out the door. It is always the perfect plot. If you no longer respect me, you won't take my advice, or if you stop doing what I need—out you go!

"Looking older. Getting fat!" His voice tightened.

"You cannot do whatever you want without consulting the King."

"I told you I was different than other men. I tried to warn you. Didn't I? I told you. But you didn't listen, just like all the rest. My women keep asking me what happened. I don't give an answer. They say I act as though I hate 'em. People make their lives miserable, not me. My hands are clean.

"You, too, deserved to be punished for what you did to me Grace. I guess you think I hate you, too.

"What did I do to you?" I screamed, forgetting he'd muted his phone.

"I gave you everything and this is the thanks I get. Just because I don't want to be in a relationship doesn't mean I wanted to break up. In my relationships, I decide who leaves and who stays. I handpicked you, but you didn't appreciate me, just like all the others. You may even say I sound like a predator, like a fox," his conscience suggested.

"Well, I know the kind of people I need to be around me. I like to associate with influential, educated, wealthy, attractive and successful people. People are simple resources in this world. God created them for this reason, to provide me with things I need."

"You're rude and show off in front of others. If I made you angry, you'd mercilessly insult and ignore me!" I shouted in tears as he continued his rant.

"If I scratch your back, you scratch mine. Bottom line. Nothing more, nothing less. But don't you forget who the King is! If you cross me, I promise you'll regret it."

"If they come after the King, they best not miss, huh?" he asked sarcastically. "I won't hesitate to use others to help me punish someone. Everyone gets the signal I'm sending. It shows all of them the consequences of not being loyal to me."

"You also have angry temper tantrums if you can't get what you want, you six-year-old! But they say you can smile in someone's face and then walk with them behind a barn and slit their throats, too."

I was glad he couldn't hear me.

"Maybe with my words," he said, as though he had heard my thoughts.

"I don't have a problem smearing you or using you to get what I want—the gullible type I can pick out of any group," he chuckled dryly.

"People say I am a liar. I just call it the way I see it. It is what it is!"

"You should know better than anyone I'll drag a man's or woman's name through the very mud. No one will believe you because loyalty is more to me than to you. You saw it, didn't you? I started building my base by doing favors while you were so in love and asleep. I knew this falling out day would come."

"I have no qualms about checking on an ex or asking about her to see how horrible her life is without me. And when she comes back begging, I also rather enjoy seeing her grovel. His voice smiled. "And I hope she knows revenge is coming. I keep my friends close and my enemies closer.

"Grace, you did not have a chance. I thought you'd be the one who would never leave me—the one I had searched for all my life who would live up to my ideal everything. I had to punish you more. You needed to learn a lesson. I couldn't let you off the hook so easy. I wanted to hurt you in every way possible. You have no idea what I will do to you," he said angrily. "I will forget what you said and did for me. But. I will never forget how you made me feel."

I trembled.

"And, I don't need to see no cocaine-snorting counselor. Counseling works for women. Real men don't need it. Does God need it? Then I don't," he growled.

A toilet flushed in the background. The line went silent.

Oh my God. This is a man without a heart.

SIX

I arrived at Dr. Sherry's office feeling as if I'd made some progress. Today we talked about my childhood.

"Grace, I want to hear a little about what growing up was like for you," Dr. Sherry said.

"Where should I begin?" I responded. There're a lot of holes. Periods I can't remember. I may have some selective memory loss. There are, however, some events of which I have vivid memories. I grew up in the country with both my parents and four siblings. I'm number three among the kids, a middle child. Do psychologists still say middle children usually tend to be more successful than first and lastborn children?"

"I don't think it carries much weight today. But I haven't thrown out the baby with the bathwater yet," Dr. Sherry replied. "What else do you remember?"

"I remember how much I hated going back to school in the fall. Summer breaks were always fun. Sleeping in and playing in the woods. I always loved knowledge and was ready to return to books and classes. My concern was my parents could only afford to buy each child one new outfit to wear back to school."

"How did you feel?" she asked as she removed her glasses.

"Ashamed," I said, looking at the floor.

"I was ashamed of everything—our house, our cars, our clothes. We just didn't seem to have enough. No one knew how miserable I felt about this. I don't understand why I appeared to be the only one who knew or cared we were poor. Perhaps everyone felt the same, but none of us were talking.

"I remember one year when Mama took me to the dollar store. She bought me a pair of one-dollar black and white plastic shoes. Not only were they too large, but they also gaped open on the sides. I tried to hide my feet when I was at school. The soles of the shoes began to come unglued from the upper part just a few days after I got them. My teacher wrapped rubber bands around the top and soles to hold them together until I could get home. Mortified best explains how I felt. The kids just stared, standing there in their new leather penny loafers with shiny new pennies tucked inside or their black and white saddle oxfords. I just wanted to disappear.

"I was also ashamed our family was on the free lunch program. However, it was so much better than the alternative of sack lunches with leftover mustard biscuits from breakfast, bologna sandwiches, or having to ask my dad for lunch money. He was never pleasant. Always angry. I hated the look on his face when I asked him anything. I wanted to shout, 'Papa, I didn't ask to be born. You and Mama did this. Now give me my lunch and ice cream money and be happy about it!' He was probably angry because we were poor, and he probably didn't have enough money for his own lunch at work. Or was he like Narcissus?"

"Well, I'll certainly have something to ponder. Psychologists say a woman is never truly happy until she has a man like her father. Not sure it applies to everyone."

"It doesn't," I said and laughed.

"Do you have any good memories from school?" asked Dr. Sherry.

"Yes," I responded with a smile. "One of my teachers, Ms. Greggs, had taught my mother, and she often spoke of how smart Mama had been in school. I was proud of her. However, it was stressful trying to live up to Ms. Gregg's expectation for me to be like Mama.

"I studied hard and was an 'A' student. I guess some positive things did happen to me. When I was in sixth grade, the faculty selected me to represent our school in a statewide spelling bee. But you know how kids are. They were very mean to me. They'd corner me in the girl's restroom with an open dictionary and force me to spell words. I'd spell those words as if my life depended on it. No one could beat me at spelling.

"Unfortunately, I had even more haters when the principal chose me as the valedictorian for my school. I had the highest grade-ranking of any student in my graduating class. We were moving from grammar to middle school. I was an adult before I even understood what it meant to be the valedictorian. I gave the commencement speech at the graduation event. I remember being scared because I had so little confidence in myself. My knees buckled and knocked together. True story—it can happen. Speaking in front of a room full of people for the first time was a frightening event, I'll tell you. But I got through it without fainting or crying."

"Why, Grace. Congratulations! What an accomplishment. I'll bet your family was proud."

"I don't recall any words of congratulations from my family or anybody else," I murmured, frowning. "Nobody said anything. No teachers, not the principal, not even my parents. They must have thought I would get a big head or something."

"I'm sorry it happened the way it did. It's difficult for children to know when they've succeeded if no one praises them. Being the valedictorian should have been quite a self-esteem boosting event for you. With no approval at such a young age and sometimes even throughout our adult lives, we continue to be achievement-driven, seeking attention or acceptance to counter our feelings of low self-esteem," the counselor said.

"Thanks for sharing, Grace," she continued. "Today, we live in a world where kids are sometimes abused. Today, many parents advise their children about inappropriate touching from teachers, strangers, relatives and even family friends. But back when you were in school, this wasn't so much the case. So, I must ask you about an important and personal issue. Can you recall any incident where you may have felt abused or when someone touched you inappropriately?"

"I do," I responded, my face flooding with heat.

"What happened?"

Suddenly, I felt a nauseating wave of anxiety. I started to twist and wring my hands and profusely perspire. My heart was palpitating uncontrollably, and I wanted to cry. Then I softly blurted, "I was molested by a teenage family friend when I was about five. I know I was still quite young because I hadn't yet started school. When I entered first grade, I thought about it every day. It was obsessive. I was a miserable child. It's a wonder I didn't go crazy. Because of this experience, I was timid. It became difficult to even look into the eyes of any adult because I felt so ashamed of myself. I didn't tell anyone.

"I talked as little as possible because of the shame, I think. He, of course, was a teenager. He touched me then tortured me. He told his other male cousins what he'd done, and when I was eight years old, one of his cousins felt he had the right to force his hands between my legs in front of others. I grabbed his hand and broke his pinky finger. I don't believe he ever again thought of touching me or any other girl, yet I felt awkward at family gatherings where he'd be for the rest of my life until I heard he died. Oh, I was glad Satan was dead. The thought of him still sickens me. At the funeral, I stayed behind and danced on his grave. I didn't have to worry about him ever telling anyone else."

"Did you ever tell your parents?"

"No, I was too ashamed. I told an older female cousin about the encounters."

"Did she comfort you or empathize with you?"

"I found out I wasn't alone."

"Well, Grace, from the little you've shared about your life, I can now see how you became a target for your ex-husband. You had low self-esteem, little confidence, and you had a secret you never shared. We might even say you were codependent. This state of mind caused you to have an excessive emotional reliance on him.

"Now do you see why you became the girl of Narcissus' dreams. He knew you would keep his secrets just as you kept your own. However, I believe when he thought the relationship would end, he feared you'd tell all his secrets. He knew you weren't strong enough to fight back, so he wanted to discredit you. What he didn't know is you didn't even know his secrets, did you?"

"Exactly, Dr. Sherry. I didn't understand anything. I thought he was real. I couldn't see who he was. I was just a good, faithful wife who supported her husband and family. He thought I knew the truth about him. The wool was pulled so far over my eyes I couldn't see my feet and thought of nothing but making him happy. You can call me dumb."

The counselor laughed along with me.

"You weren't dumb. You were trusting, and you were in love. It's a requirement for healthy relationships."

"But mine wasn't healthy. Even when I became unhappy, I still tried to rely on Narcissus. Now I see how I was co-dependent," I said.

"Precisely. Well, this concludes our session for today. By the way, have you heard from Narcissus lately?"

"I got a phone call recently. It was Narcissus. I just listened. He said he was on his throne. He muted me as he spoke. Then, I heard the toilet flush," I said.

"Don't respond to any of his antics. No contact is the best recourse. Where there is no wood, the fire goes out," reminded Dr. Sherry. "Do you want to schedule your next appointment today?"

"No. I'll call when I'm ready to see you again. It may be after the wedding. Today was insightful. Thank you."

Dr. Sherry walked me to the door with a satisfied smile on her face. However, I knew she too thought I should wait longer before marrying again. But I knew better than anyone else how to live my life. After all, it was my life. I didn't need her or anyone else telling me what to do.

SEVEN
Three Months Later

I had arrived early to the wedding venue.

"Has my dip arrived?"

"Yes, Grace, it has," said the caterer Sakina.

"Susan sent it by an Uber Eats driver. She said she is a friend of the bride and volunteered to bring it to you. Said she'd attend the wedding."

"Okay, I'll tell her thanks. Who was the driver?"

"I didn't get the name," Sakina said as she wiped her face with her apron.

"Okay, I'm sure I'll see her at the wedding. Thanks again. I must run now so I can put something in my stomach before the wedding and see whether I will need to come back for butter to slide into my wedding gown." I chuckled, walked out, and investigated the reception hall.

"Excellent job, Sakina. Everything is so . . . so majestic." I winked.

"Thank you, Miss Grace. I's did it just the way you said and added a little Sakina touch," she said in her Jamaican-southern accent. Her big smile spread across snow-white teeth, with an open-faced gold crown sparkling against her dark satin complexion. She grabbed her stomach and belly laughed. She was hilarious.

I sat on the pink satin ottoman in the upstairs bridal suite and closed my eyes for a moment, then bent over and buckled my high-heeled shoe straps. My body swayed to the sweet, sultry voice of the Hispanic singer and a string quartet I'd hired to sing at my wedding. "At last. My love has come along. My lonely days are over, and life is like a song." It was my wedding day—marriage number three.

Happiness had come at last, and I was free of my absent, mad, and often critical ex-husband. I walked down the winding stairs and stood on the terrace of the wedding venue, an old southern antebellum house in Greenville, South Carolina overlooking the location where my new life was about to begin. I closed my eyes and prayed for an uneventful day of happiness. I took in a breath of country air and exhaled it, considering my life with a bright, woke mind.

This place had so much history.

"Was the old plantation owner like Narcissus? Was he evil, deceitful, spiteful, and mean? I'd thought my amicable divorce would be . . . well, so much for amicable. It was a total sham! He'd agreed the marriage was over, and he, too, wanted out. We'd agreed we would part ways in peace.

Surprise!

I must leave the ashes of the past behind. I saw the amber-colored leaves mixed with green ones waving in the whistling wind. The historical house with its round white columns and two stories had been an army hospital during the Civil War.

Theresa had told me about this place. She knew how much I love history. I missed Theresa and regretted I didn't get to say goodbye when she died. But I couldn't cry now so I pushed back those tears. It would have messed up my makeup. Theresa had kept me grounded. She'd been my confidante. She was both Mom and sister to me. She'd been the one who'd encouraged me to be confident in my looks when I felt ugly.

"Look into this mirror, Grace. You are five feet, four inches of class. Beautiful, cinnamon-toned, with gorgeous brown eyes, and you've got prettiest legs of any woman I know," she'd say. I'd blush and look into the mirror with her, but I wondered why I couldn't see what she saw.

I began to imagine Theresa was here with me and carefully wiped the tears away with my fingertips.

"I could almost hear horses neighing, arriving with the wounded, moaning and mourning soldiers on dusty, creaking wagons," Theresa had said. "Nurses were rushing out the door to rescue their next patient. Doctors were deciding to remove limbs and bullets, close wounds, hospitalize the worst cases and release others back to the battlefield."

"You know how much I love history. You made a great choice!" I said, imagining she was with me.

"Did you see the framed, handwritten notes scrawled on the wall of the groom's dressing room once used to treat injured soldiers during the war? I knew you would love, love, love this room! At times, town folks say you can still hear eerie moans coming from the house. Boo!" said Theresa.

I looked around and dismissed the suggestion. I walked around the property. My mind took me to the history I love about the Old South—where light-skinned African servants worked at the big house for Massa and little black and white children played together under the scorching hot sun in the front yard on cracked red clay.

"Wonder how they treated the field slaves on this plantation? Were the black children Massa's, or were slaves their parents? Did the slaves whip their kids? Did anyone think about how slavery would affect their personalities?"

"Grace, can you hear the darker-skinned Africans in the cotton fields singing the old Negro spirituals? Historians said singing helped the slaves endure the toil of the work and the cruel overseers," Theresa said.

I hummed.

"Swing low, sweet chariot, coming for to carry me home . . . On that great getting up morning. Fare thee well, fare thee well!"

"The slave owner didn't understand the songs were code words for freedom. The slaves certainly had no idea future families would bear the mental scars of slavery for many generations."

I faintly heard: "Don't be late for the wedding, honey." Then, Theresa's spirit vanished. A wave of sadness passed over me as I realized I was alone.

Then I snapped back to reality and composed myself. The historical events that had occurred at this place were gone, as well. However, I would always remember both. This place was now a charming venue to showcase events. And just such an occasion was about to begin.

I opened the container of the unique recipe of chips and dip Susan's Delicatessen had also made for Octavius. I sniffed the hummus made with garlic and artichoke and hurried to get it to Octavius so I wouldn't be late for the wedding ceremony. I hoped I wouldn't have to come back for butter to get into my wedding dress. Hah! Fare thee well Theresa.

EIGHT

The chapel decorations were fit for a king and queen—what an excellent start for my new life. There was a mist of love in the room. The amber glow of the candles provided lighting for a merry gathering of close family, friends and media already seated in anticipation of the wedding ceremony of the year.

I couldn't predict what nasty wind Narcissus might still blow my way. I hadn't heard from him in a while but knew he might still have a surprise planned for me. He'd made it clear he didn't want to be married to me, and yet I knew he might stalk me for the rest of my life, according to Dr. Sherry.

The ceremony finally began.

Everyone was seated in clear, Lucite chairs with gold ribbons and pink roses strung from row to row. The anticipation of the appearance of the bride and groom filled the atmosphere. The string music, along with the scent of one hundred fresh roses and love, filled the entire property.

The best man was Octavius' handsome son Benjamin. In a gray suit, he stood erect at the altar next to Reverend Crenshaw looking like a focused and robust soldier just given his orders. The excited bridesmaids, wearing their teal-colored satin dresses, walked down the moving aisle of the chapel. They were arm-in-arm with burly, handsome groomsmen wearing dark gray tuxedoes and proud smiles.

Then the music changed as the moving walkway, glittered in mini lights, and scattered with fresh rose petals, slowly conveyed us down the aisle as the crowd stood and cheered. Octavius was my last-minute escort and groom. I was supposed to be walking with my son Cedric. However, Octavius did the honor because my son's flight had fallen behind schedule. He said his stepfather had promised to send a ride to the airport. Cedric, my tall, dark, and handsome son, had wanted the honor of giving his mother away, but all I was concerned about now was his safe arrival. Cedric was standing in for my dad, who did not get out much anymore.

At age ninety, Papa was home streaming the event, I was sure. I imagined I could see him watching the screen and saying, "Hah! I keep giving her away. She keeps coming back. What happened to until death do us part? Her mama and I were together for fifty years. I hope she gets it right this time. These young people of this generation . . . "

I knew Papa, a retired truck driver who was now a widower, would have enjoyed the wedding. Months ago, he'd given Octavius his blessing for the marriage.

Octavius and I passed each row. Our guests showered us with smiles and winks. The older ones nodded with respect. The younger ones gave weird hand signals. When we strolled past a row where my friends and coworkers were sitting, I could swear Emma rolled her eyes at me. She had yet to admit she was having marital problems. But my day was much too happy to allow one jealous spirit to ruin it.

Our walk reminded me of a clip from a British movie reenacting the wedding of Queen Elizabeth and Prince Albert—with the exception that they didn't have a moving walkway. It was quite a remarkable moment, our wedding day. I was Octavius's queen, and he was my king. It was a dream come true because both of us had felt my ex would try to make sure it never happened.

A couple of weeks ago, Octavius had called me.

"Good morning, Octavius."

"Hey Grace, how are you doing this morning?"

"Okay. We've been friends for a long time. What's that tone about?" I asked as I sat on the bed.

"You know we have always been able to be honest with each other."

"Yeah, that's true."

"I've been thinking about you and your counseling and Narcissus. "I said boy, what are you getting yourself into?" I asked myself."

I laughed because he was imitating a rooster from an old 70's cartoon character. I stopped because I knew he was serious.

"What do you mean?" I said, chuckling nervously.

"Is Narcissus going to be a problem in our marriage?"

"I don't think so," I said.

No way would I ever reveal what Dr. Sherry had said.

"I just remembered this famous murder story where the ex-wife broke into the house during the night and killed both her ex-husband and his new wife while they both slept. Hit them both in the head with a hammer. Bam! Bam!"

I was quiet.

"You are an ex-marine, and you're worried about little Narcissus?"

"I just wanted to make sure you realize the marines trained me to kill. Will you be able to forgive me if anything happens?" he asked.

"Octavius, you told me you would protect me. You didn't not say how. I expect you to defend yourself."

Later, he revealed while he still had second thoughts, he didn't want to lose me.

Sometimes God reveals something to you. However, you must wait until the fullness of time to see a revelation manifest.

Octavius and I strutted down the aisle together with heads held high. I was no longer asleep. Awakened and partially healed, I could finally see my future. Both of us had seen this day in our dreams, but life had intervened until the time was ripe.

We walked to the front of the chapel and stood in front of Reverend Crenshaw. Family, friends, and the town's local media lit up the room, blinding us with their cell phone and camera flashes. A collage of our wedding photos would fill the front page of the next issue of the county's magazine, The People's Gazette. My recent job as a TV talk show host had made us famous.

In Scripture, God promised to set a beautiful table my enemies would envy, I thought.

Thank you, God. You did not say my enemies would eat. I am glad. However, as you know, I tried not to include any of them on the guest list.

Despite Emma's warning, as I stood in front of the minister, I had complete confidence in my decision to marry Octavius. My first confirmation the marriage was meant-to-be was a dream I'd had one night. Octavius, who was a good friend and business partner, was in the dream, too. I'd wondered why he was there.

The scene of the dream was a family gathering at which my father was blessing a marriage proposal. I was perplexed when Octavius dropped to one knee and proposed to me. Then, he planted an unforgettable kiss on my lips.

Wait a minute. I was not available. I was married to Narcissus. And he was not in the dream. While I had great respect for Octavius, our relationship was not romantic. Yet, when Octavius proposed to me, cheers erupted from my family members. I was in shock.

One of my sisters rolled her eyes and said, "Why does she get all the good men?"

I woke the next morning wondering what the dream's meaning could be. I chuckled when I thought of what my sister had said. It was so Jennifer. My beautiful younger sister, who never hesitated to speak her mind about anything—even in my dream.

I, however, believed the dream was a sign something was going to happen with Narcissus and me—and it wasn't going to be good.

Octavius admitted that when he and I were just friends, he'd wished in his heart someday he might have a woman like me as his life partner. He'd said I was pretty, a lady, intelligent, kind, confident and spiritual, and someone who loved Narcissus the way he wanted his woman to love him.

Octavius was the first to perceive the dark cloud forming over my life and the dimming light in my personality. However, when he saw what was going on, he was shocked and troubled, because he'd thought Narcissus and I were the epitome of a healthy and happy marriage.

Well, it wasn't so. Our relationship was like a bird with a broken wing—an I Love Freda show!

Remember when we all thought Fred and Freda had the perfect on-screen marriage? And both Freda and I knew what was going on behind our closed doors. Octavius was one of the few people who also knew the truth, but he'd kept it to himself and remained a faithful friend. He was the loyal friend I had looked for all my life.

Octavius is handsome. He has a chiseled jawline and a toned physique from bodybuilding and protein shakes. He's an ex-marine officer who made his midnight gray, sharkskin suit with the soft pink carnation boutonniere look good. (Umm! I had a bit of a challenge getting my Adonis to wear pink. But he finally realized even real men could wear it.)

"Honey," he inquired, "What color are the boutonnieres?"

"Pink, sweetheart."

"I don't do pink."

"Okay, I'll get you a white one."

I'd crossed my fingers behind my back he'd adjust when the wedding planner handed him the pink one I'd ordered two weeks earlier. Before the wedding ceremony began, when the wedding planner gave him his boutonniere, he picked up his cell phone and

Facetimed me, showing me the pink boutonniere and a snarl. I raised my shoulders as though I couldn't understand what had happened. He rolled his eyes. I smiled.
Narcissus wouldn't have worn it.

"All y'all." Octavius gestured. I thought maybe he was shooting me a bird finger. I knew that wasn't it. He seemed so different from my ex—a kind and loving soul.

My past life experiences left me a bit skittish about people's motives. I'd learned Narcissus had badmouthed me on our wedding day. Can you believe it? It would continue throughout the marriage.

However, my situation was one hundred times better with Octavius. For just a moment, I thought of Narcissus. The counselor said it would take time. I had to allow myself time to grieve the sudden loss of the marriage.

"We love your husband, Grace. He clips our hedges if our hedges need it while he is clipping his own," said Lee Ann, my next-door neighbor.

His motives looked noble, but they were not. The grateful neighbors will never know everything Narcissus did was all about his self-validation.

One day as I approached my mailbox by the road, I smelled something. Pew! It was the stench of roadkill. Was it the carcass of a dead squirrel? I recalled I hadn't seen my neighbor's new kittens, nor had I heard Narcissus complaining about wiping their little oily paw prints from the hood of his Hummer . . . and wondered perhaps another explanation accounted for the smell.

"Narcissus, have you seen the neighbor's kittens? They are always over here begging for food."

"No, I haven't seen them, have you?" He chuckled as he polished his BB gun.

"I have better things to think about than the neighbor's mangy kittens. I don't want those fleabags in my yard."

Okay, you must shake these thoughts off.
I reminded myself of the counselor's advice.

Remember "rolling eyes" Emma? She and I had been friends since college. She stared out the window during the ceremony as if she were waiting for someone. Emma hadn't socialized with anyone before the service. I had watched her from the security camera in the bridal suite. I often wondered whether she was shy because of the cleft palate scar. This was the first time I'd seen her antisocial side.

I can't say I didn't see her jealousy coming though. A year ago, when I announced the engagement, Emma began putting space between us. I had ignored it. We both seemed to like each other when we first met. We had shared gifts and lots of girlfriend time. Emma's side gig had once been as a wedding planner, so I'd asked her to assist with the wedding.

"I don't coordinate weddings anymore," she'd said. Wasn't this what best friends did?

I learned an important lesson that day—everyone you feel is your "bestie" may not be. That's what Theresa had said.

I think Emma was really trying to control my life. She could still be sulking because I hadn't listened to her earlier advice. She can't tell me what to do. Who made her my God and spiritual guide? She's just a friend.

Oh, how I wished Theresa were here. Yeah, she'd slept with Narcissus. However, I missed her just the same.

During college, Emma and I would chat when we ran into each other at school. We had met in a music appreciation class. We had a lot in common when it came to our marriages, workplace issues and family dynamics. Then fate had its way, and my life circumstances changed for the better. Emma's situation had remained the same.

I reckoned I was seeing the real Emma. She'd dropped her shield of pretense. I somehow knew this would be the last time I would see her. Fare thee well, fake Emma.

It was a curtain-time and center stage for me. Bump Emma. The show would go on. I would not allow Emma or anyone else to ruin my special moment. It was also time for Octavius to have his long-awaited day on center stage after experiencing lopsided love in past relationships. We'd both found the "fifty-fifty" love Teddy Pendergrass sang about in one of our wedding day songs, "When Somebody Loves You Back."

Over the past seven years, I'd been through hell. My new friends would say, Grace, you don't look as though you've been through anything. Girl, you look wonderful!

"Well, looks are deceiving," I'd say. I felt as though I'd been tried in a hot, fiery furnace. No other human or companion had ever treated me with as much malice as Narcissus.
Oh God! Now look at me.

I chuckled. I was more confident, had landed my dream job, and was marrying a wonderful man—I hoped. The things I thought would kill me only strengthened me and was making me better. Now, I can afford a chic Versace evening gown. I'd bought it with my own money. I'd cleaned up my credit and my finances had improved. I could even afford my glittered sling backs. I glanced down at my sparkly shoes. Octavius had given me a beautiful, six-carat, handmade sapphire engagement ring—all the way from Israel!

Hava nagila, hava nagila, hava nagila ve nis' mecha that! Here's to Narcissus and everyone else who saw me in the ditch and thought I would never get back on the road.
Well, I was back! I even had bling rings on the heels of my shoes. I was beside myself. But I deserved every bit, after all, I've been through.

Come, let us be glad and rejoice! my fellow Jewish brothers say in this song.

Today, I feel like Cinderella. However, unlike Cinderella, I got away from the evil stepmother and sisters before dancing with the prince. I imagined I could hear Octavius singing in his soft, sexy tenor in the role of the Prince as we walked down the aisle:

"Ten minutes ago, I saw you. I looked up when you came through the door. My head started reeling. You gave me the feeling the room had no ceiling or floor. I have found her . . . "

You bet you have, you big hunk! And you put a ring on it! Then I would belt back in coloratura soprano as Cinderella:

"Do I love you because you're beautiful, or are you beautiful, because I love you? Are you the sweet invention of a lover's dream, or . . . are you really as wonderful as you seem?"

You'd better be. I accepted your proposal twice, didn't I?

"Okay . . . so my thoughts had gotten a little longwinded and carried away.

I'm sure my spitfire orange Mercedes Benz won't be turning into a pumpkin at midnight, nor will I lose one of my silver sling backs on the stairway of this old plantation house. My Benz with the sports wheels and a full sunroof said, see me, Narcissus, I found the pot of gold you hid at the end of the rainbow. You wanted me to die. Well . . . I'm still alive. I don't stinketh.

Today's celebration was a full circle for Octavius and me. It was an answer to prayer and a day we would remember for a lifetime. Crying lasts only through the night. Joy always comes the next morning. A dream can become a reality. You can find someone who loves you.

At least, I hoped I had.

"Now for the vows," said Reverend Crenshaw. Octavius got a little misty. I could barely hold back the tears beginning to form in the corners of my eyes. He looked at me with those big brown eyes and said,

"Grace, you are the key to my happiness. You make life worth living. You are a dream come true. I will be your protector and provider. I promise to love and cherish you for the rest of my life."

Then, I looked directly into Octavius' eyes and said, "Octavius, because of you I laugh, I smile, I dare to dream again. I look forward with great joy caring for you, nurturing you and encouraging you. And in all things being a faithful wife."

I smiled even though I was hurting as I thought how the path to this day had been a "yellow-brick road" strewn with many sleepless nights, broken dreams, nightmares and tears caused by Narcissus. These times had tried my soul, but I'd made it.

After hard times, I was finally on the right road. I'd also answered my call. My new job was the platform to share psychology's little-known secret. I had completed the happy formula, and my wedding day was triumphant!

As the Reverend Crenshaw spoke, Octavius reached in his pocket and took out his handkerchief. I thought he was crying, but he was not. Sweat seeped through his clothes and dripped from his temple while he continued to smile and maintain his composure. He reached for my hand with a concerned look. He said he felt his tongue swelling, and he couldn't breathe. His face and ears itched. He made a strange yet familiar sound in his throat.

Allergies.

Octavius began to sway. He said everything was turning gray. He looked at me as I tried to steady him.

"Now what God has put together . . . " Reverend Crenshaw said quickly, then paused. He'd noticed our concerned faces.

"I'm going to pass out. I'm having an allergic reaction," he whispered, then fell unconscious.

The audience stirred at the commotion. They craned their necks to see what had happened. The wedding party gathered close to prevent the audience from crowding Octavius.

Reverend Crenshaw shouted, "Everybody, please stand back and give him some air. Someone call 911. Is there a doctor or nurse here?"

A woman scurried to the front of the chapel and squatted near Octavius.

"My name is Beverly. Grace, I'm from your doctor's office. I'm one of the nurses."

"It appears Octavius is having a full-blown allergic reaction to something. He is going into anaphylaxis."

"Okay," Grace added nervously. "Beverly, I am glad you could come. He had told me this happened once when he'd eaten salad dressing. He didn't know it contained anchovies. Please do something quickly!"

"Allow me to use this EpiPen. It'll reverse his low blood pressure, wheezing and other symptoms of the reaction," Beverly said, as she quickly administered the drug to Octavius. "I keep one with me for emergencies like this, when someone is experiencing anaphylaxis. He'll still need an EMT. His tongue looks as if it's swelling. We must get him to the hospital immediately."

A guest had called 911, and the EMT arrived in minutes. Two uniformed men rushed inside, placed Octavius onto a stretcher, took him to the waiting ambulance and began working on him.

The most curious guests walked outside to watch from the terrace. The murmur of voices resonated throughout the chapel. I stood in the chapel's doorway, speaking so all the wedding guests could hear me.

"Octavius had an allergic reaction. Once they stabilize him, I believe he'll be okay. He's a champ. We're going to the hospital to be sure nothing else is happening. He is allergic to peanuts. Please don't leave. We planned a grand event for you and catered a delicious spread of food. Please stay and try to enjoy yourselves. Don't leave and miss the reception. We'll be back on schedule soon," I said, trying to reassure the crowd. I could see Emma at the back of the crowd talking to a man and pointing toward the EMT van.

The reporter onsite for the wedding pushed through the crowd and stuck a microphone inside the van.

"Is the wedding still on?" he asked.

I frowned. "We're having an emergency here, sir. Privacy, please, if you don't mind. There will still be a wedding today," I assured everyone as I heard Octavius gasp for air.

The reporter stepped away from the van and smiled at the guests.

"Narcissus won't win," Octavius whispered to me. He raised a thumb to the crowd peering into the van. The guests applauded, relieved to know he had regained consciousness.

The EMT team helped me and my wedding dress into the back of the ambulance. I sat next to Octavius and held his hand. The flashing red lights disappeared into traffic. We listened to the

muffled sound of the paramedic's report to the hospital, "We're on our way transporting Mr. Octavius Washington with symptoms of a severe allergic reaction. Standby."
Octavius looked at Grace lovingly and smiled. "Look at you," he said. "What the devil meant for evil will be worked out for good."

Meanwhile, the wedding planner Nadine directed everyone to the decorated reception hall. The guests' oohs and ahhs planted a smile on her face. They entered the room admiring the sky view, human angels with harps, gold and pink decorations, and round banquet tables with lovely crystal centerpieces. The elevated head table had two large golden chairs in the center with a private attendant.

It was a room fit for a king and queen. I later heard it had received the awe I'd intended. Several guests continued chatting among themselves about what had happened.

"Everyone be seated, please, so we can serve you," Nadine said enthusiastically.

The waiters began serving Dom Pérignon to relax everyone. The string quartet had resumed playing wedding songs. They were resetting the stage for our return.
That's when Emma stood at her table. She cleared her throat and tapped a glass with a spoon to get everyone's attention in a pretentious, shy but prissy sort of way.

"Hello, everybody! My name is Emma Matilda. I'm a friend of Grace," Emma said slowly and paused. "I am not surprised about what happened to the Groom. Karma's at work here. I advised Grace to wait before getting married again. She wouldn't listen to me. Many of you may not know it, but she has been through a lot. I began feeling uneasy when I walked in the door. Narcissus, her ex-husband, feels Grace did him wrong. He wanted to do something terrible to her. I believe he is responsible.

"Most of you knew about her devastating divorce. He tried to do everything he could to destroy her life. She's been in counseling for a while now. I thought she would go crazy. Now she is jumping right back in another relationship. I think what happened to Octavius was intended for Grace. I warned her about remarrying so soon.

"All y'all stay here and continue to play along with this charade and see her hurt again if you want. I'm out."

Later, Sakina would tell me Emma had grabbed her purse and the goblet of wine and left the reception hall. Everyone had stared at each other and Emma. Whispers buzzed through the room. Emma had thrown back her head, shook it side to side to show her disgust and had walked out the door. She'd stepped outside the door for a moment and listened, apparently unsatisfied because she hadn't accomplished what she'd intended—as though she'd expected everyone to walk out with her.

She'd gone back in and walked to the microphone, talking to herself.

"Well, Ms. Grace, your wedding day isn't going so well now, is it?" she muttered loud enough for Sakina to hear her.

When she stepped in front of the mic this time, she'd hit it with her hand. The loud crack of thunder startled everyone, turning their attention to her.

"There's something else y'all need to know," she'd shouted. "I don't think any of you know Grace like I do, or how Narcissus hurt her. He is the reason she was so determined to have this wedding. And Narcissus was so determined to block it. The wedding is her testimony she survived."

According to Sakina, Emma had taken out my manuscript.

"Grace shared her story a few months ago. She said Narcissus hated her. She wanted me to know the truth, just in case anything ever happened to her," Emma said. She also said it might become a book about her life.

"She survived what she believed to be the darkest storm of her life. He made her think he agreed with the divorce. Then bam! Just when she thought her life would be peaceful, he had another hidden plan. Most of it occurred after their divorce was final.

"Octavius' allergic reaction is the worst I've ever seen. It could be hours before they get back . . . if ever," Emma said with a sad look that quickly faded.

"No," a guest agreed. The rest of the audience moaned in disappointment. "Listen up," Emma snapped. "It's time you heard Grace's story. It started when she was married to her son's father, Leonard. As you can see, she loves being married."

"What kind of friend are you, Emma?" A guest shouted.

"Didn't you say it was confidential?" another guest asked.

"Emma, I promise you, no good is going to come out of this for you. You'll regret this tell-all about Grace," said a third guest.

"I believe she'd really want you all to know the truth. She hasn't realized it yet."

In the end, no one had tried to stop Emma. I'd been so private and secretive I guess they couldn't wait to hear about my personal life.

Sakina said it had angered her when they'd all sat on the edge of their seats as Emma began to read my manuscript.

NINE

Grace's Story of Her Earlier Life Begins

One day I found it extremely hard to get out of bed. I'd had insomnia. My thoughts were like a cinder block in my mind. I was feeling guilty, and I had the blues about leaving Leonard. I must admit the thrill for him was not gone. I was surprised he had not even attempted to get in touch with his son. I'd needed to hear from him, too.

The phone rang.

I hoped it was the call of the wild or something. Life had been quiet for the past six months and a bit boring.

"Hello, Grace. It's Theresa." She'd said her name as if I didn't know who she was.

Why does she do this?

Theresa was one of my few . . . well, my only friend from high school with whom I managed to regularly stay in touch. Theresa was a few years older than me. She was like a sister and a mother. She was tall, medium-complexioned, smart, kind and had never married. She was the school counselor at the local high school.

"Of course, I know who you are," I said.

"Hey, girl. What's up, wild thang?" she asked with a chuckle.

"I am just reading a new novel I bought. I try to read at least nine pages every day to get my daily reading done."

"Yeah, Okay. Good. You know, Grace, now you're all settled into your new apartment, what do you think about dating again? Your divorce was finalized a few months ago. It's time for you to go out on a date. My boyfriend has a charming roommate. I met him last night. Nice guy, a Christian, has a nice income, and not bad looking, either.

"Mostly, I want to get him out of the way so Winston and I can have the house to ourselves. You see, he had a recent break up with his wife and is also new in town. I think they're now divorced. He relocated from somewhere in Tennessee. He and Winston are college buddies. Winston says he's always alone and always home because he doesn't know anyone in the city. We had the idea maybe you and he might hit it off. His name is Narcissus Little. What do you think of going on a double-blind date?

"Winston and I were saying the other night we see two good Christian people who could use some companionship. Narcissus is always home reading the Bible and watching TV. He needs something to do. You're always home reading nine pages from your novels," Theresa had said with a chuckle.

"Winston and I need some time alone. The double date would be safe, and if you don't like him, you'll have me there to help you get through the evening. And you never have to see him again . . . unless you want to, of course."

"So, you want to use me? Really Theresa! I'm just not ready to meet anyone right now. I haven't gotten over Leonard. It's so difficult to trust anyone again. Also, I must be careful who I allow around Cedric.

"Did you say his last name was Little? I recently read about a man named Samuel Little, a serial killer responsible for 93 murders. I hope he's not related to him."

"Grace . . . Grace . . . Grace," Theresa sighed.

"What? A friend of mine said some of these freaky, down-low guys want to be around your tender son, not just the mother. And besides, I once said there would only be one marriage. If I got divorced, I would move to Mother Theresa's convent in Mexico and become a nun and get none. Just pray all day and all night and bake bread and clean toilets. I'd seriously do it if I didn't have Cedric," I said, slowing down, chuckling at the same time.

"Girl, you are crazy. I am serious. Are you finished with your rant? And it's not about using you. I'm killing two birds with one stone. Now, let me finish, please. Narcissus is handsome, a Christian and has a nice disability income, I hear! I think he's a little shy, however. You may have to do all the talking. When I met him, it wasn't easy for him to hold eye contact with me."

"So, what's he hiding?" I asked. "You know what they say about people who can't look you in your eyes."

"Duh, I think you're a little shy, too. What are you hiding? I don't think he's hiding anything. He's Just been hurt—like you. You both need someone to fill some of those lonely hours. I know you have Cedric there with you. But you could also use the company of a nice adult gentleman. You'll have somebody to hold you tight, talk to and make you feel like a woman again. And someone who can pray and touch heaven when you pray over meals or when you face problems. And I'll have Winston to myself."

The idea sure did sound tempting, and I had begun to feel a wee bit lonely.

"I'll think about it, Miss Selfish," I said.

I could just see Theresa crossing her fingers behind her back for good luck, clearly hoping I would accept the invitation.

"Just come with us, get out of the house on Thursday and have some fun. It'll be good for you. You won't have to drive. We'll pick you up at 7pm on Thursday, and we'll go to the new night club. I think it's called Fat Tuesday. They have an open bar, a dance floor and a live band."

"Fat Tuesday. What kind of name is this for a night club?" I chuckled. "I'd prefer to go to Skinny Tuesday. I'll admit I've packed on a few pounds lately. Just kidding. I think I've heard of it. If it's called Fat Tuesday, then why are we going on Thursday?"

She snorted. "Can you be serious for one moment?"

"Okay. And, by the way, how old is this guy? And is he wheat or a tare? Does he really love the Lord?"

"Well, Winston says he's 30 and goes to church. I thought . . . perfect age. You appear to prefer guys a little older than you. He's a member of the Evan's Grove Episcopal Church. I think Winston said Narcissus is a deacon over the Men's Ministry. Now, who gets assigned such a position without some serious integrity and brains? It'll be fun, and who knows what might come of this date? He's got a good reputation."

"I hope you don't think I can't see you're not answering any of my questions," I said.

"Because you're talking scared and being paranoid. You need to get out of the house and be with some adults. By the way," Theresa continued, "When's the last time you heard from your so-called friend Emma Matilda? You know I've never liked her. Don't think she's the good friend you believe her to be. I don't trust the heifer."

"Don't be so hard on Emma. She doesn't have many friends, and her family ignores her," I replied.

"And you can't see why," said Theresa.

"We both take evening classes at the college and talk occasionally. We reconnected recently. We mainly chat about whatever's going on with us at the time . . . only about every six months, when I run into her on campus."

"Yeah, she sounds like a bestie. All I say is be careful what you share with her," Theresa said.

I thought to myself I wished those two could be friends. I needed both women in my life.

"Winston is knocking at my door right now. I've got to go. Let me know if you change your mind. Goodnight."

Change my mind? I never agreed to go. And what is Winston doing knocking at her door at this hour of the night? Well, it's none of my business. She's my friend. Okay . . . so why not meet this Narcissus? If I was being honest, I wished someone were knocking at my door.

I went to the kitchen and poured myself a glass of light pink Moscato d'Asti wine, went back to my bedroom, flopped into my new red recliner, and threw one leg over the arm of the chair.

I sipped my favorite wine and began to think about my last job as a human resources specialist.

"I sure do miss the salary I'd made, along with some of the people who'd worked there. My boss was funny and handsome, but what a jerk! The top-level executive, Mr. Esposito, would pop into my work area. He was a gorgeous Italian, short like Napoleon, and had slicked-back hair and crystal blue eyes. And, he'd thought he was the smartest person at the company. He was a snack for the ladies in the executive office. They say he'd slept with all the female staff. I respected him, but I didn't like him much."

"Ciao, Grace," he'd said one day as he burst into my office.

"Ciao, Mr. Esposito," I'd responded, looking up from the desk.

"When are we going on a date? The ladies from upstairs are wondering why you don't have to go to bed with anyone to keep your job," he said with a wide Cheshire cat grin.

I looked him straight into his eyes and said, "Because I have brains, skills and morals. And no disrespect, Mr. Esposito. But aren't you married, anyway?"

He'd known I'd never go out with him. He'd also known I'd never repeat the things he said.

After a bad experience, my rule was never ever to date a coworker again.

"My wife is always mad at me. I have no idea why," he continued.

"Really?" I said. "I think I do," I place-marked an item on my to-do list.

"So, I just find 'em, use 'em and forget 'em" he'd said with a cocky, self-satisfied grin. Then he'd walked out the door and allowed it to slam behind him.

I still can't forget nor believe what Mr. Esposito had admitted to me.

I should have reported him to human resources. But who would have believed me? He was third in command of the largest branch of our company. He was human resources!

Narcissus sounded like a perfect gentleman compared to Mr. Esposito, whom I thought was selfish and mean. I had offended him when I didn't join his human office supply. Find them, lie with them, and forget them?

Ladies see what a one-night stand with the big boss will get you.

As far as I'd been concerned, Mr. Esposito was a crazed, high-functioning sociopath who would be divorced before the year ended. And he was.

I'd encouraged myself to go on a date with Narcissus.

It's just a date. He's not asking for your hand in marriage. And even then, probably not for a long time since he too is divorced. You have only eaten out at the local Kiddie Burger with Cedric and socialized at your parent's house and family gatherings. You read nine pages from novels every night.

Boring!

When is the last time you've been to the park, a good movie, or the museum? You could be friends and have a hangout buddy. No need to get serious right away. Control yourself. Okay? You can handle this. You'll enjoy going out. You haven't dated in a while, especially not with a swag, tall, handsome GQ man.

A woman needs to get dressed in all her girly stuff. You've been praying for God's will in your life and Theresa said he's a Christian.

Yeah, but Mama warned her girls, "Everyone who says Lord, Lord is not a Christian, nor will they enter Heaven."

But how can you know if you don't meet people? This guy may be the one you've been waiting for all your life. Now encourage yourself, take a leap of faith, tie a knot, and hold on! God won't give you more than you can handle. It's written in His Word. Now stop talking to yourself.

"Mommy! Mommy!" Cedric's voice interrupted my thoughts.

"What is it, Cedric?" I'd asked as I walked toward his room.

"I'm ready to go to bed. Can you read me a story?"

"Yes. I'll be right there, my favorite son."

He'd giggled. "I'm your only son." His smile would light up his room.

"Yeah, but you're still my favorite," I'd said as I knelt with him at the side of his bed.

Cedric and I had prayed our short bedtime prayer:

> Now I lay me down to sleep,
> I pray the Lord my soul to keep.
> Angels watch me through the night,
> And wake with the morning light.
> God bless Pee-Paw, Daddy, Mimi, Mama, and me.
> And bless everybody in the whole wide world. Amen!

Then he'd hand me his favorite book and snuggled close. While he was turning the pages to find his favorite bedtime story, he'd asked, "Mommy, has Daddy called to talk to me?"

"No, he hasn't, but I'm sure he will," I'd said, feeling his sadness. I'd started reading his story.

"And the big bad wolf huffed, and he puffed and he blew the house down." I'd lowered my voice to a whisper. Cedric had been purring like a kitten. I'd kissed his head, put cotton balls in his ears and gently tucked him in and closed the door.

I curled up on the sofa downstairs with the TV quietly running in the background. Now . . . back to this date idea with Mr. Narcissus Bentley Little.

Should I do it? What should I wear? Oh yeah—the stylish, sheer black blouse with matching camisole and the black slacks I'd gotten on sale at the store. And those black, strappy, sexy sandals would show one of my good assets—my pretty toes. This would work. When I wore sandals, people complimented me on my toes. At least there was something still pretty about me.

"It appears," I said aloud in a whisper, "that I, Lady Grace, will be going on a date with Lady Theresa, Your Grace Winston, and Your Grace Narcissus. I mean . . . we are sons and daughters of the Highest God. If people on earth can have such titles, certainly God's children can, too. He makes us royalty. Sounds good to me."

I'd quickly tumbled into my soft bed, clapped off the lights, pulled the soft covers around my neck and fell into a deep sleep. I'd dreamed lucidly.

I stepped onto a train and found myself alone in an empty car. I wasn't completely alone, though — a handsome angel stood in the aisle. He spoke to me. And he was fine. He wore a black suit and a white shirt with a red bow tie. I hoped he wasn't Dracula. While he looked like a man and didn't have wings, I somehow knew an angel addressed me.

"Don't be disturbed by what's happening in your life," the angel had said.

"You are a visionary and teacher. Go to the School of the Prophet on the wings of faith. You have an assignment. Your job is to reveal one of psychology's best-kept secrets. Now wake up!"

My eyes popped open and I sat up in bed, clutching my sheets, my heart racing. The angel had bedazzled me. Psychologist's best kept what? I pondered those words for a moment, suddenly knowing how Cinderella must have felt when told she was going to go to the ball.

Me? I decided I would keep this dream to myself.

Perhaps it was the food I had eaten for dinner, I thought—a delusion of grandeur. I'd be the first to admit I can get beside myself sometimes, although many of my dreams have been warnings. And who would believe this, anyway?

God calls men, I decided, and went back to sleep. I woke up thinking of Cedric's dad.

TEN

Emma had everyone's attention. Sakina told me you could hear a mouse pee on cotton. She sat down, crossed her legs, and continued reading my story.

"My first marriage didn't last. Things were terrible. Neither of us was happy. Our only son Cedric was a baby. Leonard was an Ensign in the US Navy. Every day he came home from work angry and would never communicate his feelings.

He had graduated from the US Naval Academy at the top of his class. During the last year of our marriage, someone had stabbed a sailor on the base under Leonard's command. It had made the front page of the local paper. NCIS never found the weapon. During the investigation, Leonard was relieved of duty and put in an administrative position. He never spoke of the incident. He loved the sea, so I wondered why most of his work projects were on land after the incident, but he wouldn't discuss it with me. Period.

He was miserable, and he made me sad. There wasn't enough love or money. He was usually silent unless he was talking about his job or his mother. I didn't have a job. While Leonard didn't earn enough to make a comfortable living, he still wanted me to be a stay-at-home mom.

Leonard came home one day drunk and vomited all over everything. I thought he was sick until I struggled to get him to the bed and cleaned up the alcohol-reeking vomit. I had never seen him drink before.

"What is going on?" I said as I gagged.

Why was he so unhappy?

These repeated evenings caused me to lose patience with his immaturity and unstableness, along with experiencing the ongoing feeling he was cheating. A woman knows when her man is cheating. Maybe this was the reason he was so unhappy, and I could not sleep. I knew what that meant. Did he want someone else? I pondered.

I went to pick up the mail a few days after one vomiting scene. An unusual letter with a lovely fragrance—my favorite scent—had arrived in a red envelope with an address from North Carolina. As I walked home, I opened it, thinking the card was from Leonard's mother. The letter was addressed to Leonard. Lucretia had signed it with a bright red lipstick blot.

"Leonard, I miss you so much," the letter read.

I stopped mid-step and put the letter back into the envelope. When I got inside the house, I tossed it on the kitchen table. It stayed there all day. Steam rose from my collar each time I looked at the envelope. In my mind, I called Leonard everything but a child of God. I pretended to have no interest in reading the rest of the letter each time I walked by, as I knew it would hurt even more if I did. The last time I passed by the envelope, Cedric's playtime was over, and he was napping. All my pretense of strength flew out the window as a voice prompted me to read it. Okay. I sat at the table and slowly unfolded the letter as my heart pounded inside my blouse.

How could Leonard do this to me?

I put my hand over my mouth and cried out loud.

When Leonard came home, he saw the opened letter and my swollen eyes. He knew he was knee-deep in trouble. He tried to weasel out by saying, "Woman . . . what do you mean opening a grown man's mail?"

"And what you mean giving your mistress our address and my perfume?" I snapped back.

"Baby, this girl is not my mistress. She means nothing to me. What perfume?" he asked with less cockiness and a guilty expression on his face.

I was too angry to listen. I took Cedric by the hand and slammed the door shut behind me.

The wall shook.

I shook.

I went into Cedric's room and felt a hint of satisfaction as I heard the click of the lock. I stayed there for the rest of the evening, coming out only to eat the dinner I'd prepared earlier.

Leonard and I ate at the dinner table. The only sound was the click of their forks and Leonard's loud smacking. While his smacking irritated me beyond belief, I smiled anyway. Leonard had always complimented me on my cooking skills. Today we ate our steaks and potatoes in silence. Cedric talked and looked from his dad to his mom to provide the usual dinner conversation.

"Mama, we had fun today, didn't we? Remember, we played with my toys?" Cedric said.

"Yes, Baby, we did," I said.

"Mama, are you sick?"

"Mama is fine. Just eat your dinner."

"Eat your dinner, buddy. Mama is acting weird again," Leonard said.

Cedric laughed innocently. I rolled my eyes and shot Leonard a bird finger. He laughed.

After we finished our meal, watched our favorite evening show, Andy Griffith. I ran baths for Cedric and myself, put on our bedclothes, read Cedric's favorite story, and went to bed. Cedric fell fast asleep.

Leonard milled around the house and the sound of music blasted from the master bedroom. I curled up next to Cedric and fell asleep in his room to, "Meee and Ms. Ms. Jones. We got a thing going on." I chuckled that Leonard could be so petty. I pushed in my earplugs, pulled down my pink sleep mask, and fell fast asleep, too.

After I'd been asleep for a couple of hours, I was awakened and startled. My heart raced like a time bomb. Leonard stood above me holding his old hunting knife, his eyes stretched wide open with a menacing frown.

"Talk to me, woman. No one gives me the silent treatment in my house but me."

He threw back the covers and lifted me by the neck of my nightgown.

"I told you there is nothing between Lucretia and me. What an imagination you have," he insisted.

"And I told you if you ever cheated on me, I would leave you. Imagine that!" I sneered. "So, let me go. And put your big, rusty knife away before you cut me or stab Cedric. Because you have lost your mind and you are about to make me lose mine. Don't you ever put your hands on me—no, don't you even think about it. I'm not afraid of you. And I will leave you! This knife gives me a further reason to get the hell out of here."

Leonard released me with a shove. I fell back onto the bed, closed my eyes, and listened for the door to slam.

Girl, you'd better pack your stuff and get yourself back home because this bro is crazy. This is Dr. Jekyll and Mr. Hyde.

So . . . this is the way we talk things over? He must think I'm a James Brown's wife.

"I'm black, I'm proud, and I will pack a brand-new bag," I said as I pushed my suitcase against the door.

"I told him not to play with me. I will show him better than I told him. When I caught my breath and my heart stopped pounding, I also pushed the chest of drawers and a chair in front of the door, too—just in case Lunatic Leonard got another stupid idea.

Leonard didn't know it, but he'd scared the Mr. Hanky out of me. I exhaled and kept my eyes on that door.

I had never seen this side of him. I wondered whether the knife was the one described in the newspaper, the one used to make the wound that had killed his subordinate. They'd never found it.

I wasn't going to stick around to find out.

"They'll never find my body in the freezer," I thought out loud.

When morning came, I heard Leonard leave for work. I decided I'd leave Leonard before the sun went down. I felt sad about the way things had developed. While Leonard was at work, I dropped Cedric at the church daycare in the neighborhood. It was Mom's Day Out, so I went downtown. I just needed to get away for a moment of me time, and to think things through before I committed murder.

When I approached downtown, I saw reporters and cameras as well as locals outside one of the stores. I wasn't sure whether the gathering was good or bad, so I peered in the window, pressing my face close to the glass. To my surprise, I saw the famous musician Santana inside the shop. He glanced at me and waved, flashing a big smile.

The shop owner had closed the little boutique so Santana and his companion could shop. This was the closest I'd ever been to a celebrity. I watched him from the window for a while. I wished I could meet him or be married to him. Anywhere but where I was, was where I wanted to be. However, I went to the store next door, picked up a few items and headed back home.

I'll tell my friends back home I met Santana.

Well, not exactly, but almost.

I picked up Cedric from daycare and said goodbye to his teacher, then went back to the house. I wrote Leonard a letter, made reservations for tickets to fly back home and packed our things.

I left behind everything that would not fit into the suitcase. When the taxi came to pick us up, I asked the driver whether he could wait a moment for me to run back into the house. He nodded. I rushed into the door and I pulled off my wedding band, leaving it on the dining room table.

Cedric and I boarded the 747 to fly back to happy Greenville. I was heartbroken. I'd wanted the marriage to work, if not for me, then for Cedric.

The flight attendant announced a storm was on the way, and the plane would not fly out until the next day. It was evening. The airline said it would pay for rooms for all the passengers in the hotel located next to the terminal.

Cedric and I walked to the hotel. Tears rolled down my cheeks. Cedric put my hand under his chin and said, "Mommy, it will be okay. Will Daddy come and get us?"

"No, Baby. Daddy won't be coming with us this time."

Cedric eyes filled with tears.

"Why? I want my daddy," he said. I held him while he struck me with his little fists.

It broke my heart even more to see my baby cry like he did. However, I knew all was left of my marriage was the band of gold I'd thrown on the dining room table. It was just me and Cedric now. I'd have to wait a while to tell him the truth.

Not today, not ever will I tolerate a man who cheats or beats, I vowed.

Cedric was not old enough to know the facts. I had warned Leonard the moment he touched me, or I found out about someone else, it would be over.

It was over.

I checked into our room. I ordered room service for Cedric and then put him to bed. He cried himself to sleep. When he finally fell asleep, I buried my face in my hands and wept inconsolably, muffling the sound with a pillow. This would be the last time I would see Leonard until Cedric graduated high school.

I had thoughts about whether I had made my move too soon and had not given Leonard a genuine chance to redeem himself. I didn't sleep much that night. We boarded the plane the next morning and were on our way to a new life. We both slept during the four-hour flight back to my childhood home.

I'd left Leonard in New Mexico. I felt cold and ruthless, but I didn't know what else to do.

"My philosophy is if he broke the marriage covenant once then he'd do it again. He was not getting a second chance when he had proven he couldn't do right by me with his first chance.

When I arrived in Greenville, Leonard called me, claiming remorsefulness about how things had turned out. He asked for another chance. He told me I was the best person in his life. However, when I compared his actions with his words, I could find little mercy in my heart for him. He'd need to take his glass slipper and look elsewhere.

He'd shown me what he was. I believed him.

The separation hurt him. It hurt me, too.

And in the long run, Cedric would be hurt the most. He'd grow up without his father and might eventually blame me.

Who would want to marry me with a child? And would I be able ever to pick the right mate?

The plane flew out of New Mexico.

Goodbye my sailor man.

ELEVEN

Starting all over again was hard, but I was happy, I had money in the bank, and I'd been hired by the local department store.

It was 5:30am when the phone rang. Once I saw the caller ID, I knew it wasn't bad news. I knew who it was this early in the morning and smiled as I answered the phone.

"Good morning, Grace," My mom said. "Baby, I wanted to be the first to wish Cedric a happy birthday. I remember he was born at 5:30 in the morning because you were born at the same time."

"Yes, it was 5:30am and believe me, I will never forget those birth pains," I said, rubbing my tummy and then the sleep from my eyes with all the perkiness I could muster. "Cedric is still asleep."

"I know. I was up and I knew you to be an early riser like I am. Stop by the house when you can and pick up the cake I baked for Cedric. How are you doing?"

"Thank you. Cedric and I will come by the house later today. I love you, Mama, and thanks. No worries. I'm doing fine."

"You're the child I worry about the least. Just be careful whom you give your heart to in the future. I can't bear to see you hurt again. See you later today. Okay?"

"Okay, Mama." I hung up the phone.

Each year, Mama called all her kids at the exact time we were born. I looked forward to hearing my Mama's voice every year on my birthday. I was glad to see her tradition extended to Cedric, her grandson. She told me the same story each year about my birth.

"I well remember the morning you were born," she'd say. "I'd had a sonogram and knew the baby was a girl. You were born at the Lee Perry Hospital delivery room at 5:30 am. Your father was there, too. I heard the doctor say, 'The baby is crowning. What a head full of hair! Here she comes. Get ready.'"

"You came out of me like you were on a Slip and Slide. You shot right through the doctor's hand like a cannonball and onto the floor. Then my afterbirth followed and fell right out on top of you. Your dad fainted," she'd whisper.

"He never wanted anyone to know, but he really did faint. Bless his heart. The nurses helped him up and took him out to the waiting room." She'd chuckle then as she remembered.

"The doctor picked you up and slapped your little bitty butt," she'd continue. "You screamed at the top of your lungs, and I was happy. My baby was fine. Thank you, Jesus. You had a head full of curly hair, black like coal. The whites of your eyes were blue, though. You were the most beautiful baby in the world to me. All of my babies were beautiful."

I could imagine Mama picking up the hem of her short, cotton nightgown. She'd wipe away the little puddles which formed in the corner of her eyes when she spoke of her children. She loved us unconditionally. I wanted to be just like her when I grew up. For a moment, I felt a wave of sadness at the thought Mama would someday go to heaven. I always hoped I would be first and quickly pushed the thought from my mind.

Long lives Mama! Hear, hear! I thought, and then said,

"Ughh! So, thanks, Mama. I think this story explains why I am so afraid I'll drown every time I get into a swimming pool.

You didn't know it, but I had enrolled in swim classes three different times, but I never got beyond the first day. Once when the swim teacher instructed the class to get into the pool, I froze, and a little pee ran down my legs. One time the water turned blue and I turned a light shade of black cherry. I certainly didn't return on Day Two." Mama and I laughed together.

I made sure Cedric learned how to swim. He started lessons when he was three years old.

It was still early, so I went back to bed for a few more winks of sleep after talking with Mama.

It was a typical cold February day. The sharp winds cut through the trees like a knife. I felt like nothing could go wrong today.

It was the kind of wind Mama warned would snip my hair unless I was wearing a headscarf or hat. When I was younger, I'd leave home with my scarf tied under my chin like a Russian refugee. When Mama was out of sight, off went the headscarf. I thought it was probably just another old wives' tale or a slick way to ward off a winter cold. However, today I grabbed a sporty hat when I went out.

The temperature was around 55 degrees, which felt quite cold to me. The leaves had just begun to turn back to green. The wind softly whistled through the neighborhood. It made small whirlwinds with the fallen brown dried leaves. It was a quiet weekday.

Most people in my apartment complex were at work, or like me, they'd stayed home to enjoy the beautiful start of spring. I stood in my doorway inhaling the fragrant scent of spring flowers and sweet honeysuckle.

I was so happy to be living in my apartment with no roommate. I'd moved up to the eastside to a deluxe apartment in the sky. My heart sang.

When I came back home from New Mexico, we'd stayed with Aunt Bea for about a month. It was a short, pleasant experience. Aunt Bea had advised me to leave Leonard if it didn't work out.

My family had never been the type to stick their noses in another family member's affairs unless asked. However, I was glad I didn't have to inconvenience her very long.

I scanned the room. The only furniture I had was a torn green floral sofa donated by my mother's girlfriend Betty and a double-sized mattress set, which I'd bought at the discount furniture store for a reasonable price. No headboard, just brown metal frame for thirty-five dollars.

"This will do for now," I thought out loud.

It was Cedric's eighth birthday.

I closed the door so Cedric would not wake. Then, I ran the vacuum and mopped the floors with a fragrant cleanser. I could smell the aroma of the homemade biscuits cooking in the oven which I'd prepared earlier. I loved the fresh smell of pine from the cleanser I used. I felt mighty fine on this spring morning in my very own two-bedroom chalet. I sang and danced with the broom as I dusted every inch of my home.

I felt so grateful to be alive and to have peace. "Oh, happy day! When Jesus washed all my sins away," I sang as I stepped back inside and stood in the hallway.

"Oh, Cedric! Sweet Cedric!"

His eyes flickered open from sleep.

"Today is your birthday. I have a surprise. You can stay home from school to celebrate. We're going to play hooky from school and work, and we're going outside to play," I said as I sang a Temptation's song.

"Yaaay! It is my birthday. We're going to play hooky! Am I having a party?" Cedric asked while yawning and stretching.

"Yes. Just you and me, buddy. We will go to the grocer and buy food for your favorite meal."

"Mommy, I love you. Can I tell the kids at school you and I played hooky today?"

"No, Baby, it's our little secret. You can't tell anybody. Okay?"

"Okay, Mommy."

We grabbed our light jackets and my sports hat and headed to the store. Cedric picked his favorite foods—macaroni and cheese and chicken nuggets.

"Mommy, you're going to love my favorite food," he said.

"Yeah, I'll bet you will, too!"

"Yeah, Mommy . . . maybe." Cedric smiled.

When we got to the checkout, Cedric placed the items on the cashier's belt.

"Mommy, can I borrow some money? I'll pay you back when I grow up," he said with a smile.

"No way. It's your birthday and it's on me."

The cashier gave him a birthday high five.

When we returned home, I grabbed Cedric's crayons and I made him a homemade card and gleefully handed it to him.

Then I sang the birthday song.

"Happy birthday to my Cedric. Happy birthday to my Cedric. Happy birthday to my favorite son! And many more."

He smiled the biggest smile I'd ever seen and said, "I'm your only son like Jesus was God's only Son," he said, admiring himself.

He was so full of love.

I thought it was the best birthday celebration a mother could hope for—to spend the day making her baby happy. The cake from his favorite grandmother would come later.

"Hey, buddy, ready to start your birthday dinner?" I asked.

"Yes," he said.

"Okay. You put the water in the pot, and I'll cook it. And bake the nuggets."

Suddenly a knock sounded from the front door

"Who's there?" I asked through the closed door.

"Papa," the voice said.

"It's Peepaw!" Cedric said with a shrill and laughter. He ran to open the door.

"Your mother said she spoke with you earlier and thought you'd be busy, so here's Cedric's cake by Papa's Delivery," he said with a chuckle.

"She didn't have time to bake one. This cake is from the bakery. Their cakes are delicious."

"Thanks so much, Papa," I said softly and looked at the floor.

"Your mother has dinner almost ready. She's not feeling well today, so I have to run right back. I like a hot meal, and she needs me there. Happy Birthday, Cedric. See you later." He lowered his voice so only I could hear. "I see the look of disappointment. She's been complaining a lot about her health lately. You'll love the cake." Papa hugged me.

"Bye, Peepaw."

Cedric called his grandfather Peepaw. The first time he'd said it to my Papa his expression was priceless. Cedric had asked, "Do you like the name I gave you?"

"Sure do!" Peepaw had said at the time. Cedric had looked at me and laughed. I'd all but dropped a lung in laughter.

The stove timer rang.

"Dinner will be ready soon," I said.

"Okay, Mommy," he'd said with a chuckle.

"Dinner is now served to the Birthday Boy! Let's eat," I said.

"The macaroni and cheese smell so good," Cedric said. "Will we eat some of my cake for dessert?"

"Absolutely! You know you are too smart for your good, don't you?"

Cedric smiled. Then he asked, "Is my dad coming?"

I stuttered, suddenly unable to breathe.

"No, I don't think so," I answered after a long pause.

"When you two got a divorce, did I get a divorce, too?" he asked.

"No, Baby," I said. "Your dad loves you very much."

"He never calls me. Maybe I can go and live with him someday."

"Maybe," I said, my heart hurting.

For about half an hour, our forks and spoons tapped and scraped against our plates, along with my classical music—Beethoven—which I always played during dinner. I wanted to make sure Cedric appreciated other kinds of music, not just rap, R&B, and reggae.

We ate our cake together.

"Mommy, this is the best birthday ever."

"Well, you have one more gift," I said happily, pleased he was smiling again. I went to my bedroom, brought out a cardboard pet carrier and opened it. Out walked the cutest white kitten with big blue eyes and a bushy little tail.

Cedric shrieked in delight.

"Is she mine?" he asked as the kitten made a beeline to him.

"Well, it's a he and he's ours. But it looks as if he has picked you."

"I love him. He's going to love us too, Mommy. I will call him Prince."

"You picked a great name. But you must promise to help feed Prince, give him water and love him. And clean his litter box."

"I will, and I already love him, Mommy. He is so beautiful." Cedric gave me a big hug.

"Now, let's do the dishes and get ready for bed."

"Okay, Mommy. I love to wash dishes." Cedric grabbed his stepstool and headed to the sink. I smiled.

I sure hope this love for dishwashing continues.

The day's birthday celebrations eventually came to an end. The leftovers were put away and the kitchen cleaned. We took our baths. The next day's clothes were ironed and laid out. Prince's kitty items were set up in Cedric's room.

Cedric played with Prince for a while and then I read him a bedtime story. That night he prayed for his dad.

" . . . and thank you God my dad will call me sometimes. Amen." I tickled him and said good night. He and Prince curled up together and were both purring.

I stretched out on my soft bed with a good book, but it wasn't long before I turned it down on my chest and began to reminisce about Leonard, wondering how he was doing. I felt lonely. but knew I couldn't turn back the hands of time. I had to be careful who I introduced into Cedric's life, I thought, as the phone rang.

"Hello, Grace. Isn't today Cedric's birthday?"

"Hi, Theresa. I was just wondering if you had forgotten about him after driving me to the hospital the morning he was born."

"Never, my friend. Just a busy day," Theresa said, chuckling.

"What are you doing at this hour?"

"Getting ready for bed. Give Cedric a belated birthday hug and wish in the morning. By the way, did Leonard call him?"

"No," I said.

"I'm sorry for Cedric," she said. "Goodnight, my friend. I'm looking forward to our double date!"

Me too.

TWELVE

I stared out the kitchen window. Dark clouds were forming in the sky, but this time it didn't appear to be over my life. I'd had a happy, normal family life and was feeling resilient. Nothing could hold me down for long.

We don't have much. I'd left it all in New Mexico. It just felt so good to be free and have peace of mind.

That day I reminisced about my childhood and growing up with Mama and Papa and my siblings. Mama was a stay-at-home mom, but she had a part-time job. She restocked greeting cards a couple of days a week at the local pharmacy. Papa was a truck driver who transported cars and other merchandise. He sometimes brought home boxes of items accidentally left on trucks. His boss would give them to him. He brought home purses, toys, and other kinds of goodies. I remembered one time he brought a box of raw almonds.

I ate so many almonds. I learned to love them. They are great for the heart you know.

I also remember how much my parents loved music. I can still picture in my mind a few people at our house, Papa in his black plaid walking shorts, ankle socks, and black leather dress shoes dancing like James Brown. I also remember watching him and Mama dance to slow music, their arms wrapped around each other, exuding the love they had for each other. I would watch from the side of the door until I was spotted. Papa didn't say much. He just gave you the eye. My siblings and I knew what it meant. Mama and Papa seemed to enjoy one another when we had visitors. The kids weren't invited to the party—unless, of course, you could do the latest dance. They would call one of us kids to come in and demonstrate the moves. Most of the time it was me.

"'Grace, get in here and show us how to do the Stanky Legs,'" Papa would say as he laughed. Those were some happy days. I always hoped someday I would find a man just like Papa.

Memories of Mama are the highlight of my young years. She played with her kids all day and nursed them all night if they became ill. I had a fond memory of the time I was sick and had to stay home from school. Mama and I stayed in bed all morning. We watched cartoons.

I'll never forget the plastic pink princess phone Mama gave me when I was sick with the measles. It made me feel loved. There weren't many doctor's office visits unless the kids had pneumonia, scarlet fever, or something serious. Every ailment would run its course, and Mama would treat it with home remedies from homemade cough syrup to cod liver oil. Mama was straight out of Africa. She would use spider webs for cuts and scrapes and salted pork to draw out splinters or shards of glass from a foot or a hand. The ancestors must have been whispering to her.

Dr. Mama was something else. She seemed to think Castor oil healed everything. Surprisingly, most of the time it did. Castor oil was a weekly tonic. Each Monday morning, Mama put us in line from the oldest to youngest to administer a tablespoon-sized dose of Castor oil with a squirt of lemon juice and a personal roll of toilet paper. I shivered at the memory and floated back to the present.

Yeah, and now I have my very own first apartment.
I didn't much mind the lack of furniture in all the rooms, but the roaches—ugh! This was a first.
I'd never had roaches in the countryside. It was both scary and crazy. Nasty little critters! We'd put cotton balls in our ears, say a prayer and go to sleep each night until I got the awful roach problem resolved.

The Bible said God gave Adam authority over all the things that crept and crawled. I figured I must take authority, too. The character in *Gone with the Wind* knew nothing 'bout birthing no babies, and I knew nothing about killing no roaches, but I'd have to learn. I wasn't waking up another morning to find a cockroach parked in my nostril. Off to the hardware store to buy bug spray, traps, roach bombs and an antibiotic. I had to TAKE AUTHORITY over these creepy and crawly things.

I also picked up a few other necessary items such as pots, pans, plates, and drinking glasses at the local Super Walmart. I was starting all over again. It was going to be tough and could be fun, but I knew whatever the situation, I'd make it.

I thought about my job at the retail store and going back to work and class after our day of *playing hooky*. Today, again, I thought of Leonard.

Will I ever get it right?
I smashed a red cockroach running across the wall. "Ugh!!"

THIRTEEN

After dropping Cedric off at school, I went to the local hardware store around the corner and found the right products for my fight, and in time, I got the roach situation under control at the apartment. I wished I could so easily keep away the human pests. Life was good. Cedric and I both were growing up and were no longer sleeping with cotton balls in our ears.

Lord, I took authority, and I have tastefully decorated my place if I say so myself.

I found many inexpensive used items from the local discount hotel store and Secondhand Rose around the corner.
The apartment looked like pictures out of a decorator's magazine, I thought as I was enjoying my second cup of coffee.

"Simply, inexpensively . . . elegant," I said out loud.

"Mama always said I had champagne taste on a beer budget. She was right."

I was finally feeling like my old self, replacing all the items I'd left in New Mexico with new-to-me things. I'd even purchased a second bed and decorated another bedroom. I thought it would encourage Cedric to sleep in his room. However, I'd still awaken each morning with him snuggled next to me.

As I sat at the table writing checks for the monthly bills, I felt grateful for my retail job at Rich Avenues. It provided medical insurance and other benefits for Cedric and me. I was also a part-time student at the local university. I didn't have much time for anyone other than Cedric. It seemed I lived at the library researching and writing papers. I didn't have time to make new friends.

My only friends were Emma and Theresa. However, my dearest friend was Theresa. She told me she had never found the right guy. She was dating this new guy Winston who was an associate pastor at the local church. She appeared relatively happy about their relationship. I had met Winston and I liked him right away but wondered why, after two years, he still wasn't talking marriage with Theresa.

Life was looking up for me. I had my own car. Papa had cosigned for the loan. It was a shiny spitfire orange Volkswagen Golf. Look out, world! Some danger was speeding your way.

I had something to do. Something I believed in. Yet something was missing since my separation from Leonard. No one had to shout it from the mountains. I knew what was missing from the happiness formula. My psychology class spoke directly to me.

Happiness is having something to do. Something to believe in. And having someone to love.

I needed God's help with number three. I'd already struck out once in this arena.

I walked out the front door of my apartment and placed the envelopes in the mailbox, enjoying the morning breeze. It was time to get ready for work. The best thing about the location of my new apartment was it was just four miles away from my parents. My mother took care of Cedric when I needed a sitter, and she also picked him up from the bus stop each day when he started kindergarten. The bus dropped him off on her street and Grandma Mimi got her daily exercise. She jogged out to meet Cedric on the main road when he got off the bus and made his day. He loved Mimi.

Mimi said, "I stand at the bus stop waiting for the bus driver. When the driver opens the doors, I get on one knee. Cedric runs down the steps and falls into my waiting, sweaty, outspread arms".

"Here comes my little honeybunch," she would say to Cedric.

Mimi would talk about how the driver smiled and how the kids stared with their faces pressed against the bus windows, waving at Cedric. He knew he was the envy of every little kid on the bus. They'd walk to her house holding hands. They'd share their day and anything that had occurred at school. They also talked about what had happened at home during the day for Mimi, and, of course, whether she had baked his favorite afterschool snack—white chocolate chip cookies. She shared her worries with Cedric, and he shared his little concerns with her.

Mimi was concerned about one of their conversations and shared it with me.

"How was your day today?" Mimi had asked when he hopped off the bus without his usual pep. He skipped alongside his grandmother, holding her hand tightly.

"It was okay. But I wish I had blue eyes and blond hair," Cedric said, out of breath, in his innocent child way.

"I don't! I love those brown eyes right there," Mimi had responded. She pointed at his eyes and hugged him real tight. She tried to squeeze the idea right out of him. She wanted him to be proud he was a black person. They quietly continued their walk to Mimi's house. Cedric held her hand tightly under his chin. She later called me.

"Thanks, Mama, for telling me this. I'm concerned. Cedric is my eight-year-old baby. What are those blue-eyed kids getting my Cedric isn't?"

When I picked up Cedric from Mimi's, Cedric crawled into the front seat and put on his seatbelt. Then he put his little hand underneath his chin and propped his chin on his knees.

"I'm so worried," he said.

"What are you so worried about?" I asked with a surprised look.

"Well . . . I don't know. Mimi says it all the time. Then I just hold her hand."

I held his little soft hand in mine.

"Mimi said you had something on your mind," I prompted him. "Let's talk about it. What did you tell Mimi today?"

"I told her I wish I had blue eyes and blonde hair."

"Why do you want a different color hair and eyes sweetheart? What's wrong with your black hair and brown eyes?" I asked, my eyes and nostrils burning. "I think your black hair and brown eyes are beautiful—just like mine and your dad's. I like mine just the way they are. Let's talk about this when we get home."

Cedric pulled a book out of his bookbag. The rest of the ride home was made in silence.

As I was driving, I recalled a case I'd had to read in a psychology class. It was the blue-eyed and brown-eyed children experiment. The third-grade teacher Jane Elliott, an anti-racism activist and diversity teacher, created an experiment to show the students how it felt to be a black person. She told them it would be hard to understand unless you experienced it.

She decided to base it on eye color rather than skin color. She gave the blue-eyed children special treatment including extra privileges, second helpings at lunch and additional recess time. She gave the brown-eyed children the opposite. Also, they weren't allowed to drink from the same water fountain.

Both the blue-eyed and brown-eyed children were white. After the experiment, the blue-eyed children became bossy, arrogant, and unpleasant to the brown-eyed children. And the academic performance of the brown-eyed children suffered. The research revealed people who received privilege, no matter what color they were, developed a sense of superiority over others. The sufferers felt inferior. So, what was going on with this teacher? I thought as I pulled in my apartment's driveway.

That evening after our dinner, during our bedtime story, I said,

"Cedric, you are a beautiful brown-eyed, black, curly-haired boy. There are some beautiful, brave, courageous, brown-eyed people in our Black history." Cedric listened intently as I told him about Frederick Douglass, Harriet Tubman and Martin Luther King, Jr. He smiled a big smile.

"So, what did the blue-eyed kid get that you did not get?" I asked Cedric point-blank. I had a finger on speed dial. Tomorrow there would be a meeting with the teacher and principal or the county school board, the President, the FBI, or whatever, based on the answer I got.

"Just hugs, Mommy . . . just hugs," he said. I un-balled my hands and exhaled. The teacher was cleared.

"Let's see what we can do about this." I said as he finished his bath and put on his superhero pajamas.

"Okay. I've got it!" I said. Cedric and I wrestled on his bed.

"Mimi and I promise to give you twenty-six hugs a day. Thirteen from her and thirteen from me. Nobody in your classroom will ever get as many hugs as you. And who else is picked up at the bus stop by a Mimi who waits on one knee?"

"No one! Mommy . . . you and Mimi are the best!" he exclaimed as I tickled his feet.

After that night, I never heard him talk like that ever again. If he had, there would have been a parent and teacher meeting, if necessary.

"Don't mess with Mama Bear's cub in the woods or at school.

Beware!

It was a typical Monday morning at Rich Avenues. Good things were coming my way.

I laughed out loud. *I just felt it in my funny bone*.

Fall had finally come to Greenville. Lots of people were coming and going from Rich Avenues looking for bargains. I looked away from the register. I was assisting one of my regular customers, Ms.

Dupont. My eyes met an extremely handsome gentleman with a warm smile. He stood a few feet from the counter. I looked up and acknowledged him with a smile. He had the most beautiful teeth I had ever seen. I could see little star lights glistening on them.

This fellow could be a successful salesman or do Colgate commercials and could be the perfect father for my next child.

"Sir, I 'll be right with you," I said with a smile.

"Okay. Take your time," he whispered. "I'm not in a big hurry today. I'll browse a bit to see if anything catches my eye."

Other than me, I thought as he swaggered away from the counter toward the ladies' accessories.

"How is little Cedric doing?" Ms. Dupont asked as she cleared her throat to get my attention.

"He turned eight years old and is becoming more inquisitive and handsome every day," I said, trying to stay focused.

"Well, I'll bet he is. Keep taking good care of him. He might have to choose your nursing home someday." She laughed.

"Ms. Dupont, you are something else, and funny. Thank you for your purchase today."

"I just wanted to make you laugh, Grace. I haven't seen that beautiful smile lately. I know you're a good mother. See you and I . . . we're from good stock. I'll see you next time. Handsome fellow over there," she whispered and winked at me.

Ms. Dupont stepped away from the counter and I walked her to the exit. She was my best customer. She donated her wardrobe each year and replaced it with the items from my store. She was my most significant account.

"See you again soon, Ms. Dupont, and I'll call you about any sales."

"Sure thing, Grace. Goodbye."

I then turned my attention to Mr. Unusual. I left the counter to find this good-looking gentleman.

"How can I help you, sir?"

He scanned my blouse, looking for my name tag.

"It's Grace, and welcome to Rich Avenues. Your name Is . . .?"

"Well, Grace, my name is Teddy. I'm looking for the perfect gift for the perfect girl."

"This lady must be special. What does she like, or what kinds of things does she like to do?" I asked inquisitively.

He looked deep into my eyes, a little flirtatiously. "She is let me see ," he said as he paused. "Well, she is just about your height and size. Your skin color, too. You two have a striking resemblance to each other. She is a spiritual friend. I want to buy a little gift to express my appreciation for her friendship. She is a friend who is always there when I need one. However, I don't want her to get the wrong idea and think I want more than her friendship. What do you recommend?"

I noted the relationship was platonic.

"What is her favorite color, or what does she like to do? I have a few special things I can suggest. Follow me. By the way, what is your name again, sir?"

"It's Teddy . . . like Teddy Pendergrass. Not sure of her favorite color, but I know she likes to read novels, and she is a churchgoing lady."

"Nice to meet you, Teddy. I can help you," I smiled and ignored the obvious come on. "Let's see. I've got the perfect, noncommittal gift every churchgoing lady can always use. A lace handkerchief with one initial monogrammed on it. What initial for this special lady?"

"G for Gloria."

"G. Same as mine. G for good." I chuckled as I searched the pile.

"I am the department buyer/manager and I noticed we had plenty in stock yesterday. Here it is." I handed him a gift set of three beautiful delicate white cotton Parisian hankies with a purple G monogrammed in silk threads in one corner.

"I think she will love this . . . I certainly do. I plan to buy one for myself," I said as I walked him to the checkout.

"Thank you for your help. I would have never thought of this on my own. What a lovely gift. Can you gift wrap it?"

"Sure can. Will there be anything else, Mr. Teddy Pendergrass? I asked with nervous laughter as we walked to the checkout.

"No, I think that's it for today."

"Would you like to use your Rich Avenues card today?"

"I don't have a card. I only use cash," he said as he reached for his wallet.

I asked the cashier to finish the transaction, and then I went into the stock room to wrap the box.

"It will take just a moment more. I'll wrap it for you myself," I said as I almost tripped over a display as I walked away.

Teddy chuckled and pretended not to see my nervousness.

I turned a soft shade of black cherry and went to the back room and returned momentarily with the wrapped box, purple paper with a gold bow.

"Great choice for the lady. All wrapped and ready to deliver to a queen," I told him. The cashier bagged it and handed it to him.

Teddy grabbed my hand to thank me and gazed into my eyes for just a moment.

"Come again . . . it was my pleasure to serve you today at Rich Avenues, Mr. Teddy." We both laughed nervously this time.

Well, if I didn't know any better, I think this guy was flirting with me and was sweeping me off my feet with one sweep of the broom. It's been a while since an eligible bachelor paid any attention to me.

I noticed other customers entering the department as Teddy walked toward the exit. There was something special about him. He had the warmest green eyes and was quite charming—and not to mention handsome!

I didn't have time to analyze my feelings. I had other duties waiting for me. When Teddy reached the doorway, he looked back and waved goodbye. Our eyes met. He didn't seem to want to leave, and I didn't want him to go. I smiled and waved to him.

I watched him as he swaggered out of sight.

FOURTEEN

I was still wearing the smile he'd given me. It was finally Thursday evening, and I was both nervous and excited about the double date with Theresa and about meeting Narcissus Bentley Little. However, I couldn't stop thinking about Teddy.

What should I wear?

I pulled several pieces of clothes from the closet to put together the perfect outfit. I didn't want to be too revealing. Neither did I want to look like Mother Teresa.

I eventually started to breathe again and remembered the sheer blouse with matching lacy camisole and pants I'd planned to wear. The night before the date, I had tossed and turned in bed, and I had dark circles under my eyes and couldn't think clearly.

"Why am I so anxious about this date? What was hidden here? It was way more stressful than I'd anticipated. I hadn't been on a date in years, it seemed!

That was it!

I looked in the mirror.

"My bags are packed, and I am going on a double date," I said out loud.

I went to the kitchen and pulled a cucumber out of the vegetable bin of the refrigerator, cut it into slices, put two of them over my eyes, and laid down for an hour. If it worked in Mommy Dearest, it could work for me. Then, I jumped in the shower and got dressed. The cucumbers had a hard job to do, so I dabbed on some extra concealer under my eyes. I stepped back from the mirror and said out loud,

"That's my girl . . . not bad at all." Then I cut a James Brown step. "Hey, Hey, hey! I got the feeling. Well, not yet. Slow it down, sister!"

The doorbell rang. I opened the door and Theresa whisked in, dressed in a plain red pantsuit with a large ladybug brooch on her lapel . . . her usual conservative look.

"What's with the big bug with diamond eyes looking at me from your lapel? I kind of like it, though." I laughed.

"I wear it because Winston gave it to me," she said. "Are you ready to go? The guys are waiting outside in the car. Come on, Girl! I'll let them know you will be right out."

"Good. I'll grab my purse and be out in a moment."

Theresa ran back to the car. I walked past the hallway mirror and admired myself one final time. Then I froze and could not open the door.

Was I ready for another man in my life?

I honestly wasn't sure. I didn't want to be hurt again.

Theresa came back inside.

"Grace, we can't keep the guys waiting. What's wrong?"

"I'm just so scared, Theresa."

Theresa wrapped her arms around my waist and walked with me to the door, locked it, and walked me outside.

"Grace, you can do this. You look so attractive! I love your outfit. Come on. You'll have a great time. Just relax. I promised you I'd be close by. Why aren't you showing those pretty legs?" she whispered with a smile.

I tried to chuckle the butterflies away as I walked like a zombie with Theresa out the door. She was the mother I needed at the moment.

It was dusk. The air was warm. I was wearing the right outfit.

At least, I thought so. *The sun had just hidden behind the clouds, and I was being dragged out of the house on a date by my best friend*.

Then I looked up, and my brown eyes met his light green ones. I saw nothing less than a black Adonis who stared back at me. He was tall, dark, and handsome with an electric smile. He was what I called Denzel chocolate with a head full of shiny black curls. He got out of the car and opened the back door to the passenger side. His black curls moved with every sexy step he took.

I stumbled clumsily into the back seat. I tried to breathe as he gently held my hand.

"Are you okay? You didn't hurt yourself, did you?" he said trying not to laugh, as I slid from the floor up to the back seat. He then reached around my waist to buckle my seatbelt. He smelled so good I just about fainted.

"I couldn't keep my eyes off this man. I couldn't breathe and my heart skipped a thousand beats. He was debonair—I mean debonair, and was dressed in a black double-breasted suit, his nails manicured, wearing "Mack Daddy" shoes and carrying a man bag.

While I was mesmerized, I thought to myself, I have seen this brother before.

Theresa didn't tell me he looked like Denzel with green eyes.

Theresa shouted from the front seat and cleared her throat.

"Grace, this is Narcissus Little."

"Narcissus, it's nice to meet you. And good to see you again, Winston. Long time no see."

"Hey, Grace. Yes. It's been a while. How have you been?"

"Considering all factors, not bad at all. Life is good. How about you?"

"Life is good for me, too!" He winked at Theresa.
Winston left my driveway and pulled his Range Rover onto the main road. Theresa and Winston chatted away in the front seat about their week.

In the back seat, Narcissus was blowing my mind with every word he spoke. He seemed to have it all. Mr. Narcissus Bentley Little!

I dare not show it or keep gaping at him. Thank you, Jesus!

"To start off right, I have a confession," he whispered in a low sexy tenor voice. I came to Rich Avenues last week because I wanted to see you before tonight. So, this is not a real blind date. I cheated. We've seen each other. I told you my name was Teddy, as in Teddy Pendergrass."

"I knew I had seen you before. Yeah, now I remember," I whispered. So many customers come in and out of Rich Avenues, I wasn't sure. So . . . since you don't like surprises . . . I guess I passed the test and didn't turn out to be the fugly duckling after all, huh?" I stared out of the window and laughed.

For a moment I thought, Can I trust this guy?
Well, he had told a little white lie and had been stalking me at work. Everybody does it! Don't get your panties in a wad.
I looked at him and smiled.

"Yes, you did. In flying colors, as a matter of fact. No, I am not a stalker. Sociopaths do that!" Narcissus said. "You were as beautiful to me then as you are now. I can still see you in your red wrap dress. And I wanted to meet you. I had also heard a lot of good things about you from Winston. I have not been able to get you off my mind," he said, as his long lashes seemed to give a mild breeze across my face.

"And no, you are not the fugly duckling. I didn't think anyone else ever used the word," Narcissus said with a sly chuckle.

"It's one of my stepfather's favorites."

I was so mesmerized by his chivalry, charm, and good looks I couldn't hear a word he spoke. He took my breath away. He had an irresistible air about him. I now better understood why Monica

Lewinsky had been taken by President Clinton. But I still wondered why he had lied about who he was when he came to the store. It didn't make much sense to me, but I didn't care, at the moment, whether he was the kind who stalked or wore a wife-beater.

This man is fine, and he has the warmest eyes—of anyone I have ever met.

We arrived at Fat Tuesday, and the parking lot was full. It was Ladies' Night and the place was bustling with fine-looking ladies who got out of cars alone or with their dates. Winston parked the car and we got out and made our way across the parking lot to the large, double-glass doors of the crowded night club.

The place was exquisite. There were also lots of professional athletes in attendance. They towered over Winston and Narcissus, making them look like dwarfs. The ladies were in awe of these seemingly gentle giants. The music was at the right volume to talk, and the red and gold décor was flawless.

And the company was mighty fine.

We started the evening with some refreshments of grilled chicken wings and fruit pieces, each of us chatting with our date and listening to the stream of jazz music.

The single ladies without a date couldn't keep their eyes off Narcissus. I was impressed he didn't seem to notice their flirtatious stares. When an attractive woman looks at some guys, they forget they are with someone else. Not this guy—he was different. Winston escorted Theresa to the dance floor. She seemed so happy. I watched them dance and the way they meshed into one person on slow songs. They had a blast.

So, she is going to help me through the date. She's got her eyes on Winston.

I was happy to see her having fun, however. Lord knows she deserved it after kissing so many toads in her past. Things were going okay right now for both of us.

"So . . . Narcissus. What do you do for a living?" I asked after taking a bite of pineapple slice.

"I'm a former FBI special agent. And before you ask, I am recently divorced. I am free and clear." He smiled. "We didn't have any children together. I have a couple of goddaughters I see from time to time. Now, I'm retired. I moved away from Tennessee, so I don't get to see them much anymore. Right before my employer asked whether I would take a position in this region, there was an accident on the job, and I was injured and hospitalized for three months. My wife left me. I moved to get away from it all and started a new life," he said as he twisted his hands together.

"My goddaughters are the daughters of two very close high school buddies. My friends thought if anything happened to them, their daughters would be in good hands and financially taken care of. I am honored, I guess. My side gig has always been computer repair. I haven't made many new friends yet, so I spend a lot of time alone watching TV or working. Most weekends, I take trips to visit my family back home in Tennessee.

"I've gone out with a few ladies. Hmm . . . let me see, what else? Oh yeah. When I decided to relocate to this area, I moved in with Winston until I could find a place of my own. What about you, Grace?"

"Well, first, what an exciting career you've had. Wow, you worked for the federal government. My job is not quite as exciting. I am a departmental sales manager/buyer for the Rich Avenues department store, as you well know." I chuckled. "It's a high-end retail store in Greenville. The pay is good. I'm also in college pursuing a master's degree in psychology. I am a new divorcee, single parent with one eight-year-old son named Cedric. I enjoy church, physical exercise, good books and spending time with my son, my siblings, and my parents when I am not in class. Classes, study and library research take a lot of my free time."

I took another bite of fruit, observing to see whether Narcissus' body language matched his words. I'd always believed success and honesty were apparent when words, thoughts and actions were in alignment. Otherwise, your life was nothing more than a little white lie. I picked up the goblet of wine.

"What about you . . . are you a churchgoer?" I asked to confirm what Theresa had told me earlier.

"Yes. I attend every Sunday, and once a month I get the men together on Saturdays for the monthly men's ministry. I guess I can say I have been in church all my life. My mother took my two sisters and me to church three time a year on Mother's Day, Easter and on Christmas Eve. She made us read the Bible daily and go to Bible study every Wednesday night. We had to pray before meals and get on our knees for bedtime prayer every night. Sometimes we prayed one-knee prayers, and some required two knees," he chuckled.

I couldn't detect any sign he was a liar. He didn't blink his eyes. He didn't look away—you know those signs the internet articles tell you to look for to spot a liar.

"You're a mess. I love the church, too!" I beamed. "Your story sounds a lot like mine."

My papa is an associate pastor in the church and took the family to church or made us go to church every Sunday. And my sisters and I would go with him when the pastor would get invitations for Sunday evening services. The truth is I was so churched when I left my papa's house, I didn't plan ever to attend another church. Well, the idea never took hold. When I moved away from home, I missed a few Sundays and was miserable. So here I am today, a church lady."

Narcissus stared at me.

What was with this?

He appeared to be looking right through me.

"What's the matter? You're staring at me."

And scaring me at the same time.

"Oh, sorry. I've just never met any women quite like you since I've been in this area. Forgive me. It just seems to me most ladies I meet are looking for someone to take care of them and their children, have on yards of hair weave, dresses or blouses split to their navels, stretch pants whether they are a size two or twenty and are chasing after me like crazy. I'm old fashioned. I like to do the chasing. I like a lady with an element of surprise. I would fit right into the Victorian era when women wore ankle-length dresses. You seem to be more that type," he said as he looked down and ate his chicken.

"You don't hog the conversation talking about yourself, either. You seem to genuinely care about others. You are a pretty lady."

I blushed a light shade of black cherry and said,

"Why thank you sir.

"What's the status of those ladies you've gone out with?" I asked assertively, waiting anxiously for his reply.

"Nothing serious . . . just phone conversations mostly," he said.

Winston and Theresa approached the table with sweaty clothes and hair. They were laughing.

"Are you two going to bust a move tonight?" Winston asked.

"I don't dance much," said Narcissus.

"I like to dance, but I'm with Narcissus and we're enjoying some good conversation. However, it is getting late and tomorrow is a workday for me. I've also got to pick up my son, who has school tomorrow, from Mama's house."

"I heard you talk about your kid at the store. I love kids. A son, right? How old is he?"

"He just turned eight years old. And I'm sure Cedric is waiting by the door for me like our cat, Prince, when we come home."

"I'll bet you are a good mother. And you are a cat lover. A cat named Prince. I'll bet he's unusual," he said doing an impression of Prince, The Artist.

"That's good," I said.

"Well, I don't like pets much myself," he continued.

"I love both cats and children," I said. *Hm! a man who doesn't like cats. What do you think of that? Nothing. Heck I don't like Iguanas! And I'm okay.*

"Yep guys, I have be at the church early tomorrow and Theresa has to be at school, too. Guys let's call it a night and do this again real soon," Winston said.

We left Fat Tuesday and headed to the car. Theresa and Winston walked together. They giggled and chatted like two teenagers. Narcissus and I walked several feet behind. We talked about the evening.

"I enjoyed tonight and meeting you, Grace. It feels as if I've known you before."

"Me too," I said.

Narcissus stared at me as though he wondered whether I was telling the truth. The ride home was quiet as we listened to 80's music on the radio.

When we arrived at my apartment, Winston and Theresa said their goodbyes to me and Narcissus walked with me to my door.

"Have a good night, Grace. Be careful picking up your son," he said as we stood outside the door.

"Yes. I will. Thank you for a nice evening. Goodnight, my little stalking Teddy Bear, I mean, Narcissus?"

"Of course," he said with a twinkle in his eye and a wink. Narcissus leaned toward me, almost touching my lips, and stared into my eyes.

"I am not a stalker. Remember, only sociopaths do that," he whispered, his voice husky.

I extended my hand to shake his and placed a folded slip of paper in his palm.

"Okay. Tonight, I end the joke forever. I didn't mean to offend you. Good night Narcissus." I unlocked my door and quickly disappeared inside, closed my eyes and leaned my head against the door.

Oh, what a man. Yes, I know he has gone on dates with other women. And he stalked me in a friendly way. But he's a keeper. There's just something about him. Yes, I just gave him my number. Theresa said he is always home alone. As my Papa would say, "Whatever is supposed to happen, you can't stop it."

I swirled around laughing out loud.

Theresa told me when Narcissus returned to the car, he unfolded the slip of paper and used his cell phone light to read the note.

She said he slowly crawled into the back seat, positioned his long legs and smiled at Winston through the rearview mirror.

"Well, Narcissus . . . will you see each other again?" Winston asked reaching over the car seat to bump fists with Narcissus. "Yeah, man. It's a green light!"

Theresa said she smiled and winked at Winston.

Narcissus and Winston dropped Theresa off. Now, I imagined they rode in silence but had a lot to talk about when they arrived back at Winston's house according to what Theresa told me later. She said Winston told her everything except the part where women were involved. When they arrived, they both had plopped down on the sofa as Winston kicked off his slip ons.

"Did you tell her you dropped by the store to see what she looks like."

"Yes, I did. I did not want to start deceptively."

"Well . . . you will also need to let her know you are not 30. Theresa told her you are 30 years old because she likes older men. And I told Theresa you worked with the men at the church."

"What? Okay. I will fix that lie in time, too. I would be angry with you, Player, but it worked. She gave me her number. I will continue to come to the meetings, so I won't look like a complete liar."

"When will you call her?" Winston asked picking up his shoes.

"Don't want to appear too desperate. I will wait a week or so."

"Alright Player, you don't want to wait long, or you might go wrong . . . Pastor Reynolds told me once and he was right." Winston laughed out loud, walking away.

"Grace's ex-husband hurt her. Theresa told me tonight she had to push to get her to go on the date. So, no slick games, okay.

I know you. You can come across as Mr. Perfect, but you know I've seen you 'rock 'em and drop 'em.' Grace is the kind of girl you take home to meet the parents and family. Behave, Narcissus Bentley Little!"

"I got this Player. Don't be sounding like my mother. It sounds to me anyway, like the pot is calling the kettle black. Remember when you use to pick 'em up and put 'em down when you were a hotshot youth pastor. Remember the girl whose heart you broke, and she had a mental breakdown?" said Narcissus, slightly irritated.

"What girl? Good night Narcissus." Winston said as he walked to his bedroom, yawning.

"Yeah, I knew you'd get amnesia."

"Player, don't forget we both have shameful dirt on our shirts." Narcissus shouted.

"All right let's put the past behind us," said Winston. "Where are you going at this time of night anyway?"

"To get something else to eat. The fruit and wings did not do the trick for me. It was just enough to make me angry. See you later." Narcissus walked toward the front door.

"Well, why did you try and eat like a bird, when you know you are a pig? I'm just saying" as he laughed.

"I had to be a man of class with this woman. But now, I need some thighs and legs," he laughed.

"Boy, you are never going to change. Are you?"

"Does a zebra change its stripes?" said Narcissus as he sneered.

Winston shook his head as he heard gravel crackling, as Narcissus backed out of the driveway.

I smiled and walked out the door, got into my car and took the short drive to pick up Cedric at Mama's house.

I couldn't stop thinking about the evening and my first date with Mr. Narcissus Little.

He was so fine. I tell you.

Narcissus seemed like a nice guy. I liked him. Cedric might like him, too. He never hears from Leonard, and he needs a strong male role model around.

I might give Narcissus a try if he's as interested as I am. I don't want to get too arrogant and beside myself. There are a lot of pretty girls in this town. *Essence* magazine says there are about seven women to every man in this part of the country.
But you're not every woman. You're a woman of God. You're the apple of God's eye. *Yes I am. And He thinks I am special.*

I laughed out loud as the porch light popped on as I pulled into my parent's driveway. Mama stood at the door, holding the screen open as Cedric walked down the steps to the car.

"Night-night, Mimi!" He yawned and threw her a kiss.
I backed my car out of the yard. There was a strange car parked across the street with parking lights on. It looked like a Hummer. I'd never seen it parked there before.

"I hope that person doesn't leave their lights on all night, Cedric."

"Me, too, Mommy," Cedric said as he reclined in his car seat and dropped off to sleep.

My cell phone rang just as I buckled up.

"Hey Theresa!"

"Well. Are you glad you came out tonight without reading those nine pages?" she said with a chuckle.

"I really like him. And you could be a little more well-read yourself."

"I knew you'd like him. You deserve to meet a live man instead of fictional characters," she said.

"And I have to read a lot of academic material," I told her. "That's why novel reading is limited to nine pages."

"Okay nine pages! Have a good night, Grace. By the way, I told Winston you don't do booty calls."

"Girl, you're crazy! Good night."

"Mommy, what is a booty call?" Cedric asked as he sat up in the front seat and yawned.

"It's a sound you make in the woods to call bears. Here Booty, Booty."

"Mommy, I don't believe that. I heard the kids talk about it at school," he said and laughed. All I could do was blush.

It had been two weeks since my double date with Theresa and Winston. I was now pacing back and forth like a caged animal in my house.

Perhaps Narcissus decided I didn't pass the test after all. Maybe I'd talked too much. Okay . . . You win some and lose some. Maybe it was because of my young child. Some men can't deal with another man's child and the possibility of the ex-husband coming around. And some mothers encouraged their sons not to date a divorced woman. Maybe it was my voice. My voice is raspy like Lauren Bacall and sounds a bit authoritative. I was feeling crazy insecurity. One guy had once told me I acted like a man. That idiot would not recognize confidence if I had smacked him in the face."

The phone rang as I got into my car.

"Hello?"

"Hello, is this Grace? It's Narcissus Little."

"Why, Narcissus Bentley Little . . . I thought of you last week. Long-time no hear." I winked at myself in the rearview mirror as I pulled the seat belt around me.

"I wanted to give you time to marinate about me and decide whether you wanted to see me again. I knew from the night we met I was interested in getting to know you better. So, I gave you space to be sure you felt the same way."

"I did have to give this quite a bit of consideration, but I think it would be nice to go out for dinner and do some other things together," I winked again at myself.

"Okay. It's a deal. Let's plan a get together soon. I'll call you this weekend," he said.

"All right. Talk soon. Goodbye, Narcissus." I hit the door lock zipped off to work.

"I still have scoop-ability after all," I said to myself as I hummed, "Somewhere over the rainbow, way up high, there's a land that I heard of once in a lullaby."

Whew! I knew I'd hear from him. I'll admit I was a tiny bit nervous he had not called. Okay, more than a little bit. Hey! Lighten up on yourself. Men have hurt you in the past.

I pulled onto the main road.

It's going to be a brighter day.

FIFTEEN

It was Saturday morning and I was still in bed. My morning breath warmed my pillow and made me frown at the same time. I needed my mouth wash, but it was hard to roll out of bed. Oprah Winfrey had once said, "There is nothing like those 600-count sheets." She was right. I had found a new, unopened set at my favorite thrift store. They felt so good. I didn't want to get out of bed.

The phone rang. It was Narcissus showing on the caller ID. I just watched it for a few rings. I couldn't believe someone like Narcissus was calling on me.

"Good morning Grace, how would you like to go on a picnic to Pastel Park today? I had my five-mile jog this morning. The sun felt good on my face, and the warm breeze was exhilarating. Today's weather is perfect for a picnic. Cedric is welcome to come along as well."

"Sounds good. Today's my day off from work and school. However, Cedric is spending the day with his Auntie Sylvia. He'll have to take a raincheck. Besides, I'd like for us to get to know one another a little better first. You know how it is with kids. When their parents get divorced, they're always looking for a father or mother to replace the absent one. They fall in love with you quickly if they like you. Then, if it doesn't work out with their mom and that person, their little hearts get broken, too. I must protect my son. Let's wait a while before the two of you meet, okay? But I appreciate you inviting him," I replied as I squirmed deeper into my soft bed.

"Okay. I understand. I just want you to know I see this as a package deal. I'm not like other guys."

I listened to Narcissus with disbelief. What did he say? This guy was reeling me in like carp, and he didn't even know it. Or did he? I thought he must be different.

"I like the way you think. Some guys want only the woman and not her children. One of my coworkers told me about the horrible experience she had. Apparently her boyfriend went into a fit of rage over something minute her son had . . . . "

My voice cracked and trailed off at the memory. He . . . he threw her son out of the window of a high-rise building. The boy died on impact, breaking every bone in his little body. It was in the news. It happened in a town in Georgia, I believe."

"Wow. I'm sorry to hear this. That's terrible," Narcissus said.

"It's good to hear you'd take the package and the challenge. I believe you mean it," I said. "If anyone ever laid a finger on my Cedric, I'd kill them with my bare hands! Lock them in a room, handcuff them to the bed and break both of their feet. I'd hammer toothpicks under their toenails and then intubate them with the straw from a can of installation foam. I'd slowly press the valve and laugh as it expanded and pushed out of his eyes, ears, and mouth."

Narcissus made a surprised sound as I continued. I wasn't sounding much like the Christian girl he'd gotten to know at Fat Tuesday. And I didn't want to. I was sending him a message, loud and clear.

"Then, I'd decapitate him with a chain saw, put his head on a stick, pour gas on it and burn it."

"Well, okay, Grace. I get it."

"Oh, there's more," I said. I wanted to make sure Narcissus did not ever think about putting his hands on my Cedric.

"Then I'd throw the blackened corpse in an alligator pond. I'd watch the gator death roll the torso in a pool of bloody water until it ate every piece of his evil body."

"It's okay, Grace. Take a deep breath," he said with a weak chuckle. "Cedric will be okay. He'd be in good hands with me."

I held the phone to my face and stared off into the distance like a psychopath. I meant every word. It was just a moment of sheer insanity.

"Grace are you still there?" he asked.

"Yes," I said.

"You don't appear to be the violent type. I just know you love this boy. I wish all mothers loved half as much, even my own," Narcissus said.

"Sorry, I digressed," I said as I wiped my eyes. "I know you'd never mistreat my son. Cedric is my pride and joy. God entrusted his life to me. Forgive me for temporary loss of sanity. I've got a few errands to run. Can we meet in Pastel Park at around noon?" I asked as I sprang from my bed.

"We sure can," he said, sounding as if he was still in shock.

"Great. See you there. By the way, I'll put together a picnic basket. I hope you like chicken. I'll get some chicken nuggets, potato salad, diet soda and chocolate cream pie. How does this sound? I have this cool picnic basket with a shoulder strap I've been waiting to find a reason to use. It even has a side compartment for a bottle of wine. I'd been saving the basket for a special occasion." I knew my voice smiled. I'd gotten my point across.

"Okay, it's a date. Don't pack the wine. I'll bring two, chilled mini bottles of pink sparkling Moscato. Okay?"

"Yes. Of course. I believe drinking wine is okay in moderation. I learned French women drink it at every meal. And the Germans, too. One of my friends is German. She's been drinking wine since she was old enough to hold a sippy cup." I laughed out loud. "And Moscato is my favorite. How did you know?"

"A little birdie told me," he said. *I did not know at the time he had already bugged my phone.*

Narcissus and I met at the park at noon. I spread out a red and black checkered picnic blanket and arranged the food, cutlery and wine glasses. Narcissus opened my wine bottle, then his. He was the perfect gentleman.

"Oh, what a beautiful day. The air smells fresh and the sun feels so good beaming on my face," I said as I leaned back on my elbows, staring at the clear blue sky.

Narcissus nodded in agreement while also bathing himself in the sun's rays.

"Yes, it is. And I brought you something." Narcissus handed me the box I'd wrapped for him at the store as he squinted in the warm sunshine. I opened it as though I didn't know what was inside.

"Thank you, Narcissus, I said as I carefully unwrapped the box. "Hankies with my initial. How did you know I'd like these?" We both laughed out loud. Then, I made a plate up and handed it to him.

"Narcissus, tell me about you, your childhood, your family and where you grew up."

"Not much to tell. I'm from a family of five. I have two sisters. I grew up in a small town. Didn't know many people. We weren't allowed to play with other kids in our neighborhood. I was a very naughty little boy. Once, I accidentally killed my neighbor's puppy.

"My stepfather would lock us in the attic for punishment." He shrugged. "I'm sure we deserved it. After the puppy incident, my parents took me to a psychiatrist, and they put me on medication. I grew out of it. I'll tell you more as I know you better. But I'm okay."

"I'm glad to hear that. However, you killed a puppy? How did it happen?" I said knowing things from Psychology training about this behavior. He averted his eyes.

"Grace, it was just an accident. I was just a stupid kid. Can we just let it go?"

"Okay Narcissus, I muttered. ADHD seemed to be the diagnosis of most of the kids of our generation. Two of my siblings have it," I said still thinking there was more to the puppy killing.

"Actually, I don't remember what the doctor called what I used to have," he said, changing the subject. I quickly put on a fake smile as he continued.

"My mother is a chef. My real dad died in an accident and my stepfather is a businessman. I love my family. Oh, yeah ... I told you I had been married and it didn't last. My wife left me. I told you about my marriage when we first met. I don't like to talk too much about the past. I'd rather keep my focus on this brown cinnamon sugar sitting in front of me," he said as he stared at me with a sexy Elvis Presley smile and I blushed. *What was the big deal about killing the puppy? When I was younger, I 'd put frogs in a box and stone them.*

"I'm from a family of six—two sons and two daughters," I said still blushing. "We grew up in the country. I'm a true Southern Belle. I pumped water from a spigot. I think I was the only person in my class without running water. Papa preferred living as if he were in the wilderness. He had grown up on a farm. He loved the country life and wanted his children to experience it as he had." Won't mention the outhouse!

"We had huge black pigs and white chickens and lived in a small four-room bungalow.

"One of the many special memories is Easter. Our parents always bought each of us a baby chick. And, yes, we ended up eating our pet chicks for dinner. We'd cry. Papa thought nothing of it. He'd ring their little necks. They'd hop around and then fall over. Now that was funny. However, the next time we saw our baby chick was on a platter next to some hot biscuits and gravy," I laughed.

"We also didn't have electricity. Unbelievable, isn't it? We used oil lamps at night. If I'm ever without electricity, I know I can survive. We didn't have much, but we learned principles. That's how my Papa wanted his kids raised," I said, smiling as if I was okay with it.

"My mother taught the girls three rules: 1) Keep your dress down, 2) Don't give men money, and 3) Don't let your boyfriend drive your car. She meant it, too!"

"I can believe the oil lamps," Narcissus said. "And, okay, I'll never ask to drive your car. But would she be okay with me giving you one?"

I didn't know what to say, so I paused and eventually said, "Maybe."

"Let me tell you about my papa," I continued. "He took us to church on Sundays. He instilled in his children a belief in God. Papa was a farmer and Mama was a stay-at-home mom, and she worked part time. All of us can plant a garden and clean a house. We'll never be hungry or have dirty homes. The things we lacked in our possessions, we bridged with love. I love my family. We gather for the holidays including Thanksgiving and Christmas. And birthday celebrations are the highlight of my life.

"My mom still bakes cakes for our birthdays and always gives us Christmas gifts, after all these years. We didn't have much, but God provided for us, and we were never hungry."

"Amen!"

"You know, Narcissus, I believe every experience we've had or will have is the hand of God preparing us for our destinies. Some situations heal us, and some of them are prerequisite life training for what lies ahead."

"Well, I believe that, too. I really like you. I certainly imagine you're going to be famous someday. I can tell. And I want to be a part of it."

Narcissus looked away, then changed the subject.

"Grace, I'm a little hungry. I didn't have much for breakfast. In all honesty, I saved my appetite for this picnic lunch with you. Pretty Lady, what you got in the pretty basket?"

"I changed our menu a little. I packed chicken sandwiches, homemade potato salad, and mini key lime pies instead of chocolate pie."

"Yum, Yum. Let's say grace and feed our face." Narcissus bowed his head. "God is great, God is good. Now we thank Him for our food . . . "

I peeked at him through one closed eyelid. I couldn't believe what I was hearing. A grown man was reciting a child's prayer. Don't judge. Do not judge him. At least he can pray. And the prayer was so sweet, sincere, and from his heart. Poor fellow.

I still wanted to laugh out loud because I remembered Theresa said I needed a man who could touch heaven.

He didn't know why I was smiling when he said, "Amen." Behave Grace.

We turned on some music and enjoyed our picnic.

"By the way, the picnic food is delicious. I see you got your mother's culinary gifts," he said sweetly.

Narcissus was staring at me again and was quiet. I got quiet, too.

"Did I say something wrong?" I asked hesitantly.

"No. I just like you. You can express yourself. You're not ashamed or embarrassed about your childhood. Most of us would never tell that stuff."

"The Bible tells us not to despise small beginnings. And besides . . . it's my history why lie about it. And, it has been said if you forget the past, you are certain to repeat it. Don't want that to happen, now do we?"

We finished eating. I packed up the basket and we laid on the checkered mat and enjoyed the warm breeze and quietness in the park. Then Narcissus reached in his pocket and took out a lighter and a homemade cigarette, lit it, and inhaled. He blew smoke circles up into the sky. He was not only handsome but talented!

"Have a puff?" he asked.

"No, thank you," I said. "I no longer smoke weed. Tried it during my teenage years. All grown up now."

"Well, I still do. It helps me to relax, and the doctor said it would heal my eye condition," he said.

"Cops come out here a lot. You might want to extinguish that. I'd hate to go to jail with you when I didn't even get high. And aren't you too young to have an eye-condition?" I asked.
Narcissus laughed and avoided the question.

"Isn't marijuana legal in our state?" he asked.

"I don't think so, not even for medicinal reasons."

"Didn't know," Narcissus said without making eye contact.

I would have never thought Narcissus smoked pot.

The real Narcissus was began to peep from behind the curtain.

SIXTEEN

Narcissus and I spent hours gazing into each other eyes. We found peace and enjoyment with one another. We seemed to have a lot in common. He'd said we were soulmates. Well, except I didn't smoke pot. So what? I drank wine. However, we both enjoyed our families, shopping and traveling. We also spent a lot of time together talking about the Bible. We'd have long discussions about my favorite novels. I visited his church and met his pastor. We met weekly for lunches, dinners and sometimes for breakfast.

Breakfast was our favorite meal of the day. Both of our parents believed in feeding their kids like royalty.

We often joked that we were King's kids. I was Duchess Grace, raised by a mother who prepared very elaborate meals. She would serve delicious fried chicken gizzards, smothered steak and gravy and always crunchy, hot buttered homemade buttermilk biscuits. Warm cane syrup and hot biscuits were a favorite staple at the Smith breakfast table most mornings.
And still is.

Your Grace Narcissus' mother is a chef, so his breakfast meals were nothing to sneeze at. His mother had often prepared salmon croquettes and grits for breakfast as well as liver and onions, and sometimes homemade pancakes and country ham with homemade syrup.

The meals at the Little and Smith homes were nothing short of royal.

We discovered we both loved visiting the museum, going to plays, hearing the orchestra and eating at nice restaurants. Narcissus liked an excellent action film and a tasty Chinese restaurant meal. My favorites were a good love story and a barbecue.

Narcissus once asked me how I knew which barbecue was good.

"I don't know, but Papa said the flies do. It's where the flies are buzzing," I said, almost embarrassed I believed the tale. Flies liked stinky stuff and sweet stuff.

Narcissus and I were also opposites in many ways. I'd often heard opposites attract but don't stay together. I was determined to change that old wives' tale.

Before long we were starry-eyed about each other. Narcissus was always staring at me. When I'd catch him, he still blushed and looked away. He was shy and so cute.

On one of our outings, Narcissus asked, "Grace, how is Cedric? You talk about him so much and of all the things you do together. You read him stories at bedtime. You sew his clothes or at least I think you told me you made him some little pajamas. I wish more mothers were like you. You love your son. I wish my mother had been more like you. And I will never forget what you said you'd do if anyone hurt him. Ouch!" Narcissus laughed.

"Yep. I do. Cedric's father doesn't stay in touch with him, so I must be both Mom and Dad. I have to protect him as a father would."

"I could be a dad to him. I'd protect both of you. We should talk about marriage. When can I meet him?" he asked as my heart skipped a beat.

"You know, I thought just the other day it might be time for you two to meet. He's been talking about wanting to go to an amusement park, which sounds like the perfect place for you to meet for the first time. He'd love it and would love you for taking him there! Now as to marriage . . . I'm not quite ready to go there yet. Let's take one step at a time. I like you a lot. But you're moving just a little too fast."

"I know you're the one for me," he replied jauntily.

"The day I first saw you, I said to myself, 'she is going to be my wife someday.'"

I smiled and blushed a light shade of black cherry and swallowed the lump in my throat.

SEVENTEEN

Cedric was in his room playing with Prince. I hoped he was ready for the angel I was about to bring into his life.

"Hey Cedric, I have a new friend I want you to meet. He's a nice guy. His name is Narcissus Bentley Little. He's kind to me, and I like him a lot. I think you'll like him, too! He wants to take us to Midland Amusement Park. I know you've wanted to go there forever," I said, sticking my head in the doorway of his room.

"Okay. Yaay!" Cedric responded and rolled over the floor holding Prince. "Midland, where the roller coaster is gigantic and high, and the bumper cars are fast. And we can eat lots of cotton candy, funnel cake and hotdogs!"

"Yeah, man! Do you think you would like to go there?" I asked.

"Yep," he chirped.

"Okay. We'll plan to go tomorrow, so you'd better get some sleep tonight. You don't want to fall asleep on the roller coaster."

"Mommy, I would never fall asleep on the roller coaster. You're just trying to get me to go to bed."

"Aren't you the genius in the room again?"

"I'm pretty smart. Right, Mommy? Do you think I'm smarter than Narcissus?" Cedric asked as he pushed his toy truck but waited for my response.

"Mommy, am I cuter than Narcissus? You won't ever like him more than me, will you?" he asked.

"Yes, you're smart for a boy your age. And yes, you're the cutest man in my life," I said as I got on my knees next to him and tickled him. "And no, I won't ever like him more than you. Why, you're my favorite son!"

"I am your only son. You always say that Mommy." He said as he rolled on the floor.

"Now, who's my favorite son?"

"I am. I am. I am," Cedric replied, fiercely laughing as I tickled his feet. Then he asked, "Mom, how do you know he's nice?"

"I just know. Don't let the bed bugs bite," I said as I picked him up and tucked him in bed.

Good question Kiddo. Good question.

It was Saturday, and Narcissus rang my doorbell. When I opened the door, he was holding a giant black and white Panda teddy bear with a big red bowtie. He pecked me on the lips and then pressed the bear's paw, causing it to speak.

"Hello Cedric, my name is Yung the Panda. Nice to meet you. Let's play?"

Cedric ran to the door eyes as big as saucers. Neither of us had ever seen a three-foot teddy bear. Narcissus had it custom made and monogrammed with Cedric's name on its vest and a special recording box inside. Both the bear and Narcissus were a big hit. He knew precisely how to win Cedric over. He seemed to be a master at it.

The way to a man's heart is through his belly. However, the way to a woman's heart is through her child.

We had a great time at the amusement park. Narcissus took Cedric on the roller coaster four times and bought him cotton candy, a hotdog, and a funnel cake. They became fast friends, it seemed. I was a wee bit jealous. However, I, too, had fallen for Narcissus. After the park, all Cedric talked about was Narcissus, Narcissus, and Narcissus.

The end of the week came quickly. Narcissus had planned to go out of town to visit his family. Cedric and I were going shopping. When Narcissus stopped by to say goodbye, he reached in his pocket and gave us two hundred dollars to spend. It was difficult to believe someone could have so much money and be so generous. No one had ever given me so much.

On Saturday morning, Cedric and I were on our way to the shopping mall. We had created a car game we loved to play. We would judge who could unscramble the quickest road signs read backwards. Each person had ten seconds. Cedric was a genius at the game. When it was his turn, he looked behind us to read the next street sign, but he got distracted.

"Mommy . . . Narcissus is in the car behind us," he said.

"No, Baby, it can't be him. He had to go out of town yesterday. Do you remember he came by and said goodbye?"

"Mommy, it's him. Look in the rearview mirror."

I looked in the mirror. I could see two men in the car behind us, but the man sitting in the passenger's seat was sitting so low I couldn't tell who he was.

"I don't think it's him, honey. It doesn't look like him to me. Now, what's the next sign?"

"Mommy, I promise you, it's him," Cedric said adamantly as he continued to look backwards.

"It couldn't be him, Cedric, sweetheart. I have to focus on safe driving. Narcissus called me from his mother's house this morning," I said as the next sign approached.

"Niotpeced Street!" I said quickly.

"Deception Street," he said shrilly. "What is deception Mom? Is that a word?"

"Yes. Someone gives you information to hide the truth or is outright lying," I commented.

"Why did Narcissus do that, Mommy?" he asked as he raised his shoulders.

I didn't know what to say, which was why I'd called out the street we passed. I'd never known Cedric to lie. Maybe that's what kids his age did to get attention. I was just a Mom. I didn't know everything.

EIGHTEEN

Theresa greeted me with a hug at lunch at our favorite restaurant.

"Grace, how are things going? Girl, I haven't heard anything from you in months," she said as we entered the restaurant.

"What's going on? Since you dropped me, I assumed you were spending all your free time with Narcissus. At least, that's what I hear from Winston. He says Narcissus likes you and is talking about settling down. What does Cedric think about all of this?"

"How many for lunch?" asked the hostess.

"Two. And we both want the lunch special," I said. She seated us in our favorite booth, and we continued our conversation.

"Girl I haven't dropped you. Stop talking like that. Just busy with life. Cedric seemed to like Narcissus at first, but he also appears to be showing some jealousy and wariness. Whenever we're out together and holding hands, Cedric pulls our hands apart and walks between us or sits between us. If we sit someplace, whether at the movies or home on the sofa, he squeezes between us. And the other day I heard him singing a song in his room."

"I don't like Narcissus. He is no superhero. He told my Mama a lie. He'll make people cry."
I walked into the room and he stopped and innocently waved at me.

"Hey, Mommy."

Theresa leaned toward me in confidence. "What did you say, Grace?"

"Nothing. I didn't know what to say, so I laughed."

"But here's something strange. Narcissus went out of town one weekend. We were driving to the shopping mall and Cedric swore he was in a car behind us. I guess he's at the age that kids tell lies for whatever reason."

"I think it's normal behavior for sons," Theresa said. "He's just trying to protect his Mom. I don't think it's anything to worry about."

"You've been spending so much time with Narcissus I didn't know what was going on. I thought you had forgotten about me," Theresa said with a smile.

"I'm sorry you feel this way, Theresa. Narcissus wants to spend every waking moment with me," I explained. "I don't have any time for my friends or family. Narcissus even took us to Disneyland in California. Girl, he paid for everything. He's spoiling me. He wouldn't let me pay for anything. And yes, we had two hotel rooms right next door to each other.

"Something awful happened during the trip, though. Narcissus called my room and asked me to come to his room one night after I had put Cedric to bed.

"I said, 'No Narcissus. I shouldn't leave Cedric alone.' He assured me we were right next door, and he would be fine. We would be able to hear him. He convinced me to come. We drank wine and listened to music.

"When I got back to my room, Cedric was gone, and the door had been swung open. I almost had a heart attack. I called the front desk. Cedric had awakened and was wandering around the hotel. Security said they found him near the pool catching lightning bugs. They had tried to call me, but I didn't have my cell with me. It was in my room. I felt like the worst mother in North America. Something terrible could have happened to my son and I wouldn't have ever been able to forgive myself. Maybe something did happen to him. I will never know. If I'd known, someone would have had to die. I don't know what possessed me to leave him alone.

"When we got back to the room , Narcissus said, "He's safe now, Grace. Forgive yourself and let it go."

"I couldn't. Sometimes I have bouts of guilt that flood my soul along with this other feeling. I sometimes feel smothered by Narcissus. We're together a lot, it seems. He's at my place almost every day. I tolerate it because he's an excellent provider for Cedric and me. Narcissus has been talking about marriage, too, but I'm afraid and I don't even know why," I said as I picked over my lunch.

"You won't believe what he bought me for my birthday this year," I continued. "Narcissus surprised me with an expensive golf cart with a gold trim package. I was so surprised and happy but definitely skeptical."

"Girl, he must love you," Theresa exclaimed. "You accepted it, right?"

"Yes, I did, and I kept it in my apartment garage. But I keep thinking of my mama's warning to me. 'Ain't nothing free, baby'."

"Just a few weeks ago, I closed on my first house and we moved out of the apartment. You won't even believe what else I'm about to tell you.

"The real estate agent told me at the closing an Angel Donor had paid my two thousand dollar closing costs. Narcissus says it wasn't him. I only told him I was thinking about buying a house. I said Cedric needed to know the experience of living in a home with a yard. Narcissus agreed. He rented the truck and helped us move out of the apartment. At the end of the day, I just don't know about him," I said as I took the last bite from my fork.

"Girl, he sounds like a saint to me. Winston hasn't offered me a thing. When we go out, it's Dutch. He also gets angry if I even mention getting engaged. Lately, I've been wondering whether Winston is seeing his ex-wife. He's never in town during the holidays. I've been spending my holidays alone or with my family.

"I think you better grab Narcissus. Ha! Ninety thousand women are waiting in line for a man like him. He loves you. He loves your son. He's handsome. He's wealthy. He loves the Lord. I hope you know there aren't many spiritual men around. He's got a good retirement income and a lucrative side gig—what more is there to know?

"Now, I've got to get back to work. Girl, if you don't want him, I'll take him. Winston gets a rash when I even say the word marriage," she said as she laid her money on the table, gave me a quick hug and walked away. "Keep me posted, honey. We'll talk soon."

I just sat there alone in the restaurant for a long time, thinking over what she had just said. Theresa was right. Narcissus was a wonderful man and Cedric would have to grow to love him. Afterall, he's the best man I'd ever dated.

NINETEEN

My money is always safe here. The tellers are fine, too," he said. I was chatting with Narcissus on my cell phone as he pulled his red pickup truck to the drive-through window of Howard B & T Bank.

"Grace, hold on a sec while I make a deposit," he said.

"Sure," I responded.

"Hello Mr. Little, how can I help you today, Mr. Good-looking?" The teller flirted as she opened the intercom.

"Hey, Helena! Just a deposit, as usual."

I heard the vacuuming sound of the capsule as it was sucked through the shoot.

"Wow, Mr. Little," the bank teller had said. "You're making a large deposit today. Have you thought about using our financial services? You could be making money on your money and other services," the teller said.

"Really," said Narcissus.

"When I send your receipt, I'll also send you a phone number. I am inviting you to a meeting on Wednesday night. You're just the type of person we'd like to join our organization. Bring five thousand dollars in cash to get started," she said.

"Okay," he said.

Wow. That sounded flirtatious. I'm not the only woman who thinks he's fine.

"Grace, I'll call you later," he said and hung up before I could say another word.

Two days later, Narcissus was driving me home after our dinner date. Before reaching my house, he said he had forgotten he was supposed to meet with the teller. We stopped by her home. He asked me to stay in the car. It was 10pm.

"Stay in the car? Why?

"This won't take long," he said as he walked away from the car without answering.

He rang the doorbell.

Why would the bank be having a business meeting at the teller's house?

A woman came to the door. She was dressed in beautiful red lingerie. Narcissus never looked back. He walked through the door like an ox led to the slaughterhouse. I stewed in the car reading email messages and the news.

He came out of the teller's house two hours later. He said he'd invested five thousand dollars and they would to meet again.

"Until I see a return on my investment, he reasoned, "I keep my friends close . . . and my enemies closer.'"

I was staring at him like he was crazy. Because he thought I was crazy.

"Narcissus!" The woman was in her lingerie.

"No, she wasn't," he said sarcastically and deflecting. "It was just fancy lounging clothes. Like ladies wear to keep their men in their corrals."

"Narcissus what just happened in there?" I asked.

"Nothing Grace. I thought you were different. I never thought you'd be the jealous type," he said raising his voice.

"I'm not, Narcissus." I said lowering my voice.

"I know what I'm doing, you just have to trust me. I am doing this for us—me, you and Cedric."

"Okay, " I said on the verge of tears." I trust you." I was skeptical but I believed him.

Narcissus drove me home. It was 12:15am.

"How was your day?" He asked with a wide yawn as he turned into my driveway. "Whew! I had a long day," he admired himself in the rear-view mirror."

"Really?" I said groggily. "You'd better head on home and get some rest then."

"Sorry to keep you out so late. I love you. Good night Grace," he replied, smacking my lips with another yawn.

"I love you, too. Drive safely," I said.

"Good night, my sweet love," he said as smooth as silk.

TWENTY

What the heck. Bungee jump! Take the plunge!
I heard those words one morning. You only live once, right? If the cable snaps, you'll survive. It has snapped before. I may never find another man like Narcissus. Cedric would grow up and move away some day, and I would be left alone.

After the talk with myself, I caved and agreed to marry Narcissus.

Narcissus came to the house for breakfast with Cedric and me. We were eating our eggs and toast and I said, "You know the question you asked me the other day? I'm ready to get married.

"Let's do it," I said.
Both he and Cedric looked surprised as they took their seats at the breakfast table.

"Well, good. I found the perfect engagement ring a few weeks ago. I was waiting for you to come to your senses," Narcissus said proudly, flashing a big smile.

"I'm going to put a two-carat ring on it. Oh! Oh! Ohh! I already picked it out. I'll take you to the jeweler so you can try it on," he said. He walked around the side of the table to hug me.

"My ring?" I said.

"Yes, your engagement ring. It's a two-carat heart-shaped diamond. You're the girl of my dreams. I had already picked it out for the woman I'd marry. I told you it was you I planned to marry. Remember? I told you in the park."

Cedric's mouth was open with food in it and he was looking from me to Narcissus.

"Don't chew with your mouth open sweetheart," I gently reprimanded.

"Wait a minute, Narcissus. I'm grateful for the ring, but I thought we could pick it out together. After all, I have to like it, too. And I haven't even met your family yet. How do you know your parents will even like me? Let's see a counselor for premarital counseling."

"I already told them all about you and Cedric and my plans. No need to worry. You'll love the ring, and they will love you," he said, then took a sip of orange juice.

"Now, here's some money. Stop worrying about nothing. Go shopping and get some things for you and Cedric. I'm taking you to meet my family next weekend."

"Thank you, Narcissus. Money is short this month, and I need to get some back-to-school clothes for Cedric," I said.

He handed me a wad of the rolled bills in front of Cedric and picked up his coat to leave.

"Thank you so much," said Cedric as he stared at Narcissus.

"Yep, buddy! Only the best for you and your mommy."

"Grace," he paused. "Also schedule the appointment with the counselor. I'll go with you." He winked with that glistening smile that always left me weak at the knees.

Narcissus's phone beeped. He glanced at the caller ID. He smiled. Threw a kiss as he stepped outside the door.

I opened and counted the wad of bills. There were five crisp one-hundred-dollar bills.

"Not charge! It's cash today!" I shouted in a singsong voice. "Come on, Cedric. Put your shoes on. Mommy is taking you shopping after school. You'll be the best-dressed kid at school next year!"

"Mommy, are you happy to get married?" Cedric asked as he slowly pushed his chair under the table.

"Yes." I said. "How about you?"

"It's okay, Mommy. Narcissus likes me better than Daddy does."

He finished tying his shoelaces, picked up his book bag and headed for the bus.

"Aren't you going to give your mommy a hug?" I said.

"You have Narcissus for that now," he said.

Theresa had said to give Cedric time. He would come around. I sure hope so. What happens if he doesn't come around?

I scheduled an appointment with the counselor for the following day.

Narcissus and I rode in his car to the counselor. We were mostly silent on the short trip. We arrived at a two-story white house in an upper middle-class neighborhood. Narcissus walked up the steps and rang the doorbell. The sign on the door read, Welcome ! Come On In and Take A Seat. I Will Be Right With You.

When we walked through the door, a strong odor immediately hit my nose. It smelled like some sort of chemical.

"Narcissus, what is the strange smell?" I whispered.

"Smells like cocaine," Narcissus said quickly, to my shock and surprise.

"We don't have to do this. We can leave right now if you want to," I said.

Shortly afterward, an attractive woman came to greet us and led us to another room where she conducted her counseling sessions.

"My name is Dr. Willow Sherry. You must be Narcissus and Grace. Please have a seat."

She left the room. When she was ready for our session, she asked whether she could speak with us individually first then as a couple. I left the counseling room and allowed Narcissus to talk first.

"Wow. Your session was quick." I said, smiling as I rose to take my turn with Dr. Sherry.

"Yep. Short-n-sweet," he said, returning my smile.

The counselor invited me in. She looked as if something was wrong.

"Grace, there's no reason for us to continue with future sessions. Your fiancé says there's no problem, and he doesn't think he needs counseling," she said. "Good luck. If anything changes, you can always reschedule. Feel free to call me in the future if should ever need counseling for yourself."

"Thanks," I said, "Oh well. He'd be the head of the house. I guess he didn't think we needed this, yet he had agreed to come. I wished he'd said something to me before we'd bother visiting."

Dr. Sherry did not respond.

She walked Narcissus and me to the door and said goodbye and then quickly closed the door.

As we walked the down the steps, Narcissus muttered under his breath, "Crackhead."

I didn't know what to say. I certainly knew nothing about crack, but evidently Narcissus did. He'd joke in the future about how I took him to a "crackhead" counselor.

"You're the reason I don't like counselors," he'd often say to embarrass me.

W*hy had he agreed to the counseling, then sabotaged it?*

TWENTY-ONE
Two Weeks Later

Cedric and I crawled into Narcissus's car and rode home with him to meet his family. I was a little nervous and wanted to make a good impression. I hoped they would like Cedric and me. I hoped we liked them.

We took the two-hour scenic drive to his parent's house. The sun was out. It was a nice day to be on the road. Everyone was quiet and just enjoying the ride and the music. Narcissus passed every car in front of him on the road. I read a book. Cedric had on his headphones and sang out loud. Narcissus glanced in the rearview mirror and chuckled.

When we pulled into the front yard of the little family home, Narcissus' stepfather rushed down the steps to meet us at the car. He was a warm and friendly man. He was tall, dark and handsome and wore cowboy boots.

"Hello, you must be Grace, my daughter-in-law to be. Pretty, too! And this handsome young man must be Cedric. I've heard so much about you two. So nice to finally meet you. We had begun to think Narcissus was lying about you."

Narcissus snorted and shook his head.

I reached out to shake the stepfather's hand.

"No handshaking around these parts. We're family. I'm Bernie." He grabbed me and hugged me tightly, almost lifting me from the ground. He was southern hospitality at its best. I noted where Narcissus had gotten his outgoing nature.

Narcissus' mother watched from the kitchen window. When I went inside the house, she approached me slowly using her apron to wipe her hands and said, "Nice to meet you. You're a pretty girl. I see why Narcissus talks a lot about you," she said as she extended her hand, not knowing how pretty she was.

As I looked at her, I saw Narcissus' cautious side.

"Hey, young man! "A long trip for you, wasn't it? I'll bet you could use some milk and chocolate chip cookies," she said, smiling at Cedric.

"Yes, ma'am, I could," Cedric replied. "But I don't like sour milk."

I gave Cedric a stern look. I was embarrassed. Now my mother-in-law-to-be would think I gave my child spoiled milk.

"Thank you, Cedric, for helping me make a great first impression," I said, rolling my eyes at him.

She chuckled but appeared to enjoy my embarrassment.

"Kids say the darndest things, don't they? Grace, have you seen the show?"

"Yes, ma'am. I need to let Cedric audition. He's a natural."

"Well, I raised three children, and I've heard them say a lot of crazy things. One time we visited one of my cousins. She was serving broccoli. Narcissus, who, by the way, hates broccoli, tried to eat it all and asked for seconds. I was so embarrassed. He didn't care everyone else hadn't yet had their first serving. He put all of the broccoli on his plate when they passed the bowl to him and smiled as he put the bowl back on the serving carousel."

Narcissus frowned at his mother and walked out of the kitchen door with his stepfather.

"Rachel, when are you going to stop telling this story? Let your son be a man," Mr. Little said as he and Narcissus walked into the back yard.

I found it easy to fall in love with Narcissus' parents. Narcissus' mom and I went grocery shopping and prepared a meal together, and we chatted for hours about our families. I made a comment about two women cooking in the same kitchen, that it did not usually work out.

"They can get along if they are two nice people," Narcissus' mother reassured me.

"Yes, ma'am, I agree," I said.

After dinner, as we sat in the living room that faced a stairway. I suddenly remembered Narcissus' unbelievable tale of being locked in the attic. Then, I heard the door open, and one of Narcissus's sisters walked in. She said, "Hey 'Evil One,' when did you get home?"

I didn't hear much else of what they said to each other. I was stuck on why this younger sister was mean and disrespectful to my future husband and her older brother.

She eventually said, "Narcissus, who is this beautiful lady? Aren't you going to introduce me?" She sneered at me.

"This is my fiancée Grace. Grace, this is my sister, Serena."

"Nice to meet you," I said kindly.

"Yeah, right. Me, too," Serena said. "So, you got yourself one of those city girls? Can she cook and mow the grass?"

"Yes, she can mow the grass, bake homemade biscuits, and she went to college."

"However, I have never picked cotton," I said sarcastically.

"What about you? You seem to have strong fingers," I asked. Serena rolled her eyes at me and smiled.

"Serena, this is my son Cedric."

"Hey, Miss Serena," Cedric said. "I'm eating cookies."

"Good little boy. My mama makes the best cookies around."

"Not better than my mommy. She makes the best cookies in the whole wide world," said Cedric as he grinned stretching his arms wide.

Everyone laughed.

"Got to go, or I will be late for work. Nice to meet you, Grace, and little Cedric. See you later. Tequila's got to work today. Narcissus' favorite sister. Bye y'all. Grace, remember Mama and my stepfather created this scalawag," said Serena laughing.

She quickly left.

"Well, you certainly shut her up. She'll respect you from now on. Serena always has to try people to see what she can get away with," said Narcissus' stepfather.

It's getting late and we have to go back home," said Narcissus.

"What's your hurry?" Bernie asked.

"Work and school," we said together.

Narcissus' mother invited me to the kitchen. We packed the food she was sending back with Narcissus. She caught my eye.

"I was a little nervous about meeting you when Narcissus told me you were a city girl. I thought you'd be uppity and all. But you're down to earth like me."

"Yep. Grace will be good for Narcissus and the family," his father chimed in from the living room.

"Did Narcissus tell you I adopted them and gave them my name?" Bernie asked.

"Maybe you'll get to meet his sister next time. Tequila is more mature. They were some bad children, every one of them," Bernie said and laughed.

I didn't know what to say. I glanced at Narcissus. He stared at the TV.

"Hey, Ms. Little, could I get a copy of your blackberry cobbler recipe? It is the best I've ever eaten," I said with a smile, hoping she wouldn't resist. However, she stepped close to me and whispered in my ear as I packed each bowl into our takeout box.

"Grace, around these parts, all a woman has is her recipe. We don't share."

"Okay. You got jokes. So now you have to cook it for me every time I come to visit," I said looking at her and thinking what a rude woman she was.

"I know I sound rude and I'm not joking. Ask any woman from this neck of the woods. Nobody shares. I don't mind having it for you when you come again. I love to cook."

We loaded the car with the food and said our goodbyes.

As the car left the driveway, I thought of Narcissus' parents. They were good people. But Ms. Little hadn't been joking. She hadn't even smiled when she'd said, "All a woman has in these parts is her recipe."

I didn't understand the comment about the recipe and could never figure it out.

But I knew, however the apple never fell far from the tree. I liked them. I knew we'd all get along just fine. The visit to meet Mom and Stepdad Little brought much-needed confirmation. The wedding was a go. Mr. Little was nothing like the story Narcissus had told me. Narcissus gave one final wave to his parents as they stood on the porch and we hit the highway.

I messaged Theresa from the car to tell her the good news, but she didn't immediately respond.

I was going to marry Narcissus Bentley Little without anyone's approval. I probably wouldn't ever find anyone else like him. Finally, Theresa returned a thumbs-up emoji. Her response was so encouraging, just when I needed it.

TWENTY-TWO

My, how time passes when you're having fun! Cedric was ten years old when Narcissus and I eventually went to the Justice of Peace and got married. It was the happiest day I'd seen in a long time. Cedric was the bride's guy.

Narcissus wanted to honeymoon in Greece rather than waste money on a wedding. It was beautiful. We sailed the Grecian Isles. I got excited when our tour guide pointed to the uninhabited island of Patmos, where John the Divine of the Bible's New Testament received his revelation. It reminded me of my dream and how God still speaks to people today.

After we returned from our honeymoon, Cedric and I moved to Narcissus' house. It was much bigger than ours and had an inground pool. There was no way he would've moved to my small place. Emma had suggested we find another house together. However, I told her I could handle my own business.

I moved from my house. I reluctantly gave away items and furnishings Narcissus said we didn't need to bring to his house. He already had furniture in all the rooms at his home. We never discussed how to merge households by the time Narcissus sent the movers to clear out my house.

Later, I would learn he gave away some of my things to the movers and put other items in the dumpster. I noticed items missing as I settled into the house. When I'd asked Narcissus about the missing items, he'd said, "I gave them to the movers. You didn't need them. You can buy new things."

I was shocked. He'd done this without asking and I wasn't happy about the discovery. However, I kept silent. I didn't want to make waves.

One man's junk is another man's treasure.

I gritted my teeth and swallowed my pride.

However, if this doesn't last, I'll have to start over—with nothing.

Well, I quickly squashed my negative thought, because breaking up was not an option for either one of us. Narcissus had previously proclaimed one night as we lay in bed, "We are in this thing together for a lifetime, Grace."

I agreed wholeheartedly and we bumped fists. As I smiled in the dark about this magnificent creature.

Life couldn't have been any better. Narcissus was always gifting me with cards and cash. He sent roses to me at work for no reason at all. Every birthday I'd get a special birthday cake as Mama had done. Narcissus was simply divine. I was the envy of my coworkers.

Cedric got lots of presents too. Gifts made him happier about living at Narcissus's house. I had never met anyone so generous, other than my parents at Christmastime. He was too good to be true.

When we celebrated our first Christmas as a family, Narcissus gave me fifteen hundred dollars to spend and many other gifts. He out gave my parents. He gifted Cedric a video game, a BB gun and cash to open his first savings account. I had to tell him to stop spoiling the boy.

Cedric and I gave him gifts, too. He was always respectful and thanked us. However, he never seemed too excited about what he got. It seemed he enjoyed giving gifts far more than receiving them.

Narcissus gave Prince gifts, too—little stocking filled with all kinds of cat toys. Prince even liked him. It was so cute. But when Narcissus wasn't in a good mood, he'd say, "Get away from me cat." Then the cat would show him its belly, as if to say, "You don't like me, but I still like you, meow!" Prince knew.

It was January. The holiday was over. It was my best Christmas ever. Things were getting back to normal. On this morning, Narcissus and I were enjoying our morning coffee together.

"Narcissus, this morning I was thinking about what you told me about your dad and how he treated you when you were little. Do you think about those times much anymore?"

"What are you talking about? My stepfather was great. I never told you any crap about him. Have a good day." He walked out the door.

I was sure Narcissus had told me the story. He now denied it, or he'd forgotten he told me and was now embarrassed about it. Or had he made it up? Or was I the crazy one?

Narcissus seemed to be the perfect mate. He was thoughtful. Everyone in the family loved him. He even offered to drive Cedric to school some mornings when I went in early to work or had morning classes. However, Cedric's jealous feelings about Narcissus were growing. Overall, though, they seemed to get along well. Mama said the jealousy was normal.

It was Monday morning, and I was getting ready for work. My fantasy world would get its first crack. I left Cedric in bed. Narcissus would begin driving him to school. I was so glad to have his help.

When I arrived at work, I called Cedric.

"Cedric, it's time to get up. Narcissus is driving you to school at 8am. You'd better get ready. Okay? Your clothes are laid out for you. Your food is ready. All you must do is pour milk in the bowl and eat your cereal and grab a banana from the bowl on the table. Don't make him wait."

"Okay, Mommy."

We hung up.

I called again a little later and the phone rang several times.

"Hello?" Cedric finally answered groggily.

"Boy, you'd better get out of the bed right now," I whispered harshly.

"I like it better when you drive me to school," Cedric said. I could picture his pouty lips.

"Boy I will come through this phone," I warned.

"Okay, Mommy." He hung up the phone and rushed to get ready. He was tying his sneakers and barely had time left to eat breakfast. He heard two loud knocks at his bedroom door before it opened. Cedric told me later what had happened.

"Are you ready?" Narcissus asked angrily.

"Yes, sir. I am."

"Well, don't stand there looking at me. You don't look ready. Tuck in your shirttail. Comb your hair and grab your bag. I have to go. Did you eat breakfast?"

"No, sir."

"Well, you don't have time now."

Cedric said he slowly tucked in his shirt, took his time to comb his hair and walked in slow motion to his desk to get his bag.

By then, Narcissus was steaming with anger.

They closed the door and got into Narcissus' truck. Narcissus slammed the door.

Cedric's head was down and twisting a button on his shirt.

"I wish Mommy could drive me to school."

Narcissus said, "Don't you ever slam my truck door again! And I wish she could drive you, too. However, she can't, and I'm going to drive you to help her out as much as I hate doing it. You'll like it. And you best not ever tell anybody I said it. I will hurt you and your Mommy. Now be a man, Cedric," Narcissus said as Cedric cried.

Narcissus then reached under the seat and pulled out a tree branch and struck Cedric several times on his legs.

"Shut your pie hole! I kept this in here just for you. I knew you would eventually start to smell yourself."

"You aren't my father!" Cedric shouted.

Narcissus hit him again.

"I know I'm not, and I'm glad. When's the last time you seen him?" he asked. "Yeah, that's what I thought."

When they reached the school. Cedric reached for the door handle and looked at Narcissus.

"I will tell Mommy about this, Narcissus," he said before jumping out of the truck. He slammed the door and ran into the school. Narcissus was steaming!

In the evening when I arrived home from work, Cedric said, "Mom, I have to tell you a secret." He was doing his homework on the kitchen table and I was preparing dinner.

"Okay, Cedric, what is it baby?" I asked.

"What happened was . . . when Narcissus drove me to school this morning, he was very angry with me. I don't know why. He hit me with a stick he had on the floor of the truck, and I told him he was hurting me. And I said, 'You're not my father.' Mommy, Narcissus is not nice to me anymore like he is to you. He doesn't like me very much, and I don't like him either. Sometimes he rolls his eyes or makes faces when you're not looking," Cedric said.

"He hit you with a stick?" I demanded, "Why are you making up this story about Narcissus, as good as he has been to us? Who do you think bought those expensive Yeezy sneakers and paid the tuition for a private school? I certainly couldn't afford them. Now you stop telling lies this instant," I said, visibly upset.

Cedric got quiet. He looked out the window.

"I'm not lying," he whimpered. I saw him wipe tears from his eyes.

While I didn't want to believe Cedric, I did, and I never forgot what he said.

❀❀❀

A few days after Cedric had told me what happened, Narcissus came home late. He had been drinking. I could smell it on him.

"Did Cedric tell you what happened?" he asked.

"Yes, he did," I said without looking at him.

"Well, he sassed me, so I whipped him because I didn't want him to turn out like me," said Narcissus. We had never discussed how Cedric would be disciplined. I was shocked by what I heard. But I said nothing.

"Turn out like you? What do you mean?" I asked.

"I never told you the story about my real dad. He was meaner than a water moccasin. He was worse than Bernie. Mama could sure pick them. He had green eyes just like me. Oh! How I loved that man. He used to play with me. Taught me to fish. He had a bizarre relationship with my sisters, though. They were not his. They told me he always hugged them too tight. When I became older, I learned he had a dark side.

"My mom and my sisters and I worked in the garden. One day my dad called my sister to come inside. After a while, my sister, Tequila screamed. I ran into the house. Dad's pants were around his ankles. Blood was all over my sister's little white shorts. I walked to the nightstand and I took out his 45 he kept in the drawer. I squeezed the trigger and I shot him. Point blank. Boom!

"My mother ran into the house screaming and she grabbed the gun out of my hand.

"Narcissus, what have you done, child? He was your father!" she'd screamed.

"I didn't mean to do it," I said almost chuckling.

"But I knew full well what I had done—no more screams from my sister. It felt just like it had when I'd killed the puppy. Dad would no longer be dirty. The puppy was dirty, and he was dirty, too. I had finally figured out how to help Mom make it stop.

I stood in the doorway balling as my mother and my sisters rolled his body in a quilt. Blood was seeping through to the outside of the quilt. Mom backed the car up to the front step. He was too heavy to lift, so they rolled his body down the wooden steps into the trunk of the car. Mom looked at me with tears in her eyes and said, "Narcissus, I want you to pretend this never happened. Now, go put up the hoe and come back to the kitchen to eat your dinner with your sisters. She quickly hopped into the car and sped out of our yard. I watched the car until it disappeared down the highway. The three of us siblings sat quietly and ate our dinners. My sisters hummed and I cried. Mom returned later and sat at the table and stared into space.

After my daddy left, I cried all the time. It happened whenever I thought about what I had done to make daddy go away.

"You must promise not to tell anyone. I could go to jail," Narcissus said.

"I promise honey," I said reluctantly.

Narcissus fell to the floor and vomited, and I helped him to our bed.

Was this Leonard all over again? I couldn't quite tell the difference.

Now how would hitting Cedric with a stick keep him from turning out like him? What had I gotten myself into? I thought out loud as I closed the door to the bedroom.

"Mommy, I told you he was bad." Cedric said, startling me as he peered from behind the open door. He had overheard the entire conversation. All I could do was stare at him.

"Mommy, I won't ever tell anyone either Narcissus is evil to the core," he said.

Out of the mouths of babes. More and more of the real Narcissus was seeping out.

TWENTY-THREE

In the spring of the year, I finally graduated from college with my master's degree, and Cedric graduated from high school. Mama was so happy for both of us. Cedric decided to go away to college. He planned to study Architectural Engineering.

I reached out to Leonard to tell him about Cedric's graduation from high school. He said he would come. He did. Cedric wasn't too excited, however, about his dad coming to his graduation. He had not heard from him in practically a decade.

"Mom, I don't know him. Not like I know Narcissus," he said.

"I know, but you have two fathers who love you. Some teens don't even have one. One had to love you and the other one chose to love you."

"Well, I don't feel a lot of love from either."

I didn't know what to say.

"You've graduated from high school. I'm so proud of you and I love you. We're going to celebrate big! You, my favorite son, are going on a 15-day trip to Egypt."

One evening at dinner, Narcissus offered to pay for the trip and continually bragged to everyone about it. It was his graduation gift to Cedric. Leonard would not be able to top that gift.

Nonetheless, after graduation, Narcissus had started to say negative things to me about my son. He also always set a strict curfew and wanted to know his whereabouts. Cedric stayed away from home as much as he could.

Narcissus found something wrong with just about everyone around him, especially me. He had changed. Cedric had lost respect for him over the years. I was glad Cedric was going away to college and he'd get to go to Africa with his friends. I certainly didn't want to see a scene from the movie Baby Boy at the house. I would have to deliver on the promise I'd made when we first met. Point blank. I laughed a little.

There was nothing Narcissus Little could ever say to make me give up on my son. I often reminded him of one of the quotes I lived by as it related to raising my son by Johann Wolfgang Goethe: Treat a man as he is, and he will remain as he is. Treat a man as he can be, he will become the man he should be.

"Nice quote. It sounds good in theory," Narcissus had said. "But is it true? I don't believe it is. Sometimes, you have to be cruel to get your message across to children."

Cedric wasn't a child anymore. I stared at Narcissus and remained quiet. I had begun to fear my husband and did not ever seem to be able to win an argument with him.

TWENTY-FOUR

Narcissus continued to be extremely generous with me. The one thing he didn't seem to be able to give, however, was Narcissus. He just kept giving me everything but him, and yet I just wanted him. Even as he began to stay away from home more and more, he also kept silent most of the time at home unless he spoke about work. He knew his gifts kept me obligated to him. He seemed happier since Cedric left home.

At Christmastime, it was just the two of us. Narcissus gave me a pair of expensive Lucchese boots and perfume. We often dressed alike, wearing matching boots and color-coordinated outfits. We were the neighborhood's power couple. While he was never home, however, there was no doubt in my mind I was loved and adored. Narcissus even said people were envious of us.

Since Cedric had been out of the house, we'd often send him a card and cash. Most years, Cedric spent Christmas with his friends. I wanted to spend Christmas with him during his school breaks. There was, however, no opportunity for me to create a holiday tradition that would include Cedric. Narcissus controlled our holiday plans and never thought to include Cedric's wishes nor mine. I was brainwashed and fearful. I stopped questioning him after a while or trying to stand up to him. Besides, I was a submissive wife. I was doing my duty.

Narcissus had changed. He was not much fun to be around, but I was determined to make our marriage work. I saw him transform from an angel of light into Lucifer. I had once believed he was a genuinely honest and loving and worth all my attention. I was now staring at the shell of the person in which I'd fallen in love. I did not want to believe I had been the buyer who was deceived into to paying top dollar for a knock-off Gucci bag.

One day, I thought I'd surprise Narcissus. When he came home from work, I had put a trail of red candles and red rose petals on the floor, creating a path to his queen lying in our jacuzzi tub. I had cooked his favorite meal, pan-seared salmon, baked potato, a tossed salad and Crème Brule. His favorite music was streaming over the sound system.

I thought it was dope!

"Grace, what are you doing? You're going to burn the house down," he griped when he entered the house and walked through the house frowning. He turned on the lights and turned off the music.

"Get out of the tub and fix my plate," he snapped as he sniffed the air and blew out candles..

I slipped out of the tub. I dried myself and put on my sexiest robe, then walked into the kitchen. The house was clean. My hair and nails were banging. However, I felt as low as a spider. Still, I tried to make a conversation with Narcissus, who appeared unable to perceive I was trying to make him notice me.

"Hey, Narcissus. I spoke with Cedric today." I said.

"Does he need money?" he asked, his voice dripping sarcasm. "He needs to get a job. Is he failing in college?"

"No, no, he's doing fine," I tried to say without cracking.
At that moment I hated him.

Narcissus grew more negative and distant with each passing year. He increasingly gave me the silent treatment and threw very few words my way. I would be envious when we were around other people. He was so talkative and friendly. I wondered if I needed to learn sign language since he would become a deaf-mute when alone with me.

He often took weekend trips with "the boys" to go skeet shooting. He would give me spending money and leave me alone to entertain myself. He didn't think it was his responsibility to be a companion to me or to be my date. Since he was rarely home, no one called from his side of the family nor mine anymore.

"They're just all jealous," he'd say to me when I'd express concern about it.

I was confused. He seemed to treat other people and both our family members better than he did me and Cedric. I couldn't figure out what I had done wrong. He was annoyed by anything I did, whether it was the meals I prepared, or the house, my hair, or something I'd say to a relative or stranger. He said it was my fault when any misunderstanding took place with anybody.

He was angry all the time—well, except when he wanted me to run an errand, be his arm candy at an event or visit his relatives. At those times he was as sweet as honey. When he was kind, he was charming. When he was nasty, he seemed evil. I walked on thin ice all the time. I never knew what to say to him.

Oh, I'm sorry. I forgot I only exist to you when you need something, I often said to myself. I was too afraid to tell him so.

One day, as I made myself a hot cup of tea and sat by the window staring into the back yard, I suddenly remembered something Cedric had told me when he was younger. "Maybe he'd been telling the truth," I thought out loud.

Mommy, Narcissus, hit me with a stick.

At the time, I hadn't believed my child was telling the truth about someone who had been so good to us. It had to be a childish lie. I found it hard to believe even when Narcissus admitted to me he had hit Cedric. On that regretful day, my response had probably broke Cedric's little heart. I wanted to scream. Now, it was clear. I understood why his sister Serena called him "The Evil One."

Evil was no longer peeping from behind the curtain. It was standing on center stage with a pitch fork!

TWENTY-FIVE

I arrived to work at the store. It was a warm summer Monday morning and a day to be optimistic about everything. I rolled down my car window as I left my driveway. The sound the birds made was melodic and uplifted my heavy spirit. I decided to focus on work instead of Narcissus.

I had learned a few days previous a new chief officer was finally coming to Rich Avenues. His first stop would be my department. I was the longest-tenured department manager. The district manager's directive was for me was to introduce him to staff and show him the ropes until he acclimated to his new role as store manager.

When I arrived in the parking lot, I noticed a tall, handsome dark-haired man approaching me. He entered the building at the same time I did. I wondered whether he was the new boss. He approached me and extended his hand to greet me.

"Good morning, my name is Joe Earley. I'm the new store manager. Today is my first day."

"Good morning. I'm Grace Little."

"So, you're the one who will show me the ropes and introduce me to all the department managers."

"Yes. The DM called me on Friday to tell me you would be here this morning and told me to be your right hand literally to get you started. First, I'll show you to your office," I said, walking with him to the executive suite.

"Well, young lady, you and I are going to be working very closely the next few months. Let's start my orientation at 9 am," he suggested with authority while smiling widely.

I took my purse to my office, grabbed two cups of my favorite brewed coffee from the breakroom and hurried back to Mr. Earley's office.

"I hope you like regular coffee," I said as I handed the cup to him.

Mr. Earley took a sip of his piping hot coffee.

"Yes, and hot! Thank you. Please take a seat," he said. "Let me first tell you a little about myself, and then I want to hear more about you and your career with Rich Avenues. I have been with Rich Avenues since I was a teenager. I'm in line to become a senior district manager over the northern region of South Carolina. I'm married and have twin sons Nathan and Nathaniel and my wife's name is Pauline. What about you?"

"I've been with Rich Avenues for about eight years. About a year ago, I became a manager. I, too, am married and have one son. My husband's name is Narcissus, and he's a former FBI special agent. Since retiring, he hasn't been able to sit still and does computer work as his side gig . . . it's almost as if he's still an agent. My son Is Cedric, and he's away at college studying architectural engineering."

I don't know why I was always protecting Narcissus. I never told anyone he was disabled. My perfect husband certainly would not want my boss to know.

"I know you're proud of him. Listen, I've heard a lot of good things about you, Grace, and it's nice to meet you, finally."

I noticed he was staring at my boots—and looking at me from head to toe. Awkward.

"Nice looking pair of western boots you're wearing. I see we both have something in common. I love western boots, too. A cowboy at heart."

"Thank you, Mr. Earley. Me too . . . a cowgirl, I mean! They were a Christmas gift to me."

"You can call me Joe. Let's plan to meet again after lunch today."

"Okay," I said shyly and left his office.

"Hey Grace," I heard a woman's voice as I turned into my work area.

"I understand you'll be working closely with the new store manager. You know I am so happy for you," said Megan. "However, I've been at this company longer than you. I don't understand why I wasn't asked to work with him."

I looked at Megan, who was petite with large yellow front teeth that looked like chiclets. Her hair was bright red and she was wearing a short yellow skirt with size 11 clunky combat boots. I felt sorry for her as I slowly looked from her feet to her face.

"Well, Megan," I said. "I certainly understand how you might feel. But I didn't ask for this role. Headquarters chose me. It wasn't like I could decline and ask them to give it to you. Take it up with them."

Which they wouldn't have done even if I'd insisted.

"I guess you're right. I should be grateful for the job I have. Forgive me, Grace. I'm happy for you. He sure is handsome," she said as she turned to walk away.

"I didn't notice," I lied, smiling as Megan clunked out of my area.

The morning quickly passed and soon it was time to meet with the new store manager again.

"Come right in, Grace," he said as I lifted my hand to knock on the half-opened door. "Let's meet at the conference table."

"We should review sales quotas and sales reports for the past week and the previous year," I began, "to determine new goals for all the departments. All the reports are in this folder."

"Good job. I know your husband must feel lucky to have a woman like you in his life."

"He probably does. I don't know because he never tells me," I said hesitantly.

"Likewise. Pauline is the same."

"I'm sure she feels lucky to have you. She called twice this morning. All calls were being routed to my department until you arrived. Did you get the transferred calls?"

"Yes, I did. Thank you. Pauline is a good woman, but she's addicted to opioids. I've been trying to get her some help, but she refuses."

TMI . . . too much information. Whoa!

"Joe, I'm sure she'll get some help when she's ready. What about . . . ?" I said attempting to change the subject.

"I hope it's soon. I don't think I can endure another company event where she embarrasses me. One holiday she was dancing with one of my managers and came out of her wrap dress. Dancing in her lingerie. I've never been so embarrassed in my life. I was the boss of an out-of-control spouse. I didn't think my staff would ever stop talking about it. Okay, sorry, Grace, way too much information. I'm sorry." He blushed.

"No need to apologize or be embarrassed," I assured him.

"Life happens to everyone. Even chief officers. I won't share this with anyone, and I'll help you out when she calls at work for you. Good first meeting. Call me if you need anything," I said.

I didn't tell Joe everything about the earlier call from Pauline. He didn't need to know she was incoherent, and her speech had been slurred. She was upset she couldn't get a squirrel out of the house. It had come in through the cat door. I had calmed her and had given her the phone number of a local business to call. She knew this was Joe's first day. Her situation was so easy to handle. She must have been high. Nonetheless, she thanked me and asked me not to mention it to Joe.

Over the weeks that followed, Joe would often stop by my department to say hello or ask questions about issues for which I felt he already knew answers. Other associates stared and some whispered when he came by my department, especially when we would meet in my back office. In my gut, I always felt like he was hiding something. I couldn't put my finger on it.

One Friday morning after our weekly staff meeting, Megan dropped by to chat.

"Grace," Megan said, "I thought you might want to know people are talking about you and Mr. Earley. Rumor has it you two are having an affair. You're the only one who calls him Joe."

"What . . . no way," I said as I closed the door.

"Way. They say you and he are always in this back office. You're always laughing, standing close—lovers undercover, they say. You know the Bonnie Rait song, Let's Give Them Something to Talk About? They say you and your husband knew him before he came to the store."

"Well, that's two lies, and nothing is further from the truth. Nothing is going on. We have a great working relationship, and people are jealous. Haters will be haters."

"Girl. Exactly," she said.

I didn't believe Megan's reassurance. I had seen her with the group of gossipers, too, who would stop talking when I came around. I could also not forget her reaction when the home office didn't choose her to work with Joe. And never mind the old saying A dog which brings a bone will carry one, I thought.

I didn't care much about what others were saying. I knew nothing was going on between Joe and me. Now, if he and I had both been single—I'm just saying. I knew the truth. I just liked working for him. He was the kindest and best boss I'd ever had."

Unlike Narcissus, he respected and valued me.

I knew our relationship had become extraordinary. However, I was married and faithful to my spouse, and so was he. It was a line neither of us would have ever crossed."

"Okay, I Just wanted to give you the heads up," Megan said and walked away.

"I had tried to tell Narcissus what was happening at work with Mr. Earley. His response was,

"You can handle it." I was surprised when he wasn't jealous. I would later learn the reason.

I became more worried about my reputation and I couldn't handle it. I knew Joe had a crush on me, and maybe I had one on him, too. I certainly was not getting any attention at home. However, Joe was a perfect gentleman. He was doing a great job. I knew he didn't have to lean on me as much as he did. I was leaning too—he just didn't know it. Or did he? I said very little in morning meetings as all eyes were on me.

Joe had been with the store for six months when one evening he called me into his office. We were both working the evening shift. We'd close the store that night. At 10pm we locked the doors. All the salesclerks had closed their registers, counted the money, turned in their money bags and walked out with the managers on duty. I was left alone to escort Joe and the deposit to the bank depository.

I picked up my extension and called Joe, as I kicked off my shoes and rubbed my aching feet.

"Hey Joe, the store made a killing and we met our goals today. Let's head home. I'm on the schedule to open in the morning."

"Come to my office for a moment. We can walk out together."

I had no problem with walking out together. I always liked being in Joe's company.

I walked into Joe's office. He was standing there with his coat and keys in his hand. I thought he had some bad news or something. Then he walked into my personal space. I was feeling extremely uncomfortable and wanted him to back up and hold me at the same time.

He looked deep into my eyes and said, "You know I am crazy about you, don't you?" He bowed to look into my face.

"I know how you feel, Joe. I've tried to ignore our feelings," I said, looking away.

"Well, I can't," Joe said. He grabbed me and we kissed. I was lonely, too.

After a moment, I pulled away from him and ran out of there as fast as I could run, tears streaming down my face.

I went to bed that night thinking about Joe all night. I didn't sleep a wink. I hoped he'd made it home safely. I felt guilty. I was supposed to accompany him to the bank depository. I knew I had to do something to save both of us.

When Narcissus came in a midnight, he waved at me and slept in his recliner. If I'd had a rendezvous with Joe, he would have never even been suspicious.

I worried our next meet-up would be awkward. When Joe arrived, he came to my department first.

"I'm sorry, Joe I . . . . "

Joe placed his finger over my mouth and said, "Shh! No. Let's not speak of what happened last night ever again. I just wanted to let you know the deposit and I were safe."

"Okay. I'm sorry," I said as he walked to his office. He never looked back.

The following week, I applied for an opportunity as a district trainer that was posted on the job board. Leaving the store would be best for both our careers and reputations. After all, I had a master's degree and could demand a higher salary. I could certainly use the extra money for Cedric's college tuition, I thought as I ate my lunch.

Joe was never the same after that night, and I didn't completely understand the reason.

TWENTY-SIX

It was the end of the day and Joe stopped by my work area to chat about filling the new manager's role that was open. I tried to think of the right words to tell him my news.

"Joe, I've something to tell you. I wanted to be first to tell you I applied for a district trainer position and will be transferring to Headquarters. I'll be leaving the store in two weeks," I said.

"Okay, I'll see you tomorrow," he responded and laid the job description on my desk.

He acted as though he hadn't heard nor understood what I'd said. And he didn't bring it up again.

Two weeks quickly passed. Megan and the rest of my coworkers told me they hated to see me go. I knew most of them didn't mean it. They'd been envious, and one or two downright jealous of me since Joe came.

It was my last day. I hated to leave Joe, but I was clearly ready for a change. I was gathering my things in the one small box I had when Joe stopped by my office. I thought he'd come to say goodbye.

"Would you drop me off at the bus station? My car is at the repair shop," Joe said.

"Sure. How are you doing today?" I asked.

"Better than you," he said.

I was somewhat stunned by his childish reply and thought perhaps he was a little angry I was leaving and wouldn't be there to help him and cover for Pauline. They'd be on their own.

I walked toward the employee entrance, saying goodbye to coworkers. Then Joe and I climbed into my car. Joe put on his Aristotle Onassis swag shades. Some workers kept their eyes peeled at the windows as we left the parking lot. I didn't care. I wouldn't be back. We rode in silence to the bus station.

Was he angry because he knew I'd applied for the position before I had told him? I could feel his fierce energy. When we arrived at the station, I glanced at him and saw a tear dropping from the corner of his shades. I wanted to comfort him. However, he opened the door and got out of my car, quickly striding away into the bus station.

He didn't look back. Joe surprised me.

There had been no affair, but two human beings who I thought had respected and cared for one another. Neither one of us wanted to say goodbye. Well, I did, but he didn't. Not so much as a thank you. Such is life. Goodbye, Joe, I thought as I accelerated my engine and squealed out of the parking lot feeling sad.

I called Theresa to update her. We were having a celebration dinner that evening for my new job and I needed someone to talk to. We met at our favorite eatery near Rich Avenues. We walked in together and were seated by the hostess.

Theresa immediately looked behind me and whispered,

"Don't look now, but your husband is on the other side of the restaurant."

"Oh yeah? Is he with a woman? His behavior of late is making me suspicious."

"No. It is a man," she said.

I looked for myself and my heart dropped like a stone.

I thought my eyes deceived me.

"I can't believe this. That's Narcissus seated across from my now former boss Joe Earley. I didn't know they even knew each other. Exit stage left," I said.

"Let's get out of here."

We both grabbed our purses and scrambled for the rear door of the restaurant that lead to the back lot where we had parked our cars. I hugged Theresa and we walked to our cars.

"Hmm better than you" Joe had said.

TWENTY-SEVEN

Mama had a stroke. Something strange had happened at my house. I had discovered the cut-up wedding shoe and had seen him spin out of control. Narcissus was still freaking out because I'd spent a few days at the hospital with Mama.

I had known Mama's time was close. Cedric came home from school. He stood at her bedside weeping and thanking her for helping him, for all the hugs and for taking care of him.

As she was floating in and out of consciousness, she said, "Take care of Papa."

"I will," I promised as I dried the tears from both our eyes. Within hours, Mama's condition worsened, and she died.

When a parent dies, it hurts deeply because you are the flesh of their flesh. It takes time for the pain to stop. I am not sure it ever does.

I was both saddened and relieved. I didn't want to see her go to the horrible elephant's graveyard. I was at peace.

Mama's death was the most horrific loss I'd ever experienced in life. Little did I know more heartache was on the way.

"See you again someday, Mama," I said as I bowed over and peered into her coffin without any regrets at her home-going service.

Narcissus couldn't attend her funeral. Chicken!

Cedric had stayed for the funeral but then returned to college.

Three days after the funeral, I quit my training position at Rich Avenues. Narcissus had previously told me I could do better, but I didn't find out until after the fact that he didn't want me to leave my job.

He was so confusing sometimes. For example, I'd once told him I didn't like my dark skin. We spent four thousand dollars to lighten it. I was so happy the day the treatments ended.

"Did you ever stop to think maybe I liked the darker tone?" he asked when I walked in the door from my last trip to the dermatologist.

"Did you ever think to tell me?" I said, instantly regretting my decision. But this was who Narcissus had become. He didn't think like other people. You just could not please him.

Most of the time, I called myself a submissive wife. That had been a mistake with Narcissus. For him, it gave him permission to do whatever he wanted without objections. He knew I had no choice but to forgive him or obey him. This time, however, I decided to follow my heart.

After leaving Rich Avenues, I started my consulting group. A college friend joined me in the business. I invited several other consultants who didn't work out. They left one by one when they discovered they weren't going to become famous or get rich quick.

Then I met Octavius Washington at an exercise class. The instructor divided the class into teams of two. Octavius and I were a team.

"My name is Octavius," he said in his smooth tenor voice as he introduced himself.

"I'm Grace," I responded. "So, what do you do when you aren't in the exercise class?" I asked.

"I'm a community volunteer," he said standing six feet five, bowlegged and muscular. "I'm about to give this up and look for something else to get involved in. I'm an ex-marine," he said proudly.

"Thank you for your service," I said as he held my knees for my last set of sit-ups.

"My background is coaching in small business development. I've been doing this since I left the military," he continued as he reclined for his three sets of sit-ups. He worked out like a machine without any help from me.

This guy was just who I needed on my team. I shared my vision and asked him whether he'd help me launch my business and stay with me for about six months until things were up and running.

"Sure," he said. "I have some free time on my hands. I like your vision and energy. When do I start?" he asked.

"Tomorrow," I said without hesitation and laughed. We finished our task in exercise class, exchanged numbers, and promised to connect in two weeks.

Octavius arrived for work as promised. He quickly took over ropes as a partner and hit the ground running. With his military discipline, he did not disappoint. He didn't try to advise me on how to run the business. He just grabbed hold of the vision and did whatever he could to help make the business a success. He helped me define my lane and stayed in his. He turned out to be my most valuable associate.

I often told Octavius, "You are a good man, Charlie Brown."

I didn't know what I'd do without Octavius. He was kind, spiritual and knowledgeable. He had no idea how much I depended on him.

The day at the office had come to an end. It was Monday evening and I was finally home from a long day. Octavius and I had signed a new contract after just three weeks.

I called Narcissus with the good news about the day's accomplishment.

"Hey, Narcissus. Just a call to tell you to come home early if you can. We need to celebrate. I have good news."

"Okay, Grace. As soon as I finish."

"You say the same thing every time I ask you to come home. Then I wait for hours or I go to bed, and it's sometimes morning before you show up," I complained.

"Don't start with me," he shouted.

"You know we need the money. Your business doesn't generate much income. And besides, I'm a grown man. You don't tell me what to do. You'd better have dinner on the table when I get home and the grass cut," he sneered.

He showed little interest in my news, and I looked at the floor.

I could hear the guys laughing in the background as he hung up the line.

"Fellows, I wear the pants at my house," he said.

I knew it was not a joke to Narcissus. He let them know he was Mister and I was Celie.

One day Narcissus had guys over to the house. They stood in the driveway, drinking beer and talking about their wives and lingerie. He had never introduced me to them. So, like Celie from the movie The Color Purple, I eavesdropped and overheard Narcissus speaking.

"My wife knows I don't play. Her bra and panties better match," he said.

At the time, I leaned against the wall, covered my mouth with my hand and snickered.

He was so full of himself, little lying controlling twerp. He'd never spoken one way or the other about the lingerie I wore. I didn't think he had ever even noticed my underwear.

I shook my head in disbelief. My better half was telling little white lies to his buddies. I could tell he believed what he was saying about wearing the pants in his household.

When he got home. I couldn't wait to tell him my good news. So, as soon as he walked in the door, I said,

"Narcissus, I have a new partner. His name is Octavius. I'm so excited for him to join my company. He's been with me for a month now. He has a load of experience and knows how to run a business."

I thought he'd be excited, too.

"Yeah. Okay. Good luck. I have another job. Bye."

I tried to ignore his flippant attitude as usual and pretended it did not bother me. He was so busy with computer work he barely registered what anyone said anymore.

About an hour later, the phone rang. I stopped stirring my pot to answer it.

"Hello. This is Grace."

"Hello, Beautiful." It was so nice to be given a compliment.

"Hey, Efren. Narcissus isn't here right now. I'll tell him you called."

"Grace, why are you two getting a divorce?" Efren said frantically. "Stay together. You can work it out."

"Wait, Efren. Slow down. I don't know what you're talking about. Narcissus and I aren't getting a divorce."

"Okay. I know it's hard being married. I sure miss Anita. I wish she were still alive. But I'm telling you. You can work it out. I wish you two could chat. She'd tell you. We had lots of fights, but I miss her every day. Just tell Narcissus to call me. I will straighten him out."

"Okay, Efren. Goodbye." I hung up, wondering whether Efren was drunk. He'd recently lost Anita to a massive heart attack. He spent a lot of time alone after she died. Narcissus had said he'd been drinking a little more than just socially since the funeral. I'd heard at the memorial service Anita had really died of a broken heart.

They'd said Efren was something else. He was handsome, sexy, financially secure and irresistible to the ladies.

"Efren must have drunk or smoked something," I said to myself, "Narcissus and I aren't getting a divorce."

Narcissus came home later in the evening.

"Hey, Narcissus, honey. Efren called earlier. Said to tell you to give him a call. He said something strange about us getting divorced. I told him we weren't getting a divorce. Crazy, isn't it? I thought perhaps he'd been drinking," I said as he shut the bathroom door.

"Could have been," he said as he peered through the cracked door, looking at me like a deer caught in headlights. I was clueless as to why.

"Efren told me the other day how much he misses Anita. You know it wasn't long ago she died," he shouted from the closed door.

"I'm going to watch some TV before bed. Good night, Grace. You need to listen more carefully next time. Maybe he was saying today was the worst day of the week. You know you don't listen well, don't you?"

I built up enough courage to ask Narcissus about Joe before bed that night.

"Narcissus, did you know my old boss Joe Early?" I walked into the den and asked.

"What? No! Of course not," he snapped as he turned off the light next to the couch shaking his head.

I'd caught him in a bald-faced lie.

TWENTY-EIGHT

It was 7am, I heard Narcissus tinkering around in the kitchen. I walked in there with hope in my heart. While he was cranky and criticizing me most of the time, I was always happy to see him and was still praying he would come back to his old self. I had just got out of the shower and had on a t-shirt, sweatpants and a smile.

I was also thinking about what Efren had asked me. It was so strange.

I rushed into the room to show him I was excited he was still home. He was underneath the sink, fixing a busted pipe. He slowly pulled his head out from underneath and looked at me, then sighed with a smile. I could feel his eyes on me, checking me out from my hair to hips.

"What?" I asked and smiled back. Maybe he was finally back to his old self.

"You look like a hag," he said as he continued to look me up and down.

My smile faded as I stared angrily at him.

"What did you say to me . . . you, you trailer park trash," I snapped back.

We both paused then laughed in shock at each other's response. I'd stood up to him that one time. I could not believe I had dared to say it and shook a little as I awaited his response. His comment had hurt me. Something was seriously wrong with us.

Why had he said something so mean? Why did he attack me then pretend it was a joke? He used to act as though he adored me, I thought as I slowly walked back to the bedroom. Now I felt old and ugly.

Yes, I was older. My breasts weren't as firm as when I was a teenager. I couldn't win a wet t-shirt contest. Well, he certainly didn't look as if he'd dipped in the pool of eternal youth himself. It would be mean for me to be the first to tell him he had a bald spot at the back of his head. It wasn't there when we'd first met. From the back, he looked as if it was about to give birth. I pressed my lips together, feeling ashamed at the same time for thinking ugly thoughts.

I won't go braless at home anymore or anywhere else. And neither should he go hatless.

However, he wants me to be perfect. Let's see how perfection works for you!" I said out loud after he went into the yard from the kitchen.

While I was loading the dishwasher, I remembered something else strange had happened. I had a flashback of meeting my brother-in-law Pembroke and Narcissus' sister, Tequila at a restaurant a few weeks back. It had rained cats and dogs that day. Narcissus had driven me to the door of the restaurant and then parked the car. Occasionally he'd act like a gentleman. I slipped into the restaurant alone and overheard Pembroke and Tequila talking about me as I approached them from behind.

"She isn't attractive anymore . . . just like Narcissus said," I heard Tequila's husband say about me.

When they looked up and saw me, Tequila gave me an overly friendly greeting. Both, however, looked like the cat who had just swallowed the family goldfish. It didn't matter how friendly they acted—I had heard every word Pembroke had spoken and would not forget them. I knew they had never been real friends—just in-laws. I wanted to read them, write them, and permanently erase them from my life. I never knew Narcissus and his flying monkey could be so mean and two-faced.

"Hey, sister-in-law, good to see you. You're looking good," Pembroke said.

Two-faced gargoyles! I hugged them both as I flashed my most attractive smile and extended by claws.

Narcissus left the house, jumped in his truck and sped away. I heard the door lock. Then the phone rang.

"Hey Narcissus," I said.

"Hey Grace. Want to meet me for breakfast in about 30 minutes at the Big Waffle?"

"Sure," I said as my eyes lit up.

I raced into the bedroom to get dressed. I was so excited he wanted to spend some time with me even though he had just insulted me. Yet, I was humming the song,

"It's been a long time coming. But I know a change is going to come."

I picked up my purse and rushed to the door. I turned the doorknob, but the door would not open. The deadbolt was locked. I was locked in my own house and I couldn't find my keys.

I called Narcissus and the call went to voicemail. He must have accidentally picked up my keys, so I went back to bed and watched TV.

A few hours later, there was a knock at the door.

"Who is it?" I asked peering through the peek hole.

"It's the locksmith. Your husband said you locked yourself in the house and misplaced your keys," the man said.

"Oh, okay. Thank you," I said shaking my head.

When the locksmith finished, he handed me some keys.

Mr. Little said to give you these. That will be $150," he said with his card reader in his hand ready to swipe my credit card.

I looked in my hand. It was my lost keys. I wanted to cry.

"Mr. Little will pay the bill. He requested the service," I said and walked him to the door.

I could hear him laughing. He could be so cruel at times under the guise of humor.

TWENTY-NINE

I am glad to be at work, out of prison and away from Darth Vader. The phone rang and the call went to voice mail. I looked at the caller ID.

"Octavius, I just missed a call from Narcissus. Remind me to call him back when we finish our meeting."

I called Narcissus back in about half an hour.

"Hey, Narcissus. Where are you? I'm with Octavius. We're putting the final touches on our project. We have a presentation tomorrow at Executive Enterprises," I said cheerfully.

"I called you yesterday—the same thing. You were with your pretty boy. You used to answer on the first ring when I called. Something is going on. I know it. You say it's business, but you two are certainly spending more time together. And his phone number is listed on our cell phone bill more than it was on past bills. You must think I was born yesterday, Grace. I know you're cheating on me."

Narcissus hung up the phone.

Grace looked at Octavius. "Narcissus thinks I'm cheating on him with you."

"What?" said Octavius, his eyes flashing.

"Well, he certainly got that wrong. Grace, let me school you a little about some men. When they do wrong, they'll deny it exists in themselves and attribute it to their wives. It's called projection."

"Thanks, Octavius. Duh! I am familiar with this. He's delusional about you and me. But I don't think he's cheating on me. He said he wasn't that type back when we were dating," I said sharply. Octavius dropped his head and shook it. I saw him.

Later, at home, I thought I could soothe Narcissus' insecurities about Octavius by inviting him to go with me on a business trip. I walked into the family room. Narcissus did not look up.

"Hey honey, there is a three-day conference I need to attend. Why don't you come with me? I will be in class during the day and you could rest. Then we would have the evenings to rendezvous and spend some time together in San Francisco. We could make it a short vacation. Both of us have been working long hours, and it's been a while since we've spent any quality time together like we promised to do before we got married. Do you remember when I had to attend the three-day leadership conference in New York City two years ago?" I asked jovially.

"Of course, I do. Do you think I am an imbecile? And no, I can't get away. I've got too much work. Anyway, I never told you I didn't enjoy the trip at all. Why don't you take Octavius with you? I trust him. You had said he was like family. Remember when his daughter went to the emergency room and you went to check on him—I mean them. You said he was like family to you. I can't stand him," he muttered.

"What did you say, Narcissus?" I asked.

"There's a bake sale at the IT meeting tomorrow," he said in an impatient voice.

"Okay. Do you want me to bake something?" I asked.

"No. Thank you. The last time you baked me cookies, they were hard and tasted like you'd forgotten the sugar. I told everybody baking wasn't your thing. I mean, cooking isn't your thing. Who told you you could cook, anyway?" he said meanly.

"Well, I'll fix that. The cookie recipe didn't require much sugar. Next time I'll put in eight cups just for your associates. Call them Grace's Sugar Cookies," I said and smiled. "I wish you would come with me to the conference. You're wrong about Octavius and me. He's a great business partner. But I will ask him."

He would undoubtedly be more fun than Crabby Narcissus.

Narcissus walked out the door as if he did not hear what I said.

"And don't lock yourself in the house today!"

I just stared at him. He was nuts.

The next day at the office, I asked Octavius, "You know the conference I want to attend in San Francisco? Would you like to go with me? I've rented a three-bedroom condo. You can have a whole side to yourself. I can hire temporary staff to answer the phones until we get back. I asked Narcissus to go with me, but he can't. He said I should ask you."

"Whoa! No, thank you, ma'am. I would love to, Grace, but I can't take a trip right now either. I have a guest in town that week." Octavius paused, then quickly walked back to his office as I followed him.

"No way am I going off to a conference with a married woman. We are great friends. Grace, this sounds like the quintessential setup. Does Narcissus not realize what an attractive and wonderful wife he has? No way I'd let my woman go alone. Is he crazy, or is he plotting something?" Octavius asked.

"I don't think he's plotting. He just doesn't want to go with me—that is. He'd send me with a frog if he could find one. He'd rather work." I walked back to my office.

That shocked look on Octavius' face spoke volumes. He was disappointed in us. He thought Narcissus and I had the perfect marriage relationship. Now he knew what I could no longer hide. Our life was leaking. And so was Narcissus' façade.

THIRTY

I took an Uber ride to the airport. Getting out of town felt so peaceful. I was on my way to the conference in Cali-for-ni-a and would have some peaceful time alone.

I arrived on a Sunday night. The large, three-bedroom condo felt empty and lonely, much like home lately. However, I'd make the best of the week ahead. It was a little scary being there alone. The news report indicated crime had been unusually high in the city.

Before bed each night, I'd place an ottoman in front of the main door. I slept better knowing if there was a break-in, they'd make lots of noise and I'd have a chance to escape through a back door or window. I tried to get some sleep because 8am Monday would come before I could say, *"jackrabbit."*

I switched off the soft bedside lamp and then massaged the white ring on the skin of my wedding ring finger. I missed wearing my diamond rings. However, Narcissus said to be safe I ought to leave them at home.

I'd done what he'd told me to do. I was being a *submissive wife.*

The first day at the conference was a barrel of boredom. I could hardly wait to get out of class and back to my room. The conference was not meeting my expectations. Or maybe I was feeling that way because other attendees had come with coworkers. I was there alone.

The day was finally over. I was thinking about my life, the conference and Narcissus as I drove the hilly streets back to the condo in San Francisco's rush hour traffic.

When I arrived and put my keycard in the door, I immediately felt someone had been in my room. *There was also the familiar scent of a man's cologne and a strong, sweaty odor, like someone who had just exercised or jogged. It must have been someone from Room Service*, I thought.

Also, my medications were arranged on the counter with one pill on top of each bottle. I figured I must be a little more tired than I realized, along with some jet lag.

"Did I do this so I wouldn't forget to take my meds? I must have," I said as I inspected the condo.

I still felt something was off and that someone had gone through my luggage. Things were out of place. Something was not right. Perhaps I was just a little paranoid or the maid had been curious.

I'd order room service. A nice dinner would make me, and my hypoglycemia, feel better.

"Yes. Food is what I need," I said out loud, kicking my shoes off.

Room service delivered a delicious lambchop and a green salad. Afterward, I showered, put on my floral cotton pajamas, and slid into bed to watch a movie. I never did much TV watching; however, I was always game for a forensic science show, so I turned to a detective story.

That night's episode was about a woman whose husband was having an affair. Her best girlfriend had encouraged her to hire an agency that would help persuade him to return home with the use of FBI tactics. She'd paid people to gang stalk her ex. They broke into his house and moved things around, followed him everywhere he went, poured out the content of bottles of liquids, and stole small items from his home. This episode was going to be interesting. This time it was a woman trying to drive her ex crazy.

I napped on and off as I watched the episode. Then, I woke up at the end to learn the husband had been murdered by her best friend, who was also one of his mistresses.

Hmm, I thought to myself. The show had left me feeling a little strange. I couldn't get back to sleep, so I opened my carry-on bag and took out a book Emma had given me, *Will I Ever Be Good Enough? Healing Daughters of Narcissistic Mothers* by Karen McBride. I slid back into my soft bed and woke up with the book lying on the floor. Well, Emma, I guess I didn't need it. Reading it was like a sedative.

Worked like a charm every time, I thought, and chuckled.

THIRTY-ONE

I jumped into the shower and prepared for the second day of the conference. I closed my eyes and tried to scrub away some of the pain I felt with each motion of my washcloth, wondering whether I would ever feel happy again. As the warm shower water hit my body, I heard the faint sound of a door closing. First, I was startled, then quickly decided it must have come from next door or the TV.

I dried myself and I laid out my clothes. I searched for my red panties, but they were missing.

Hmm. I'm sure I packed my power panties. A woman and her secrets. I know I packed them. Wearing them just makes me feel confident and sexy all underneath. Well, it looks like I forgot to pack them.

I opened a drawer of the nightstand and there they were, perfectly folded in the center of the empty drawer. A new shiny penny was lying on top. I picked them up and found holes pushed through the lace I had never noticed before.

Oh no! They probably ripped in my washing machine. After all, the manufacturer's tag indicated hand washing them. Who had time to handwash anything?

Sometimes I'd find screws, razor blades and nails in the washing machine basin, stuff that must have been in Narcissus' pant pockets. That was it.

I decided that accounted for the holes. But how did the penny get there? I felt a headache coming on.

This was strange. I was beginning to freak out. I decided to report to the front desk Room Service had rummaged through my suitcase. I knew I didn't fold those panties and put them in the nightstand, and I certainly didn't place a penny on top.

Were the panties torn when I'd packed them? Somehow I felt Narcissus was involved but how? He was at home. However, I was feeling quite confused and scared.

I left my room once again knowing that something was off. The ottoman I'd pushed in front of the door last night had also moved. Had someone come into the room while I was in the shower? Were there ghosts in the hotel? Had my underwear been torn when they'd inspected my luggage at the airport, or had it been something in the washing machine?
Yeah! That was it . . . one or the other, I thought nervously.

I tried to change my attitude so the second day of the conference would go better. I did more networking with other participants. I also looked for a new nugget of wisdom each day which I could apply to my business.

Of course, getting back to my room was still the highlight of my day. I hoped it would get better and better. However, on the second night when I went for a walk to get some exercise, in a safe area near the hotel, I swore I saw a car that looked exactly like Narcissus' Hummer. The silhouette of the driver's head had a remarkable resemblance to his. I'd recognize his hammer shaped head anywhere.

It was possibly just someone who looked like Narcissus, I thought. What was crazier was the man on the passenger side looked like Winston, who wore a goatee. He waved at me.

It couldn't be them. I knew Narcissus was home because he'd said he couldn't get away. But who is trying to make me feel I am going stone mad?

I cut the walk short, jogged back to my room, had dinner, and prepared for bed. That night, I got on my knees by the side of the bed and poured out my heart to God. Theresa said she always got answers when she prayed on her knees.

I ended my prayer with, "Lord help me with this paranoia. But if it's real, kill my stalkers by any means necessary. And the church said, Amen."

I would learn later that, meanwhile, back home, Narcissus had lunch with his young niece, Sadie. He had asked her to do him a big favor.

"Yes, Uncle Narcissus. Anything you want."

"Good. I need you to steal something from my house for me." He handed her a door key and a small slip of paper.

"Here is the code to the alarm system and house key. Aunt Grace is out of town for a few days this next week. She left her wedding rings in a cup on the middle shelf of the entertainment center in the bedroom. Wednesday around lunchtime, I want you to go into the house and take them to Freddy's Pawnshop downtown. A buddy of mine owns it. He knows you'll be bringing them and will set them aside for me. I will pick them up later. We're just playing a little practical joke on your auntie, Miss Better than Everybody Else. I want to teach that shrew who really wears the pants in this house," he said to Sadie.

"Okay, Uncle Narcissus. I understand," Sadie said, appearing surprised. "I didn't know Aunt Grace was like this. She seems so sweet and loves everybody," Sadie had said.

"Yeah . . . the side she shows to other people. I know the dark side of the real Grace. Here's a few dollars for your trouble. Leave the alarm off. Any questions?" Narcissus handed her a crisp fifty-dollar bill.

"Nope," she said, smiling as she tucked the money inside her purse and walked out the door.

THIRTY-TWO

He's still at it. Working behind my back I was told. Narcissus stood at my father-in-law's front door, thinking of the best way to tell him about my supposedly crazy behavior. My father was losing his hearing and the TV's volume was loud.

"Long-time no see," my father said. "Let me unlock the screen."

"Hello, Papa," he shouted

"Hey, Narcissus. Come on in. I am just watching a little TV. What are you doing on this side of town? Can I get you a Coke or some cold water?"

"No thank you, Papa."

"Huh, what's that?" he shouted. "Let me turn this volume down a little. Is that better? How is Grace? I haven't spoken to her this week."

Narcissus looked at the stained sofa, trying to find the cleanest spot and sat.

"She's doing okay, I guess. She's out of town right now in San Francisco. I went on a fishing trip and just got back this morning. But Papa, I'm a little concerned about her," he said.

"You don't say?" Papa said as he turned his head toward Narcissus.

"Yep. Grace constantly loses things—important things like her wedding rings and she talks about hearing noises in the attic. She recently accused me of stealing money from her purse, and she's always questioning me, even though, I am a grown man. And she's always talking about how no one likes her. I've tried to convince she's being paranoid. She won't listen to me."

Papa turned back to his TV program. "She has always been stubborn, Narcissus."

"Narcissus, have you seen this episode of the Andy Griffith Show?" where Barney locked himself in the jail cell? It's my favorite part. As humans, sometimes we all do dumb things. That doesn't mean we're crazy."

Narcissus rolled his eyes, and he and Papa watched the rest of the show together, laughing at the hilarious scenes. Narcissus sat there thinking of the best way to respectfully leave since he hadn't received the reaction he'd sought.

Trying to turn my own dad against me.

"Good seeing you, Papa. I must get on down the road. I have a computer customer at 4:00 pm. I will see you another day." Narcissus stood and headed to the door.

"What's your hurry about? You just got here," Papa asked as he stood and stretched.

"Well . . . you holler at Grace for me. Tell her I love her and to call me. Since Mama died, she helps me with just about all my business. Did you know? She's a good daughter. Should have been a doctor, criminal lawyer, actor or something," he said as he yawned.

"Yes, Sir, I will. And yes, I did. I told her when we first met, I thought she'd be famous someday. I saw it, too."

Narcissus rolled his eyes again to the ceiling and continued toward the front door. He grabbed Papa's hand to shake it while slipping something into his palm of his hand. He then walked out the door with a Cheshire Cat grin.

"See you later, Papa."

My father opened his hand and found a rolled-up one-hundred-dollar bill. He smiled from ear to ear, showing his gums, too.

THIRTY-THREE

Narcissus drove about thirty minutes to Efren's Sandwich Shop after he left his father-in-law's house. He was looking for someone who would listen to his smear campaign about me.

"Hey Narcissus, where you been lately?" Efren asked as Narcissus walked through the door. "That pretty wife of yours is keeping you busy with her honey do list, huh?"

"Man, she never asks me to do anything anymore. I made sure. The last time she asked me to rebuild the deck, I told her to do it herself. I am not about to rebuild any darned deck. I had other important things to do. All she wants to do is eat out on the deck, as if we are still newlyweds and she's Queen Elizabeth or somebody. Those days are long gone. I think it's so bougie . . . you know uppity anyway . . . wine glasses, placemats, and gold knives and all. I hate this kind of pretentiousness. My cousin asked me to help her with a project way more important than the wifey project."

"Narcissus, I heard she started a business. How is it going? I know you're proud."

"Proud! Well, Efren, there is nothing to it. I'll tell you the truth. I told her since she had supported me when we got married, now it was time for me to help her. It was the right thing to say.

However, I didn't mean it. Her business isn't anything new; she's always coming up with ideas." He grabbed a bar stool at the counter.

"When she tells me stupid ideas, I stare at her, shake my head, or say nothing, "Narcissus continued. "Sometimes, I talk about how successful my business is to just make her feel bad. This so-called business she started isn't making any money—not like mine anyway! And she is always with her business partner, Octavius, who needs a wife, if you ask me."

"Lots of men and women, are incredibly successful business partners, sometimes getting along better than two men. Do you help her by telling people about her business or giving out her business cards? And keep the home fires burning?"

"Nope, not really," Narcissus said as he thumped on the counter.

"Man, I told you there was nothing to it. My time is valuable and her business is not worth my time. I reported to the IRS she was not paying taxes. I think she's slipping, and I am not interested in home fires. That's over."

Efren looked surprised.

"Narcissus, you are a dirty, lowdown dog. She's your wife, man."

Narcissus shot Efren, the evilest grin he had ever seen on his face, then he walked out the door. He got into his truck and pulled out of the parking lot, splashing mud on Efren's building.

Efren stared at him and shuddered as he drove out of sight, then looked over at one of his customers sitting at a nearby table.

"Narcissus is going to lose the best thing he has ever had. Mark my word, he is going to regret this," said Efren as he cleaned the large glass window.

"I remember the day he and his wife Grace got married. He told me he had finally met the girl of his dreams. It was a most joyous occasion. Grace was a beautiful bride. It was a nice wedding. About 200 people were there. Narcissus had his chest stuck out, strutting like a rooster at his wedding. You could tell he was a proud groom. Their families got along. It was amazing. Now he acts like he wants a divorce. He doesn't know, I heard through a close friend he is secretly planning to end his marriage. His wife has no idea, either. I don't know what troubles this brother. He has changed," Efren said, walking back to the grill.

"Maybe, he hasn't changed. He sounds like my sister's husband. Now, you're getting to know the real Narcissus. He's letting the cat out of the bag, and it's hissing. He didn't change. This is who he was hiding," the customer said.

Efren said he stared down the road for a moment, totally flummoxed. Maybe the man was right.

THIRTY-FOUR

I arrived back home from the conference hoping Narcissus would be back to his old loving self. It was so hard to give up on him. My plane touched down at noon. I called Uber for a ride home.

While I waited for my ride, I called Octavius to let him know I was back and to tell him about the conference. Of course, I preferred to call Narcissus, but I knew he had no interest in me or any of the details of my trip. He was too busy.

I found it hurtful because I was one of his greatest fans in anything he did. Wasn't that what a successful marriage was all about? I had created a website for his computer service, took service calls for him, and handed out his business cards everywhere I went. I'd hoped I'd receive similar support from him. And I had always kept information about him confidential, too. He was not able to return the favors.

Narcissus also encouraged me to talk to Octavius or my other friends when I needed support or advice instead of bothering him with my trivialities. Everything was always about him. Nothing about me.

"Hey, Octavius, I'm back on the ground," I said, standing at baggage claim.

"The conference started slow but ended on a high note. I can't wait to share some of the new ideas and cost-efficient strategies we can implement right away to drive up sales. Also, I made a lot of contacts. They'll be good for us to have in our arsenal."

"How was your week?"

"The week went well. I sure did miss talking to you. I wanted to call you," I said.

"What happened?" he asked.

"Some strange things happened at the condo. I believe the guest room service plundered my suitcases and moved personal items, or it happened at the airport. I wasn't sure. Then someone put a shiny new penny on top of my underwear." Octavius chuckled.

"Sounds like you had an admirer there. I heard my dad say when a man saw a woman of interest, he'd give her a shiny, new penny. And she knew precisely what it meant. However, it is creepy. I hope you reported it to the hotel."

"It was certainly scary, and I have reported it," I said. "How was your week?"

"I, too, had a strange occurrence. Mine was a phone call I received at the office.

"Oh, yeah? About what?"

"Remember the woman we met named Leesa who rented a booth at our last charity event?"

"The tarot card reader and spiritual counselor who couldn't keep her eyes off you?"

"Yes. She's the one." Octavius chuckled nervously. "Anyway, we told Leesa to call us if she should ever need us. Well, she called me last week. She said it was a non-business call. She said she had a strange premonition about you and me."

"You and me? Really. It sounds like some gossip. But go ahead. What did she say?" I asked, curious.

"She said something bad would happen at your house. You would be in trouble, and I would help you move."

"Just what I thought. Some mess. People cannot stand to see a man and a woman who aren't married to each other be happy and get along, in business or otherwise. Neither can they stand to know two happy people who just might be considered a power couple are getting along well. Octavius, it sounds like something we should put out of our minds. Someone is always trying to start gossip about things they don't understand. N-Narcissus and I are doing fine. Just f-f- fine," I said as my rising voice stammered.

Octavius told me later he had stared at the phone in disbelief. He remembered the night he'd banged his fist on his headboard, wishing what he sensed was not valid. He, too, was an empath and knew Leesa was receiving the same vibe he got.
He knew I was living a lie.

"Well, Charlie Brown, I missed being around you. I think this is my Uber ride approaching. See you tomorrow. I have so much to share with you. And let's forget all negativity." I hung up the phone.

During my Uber ride from the airport, I thought about my weekly date with Narcissus. Before the wedding, we'd agreed with the minister we would have weekly dates and quarterly getaways to keep the home fires burning. I was growing tired of being the only partner who tried to keep the commitment. I knew Narcissus could care less.

Each week, I'd remind him, and most of the time, he didn't remember, or he was late meeting me. Every time we met, he would arrive on the phone and would talk throughout our date or asked the server to move us to a table near the restaurant's big screen TV so he wouldn't miss his sports TV program or the daily news. I was beginning to hate seeing date night come.

I laid my head back on the headrest and drifted off to sleep. As soon as I closed my eyes, the Uber driver honked his horn. He was at my house.

"I hate to wake you from a good nap, but we've reached your destination, ma'am." He opened the door to let me out and placed my luggage on the porch. I tipped him.

When I turned the front doorknob. It was already unlocked. I reached for the alarm system panel to disarm the alarm, but it, too, was in off mode. I guessed Narcissus had come home during the day and had left in a hurry.

I took the luggage inside the house. As I walked by the curio cabinet where I always kept my wedding rings when I wasn't wearing them, I noticed the cup was not there.

Hmm!

Narcissus must have put them in the safe while I was away. I rolled the bags to the bedroom, kicked off my shoes, and laid down on the bed to finish my nap. Narcissus would be home in a couple of hours.

I fell fast asleep and began to dream.

Narcissus and I were on our date, sitting together at a restaurant.

"Narcissus, you don't have anything to say to me," I said.

"No, I don't," he agreed. "You get on my nerves, and you're not much fun. What happened to the sweet, fun girl I married? Where did she go? Florence, Jefferson's maid, replaced her," he said bent over laughing like George Jefferson from *Good Times*.

I woke up when the garage door opened.

If I was not much fun, then who was fun? And, Florence, the maid? He wouldn't say anything positive to me even in a dream.

THIRTY-FIVE

Narcissus walked quickly into the bedroom, shouting. I woke up and was so glad to see him no matter how he treated me. I was about to smile . . . then realized his words weren't, Welcome home, Baby. I sure did miss you.

"Why did you leave your wedding rings at home when you went to San Francisco? He snapped.

"Because you told me to! By the way, did you put them away for me?"

"I don't know what you're talking about. They are where you left them, aren't they?" he asked angrily.

"Narcissus, I checked when I got home. They're not in the curio, where I left them, the cup is missing, and the alarm was not on. The door was unlocked. I think we've been robbed," I said as I sat up on the bed and rubbed the sleep from my eyes.

"Robbed? You know how forgetful you are. You probably don't even remember where you put the rings. And nobody's been in this house. I know I armed the alarm and locked the door when I left this morning. You probably can't remember disarming it when you came in." He stormed out the door.

Lately, this was the way it had been.

The silent treatment. Or criticism if I misplaced something. Or telling me my memory wasn't working. My thoughts were all over the place recreating his pokes at me.

He no longer liked the way I styled my hair, dressed, cleaned the house or cooked a meal. He'd minimize any concern I voiced. It seemed I couldn't do anything to please him. No one knew we slept in separate bedrooms. He said it was because of my snoring. However, he was the one who snored.

I would spend a ton of money at the hair salon, upwards of $300. He always wanted me attractive 24/7. My life was as if I always had on a girdle I couldn't take off.

He once said to me, "I work with some beautiful and intelligent women. I don't want to come home to a wife looking tattered and torn. Spend what you need to keep yourself up."

Last week, I had my hair done and paid more $350 for it. When I got home excited about my new hairdo, I'd asked Narcissus how he liked it.

"Typical insecure females. Hair all down their backs. It makes me want to choke them," he said.

I never knew from moment to moment what he would say. I'd liked the hairdo, so I'd just ignored him. His words and actions were negative. His rare moments of sweetness lasted only until he got what he needed. It could be a listening ear, sex, or advice he could pretend was his or arm candy for an upcoming event. Then it was back to his wicked ways.

"I am going to get you, my little pretty," I imagined him saying but didn't know why.

When we went out among family and friends, we put on the right front and hid the unhappiness we both felt. We were like the little whistling bird wanting to get out of the cage.

He was whistling loud and pushing me away. I didn't want a divorce. I was willing to begin counseling or do anything necessary to save my marriage. However, I couldn't do it alone.

We attended a black-tie event for IT contractors to which he was invited every year. That night, he was unusually attentive to me and proudly introduced me to his fellow contractors. We talked together all evening and seemed to be enjoying each other and were having a great time. He was even flirting with me.

"Look around. You're the prettiest girl in the room. Not prettier than me, however," he said, chuckling. The light had returned to his eyes. His words made me feel special and loved, and he appeared proud to say them. We were two Cheshire Cats smiling from ear to ear and exuding our love.

He was back and I was smiling again. When the evening ended, he helped with my coat and put his arms around me in the elevator. We left the event walking together and holding hands. He even opened the passenger door and helped me into the car. It was just like when we first met. We were smiling and saying good night to other people as we drove out of the parking garage. I was in the third heaven.

Then, once he turned onto the street, the channel changed to a scene from Tyler Perry's Diary of a Mad Black Woman. His smile faded to a frown. He stopped talking. He loosened his necktie, turned on the music, increased the temperature of the AC (it was December) until there was frost on the windows and did not speak another word in the car as he sped home.

"Narcissus, it's very cold in in the car," I said timidly.

"I'm hot," he said as he looked ahead as though his mind was elsewhere. I wrapped my hands inside my fur coat and prayed until we got home.

He had put on a good show that night. Nothing had changed. He was the same angry man.

Narcissus pulled the car into our garage, jumped out quickly, and left me in the garage to get myself out of the car. He disappeared into the house and changed out of his tuxedo, throwing it over a chair. He put on a sleek black jogging suit and did his mirror thing and jogged out the door.

I watched him from the den.

"I have a computer job," he said.

I heard his truck door slam and the engine start.

"Okay," I said as usual and went to bed wondering what had just happened. No one ever had service people at their house at 11:30 at night. I went to bed. He came in around 3am and slept in his beloved recliner.

The next morning as he was going out the door. I was shocked and confused by his words. "You don't respect me. When I told you not to go into business, you didn't listen. This is the reason you aren't as successful as I am and bad things are happening to you. You are a failure. You also think you're better than other people. When people ask me what you do now, I tell them—nothing. I say you are unemployed. You've been in business now for a while now. What do you have to show for it? Nothing!" he shouted.

Businesses don't become successful overnight. It generally takes time. you've been in business for ten years," I said mousy.

I now know he used a smokescreen tactic so I'd be so confused, I couldn't ask any questions. Like where were you last night?

"Narcissus, you're a little ignorant about business growth. Most businesses take about five years to see a profit. Even a flower needs sunlight. And all things take time to grow. Why don't you ever have anything good to say to me? I dare you to say something positive! Go ahead say it," I said as I shook

He left the house, he slammed the door, and I could hear him mumbling something. It was hard to make it out, but I was sure he said, "You have lost your mind .No one likes you, not even your family. You're weak. We'll see who is ignorant. Why do you believe everything you read in those books and magazines? You think you are so smart because of that little college degree. If you'd listen to me, you'd be better off. Things are going to change around here, though, when the New Year comes. The ignorant one will have a roof over his head and the Miss Smarty Pants won't."

What is he talking about? I thought as I hurried out of the house to get to my class on time.

Today I saw Emma at school.

"Hey, Emma," I'd said.

"You look like something the cat just dragged in. What's going on?" she'd asked, smiling.

"I am in a daily fight for my self-esteem in this relationship with Narcissus," I said, leaning against the open classroom door.

"Narcissus seems nothing like your description of him. It's hard to believe he does the things you say. Are you just being the quintessential drama queen?" Emma said and stared at me. Yes, she did.

Lord forgive me. I called her a B with an itch for siding with him!

I regretted opening my mouth and had run as quickly as I could to my next class.

Hmph! Emma emoted as she cleared her throat and looked up at the audience. She continued reading although she was visibly angry and could also feel the glaring eyes of the wedding guests piercing her. I'd called her a female dog in my story! Sakina said she broke up and held her stomach laughing as Emma fumbled to continue the reading.

THIRTY-SIX

I stood in the doorway of kitchen waiting for more vitriol to pour from Narcissus' lips. I hoped he would disappoint me because I was at the end of my rope. Narcissus walked into the kitchen, rubbing sleep from his eyes.

"Good morning. Are you in a better mood?" I asked.

"No! You're still here." He laughed.

"You don't get it, do you? You are no fun, Grace. No one likes you," he said as he walked past me, buttoning his shirt.

"Oh well, here we go again," I mumbled. Who pressed the insanity button?

"You think you are better than other people, but you're a failure. Fix yourself up. Use some collagen or something. You don't look the same. Where is the young, fun and happy girl I married? I'm not going to put up with you and another man, either. Don't you think I don't know what you are doing?"

He walked out.

Narcissus' words repeatedly raced through my mind like a broken record.

Where is the sweet, fun and happy girl you married? She's gone crazy, I said to myself.

I was confused and tired of his broken record.
Crushed. I knew what I had to do or I would die. He left through the garage door. I would leave through the front.

This was the last morning he'd criticize me, accuse me, and threaten to throw me out of his house. Now it was clear why he never wanted to co-own the house.

I packed a bag and left shortly after he did that day.
I was moving out. I walked out the door with a suitcase. However, when I stepped out onto the porch, I screamed as the porch detached from the front of the house. I fell through the large crack. My suitcase fell to the ground and I was hanging from the doorway and landed on top of it. I reached for the broken planks and was able to pull myself up. I had a few scrapes, but it was not as serious as it had been scary. How did the porch detach from the house? Had Narcissus done this? Should I call the police or just meet him for dinner and act as though it didn't happen?

I called Octavius and told him what had happened asked him to come and help me. I was disheveled and dusty, shook like a leaf on a tree and cried when he arrived. He hugged me and cried with me. He followed me in his car to a local storage unit. He then offered me a room in the basement of his house until I could rent an apartment. The move is what Leesa, the tarot card reader had seen.

It was dinner time and thoughts of Narcissus' words and the porch raced through my mind as I unpacked a few of my things at Octavius' house and dressed my scrapes. I'd tell Narcissus goodbye after our weekly dinner—if he even showed up.

I dialed his cell phone.
Maybe he will show some empathy and excitement about our date today. This is the last straw.

"Yeah," said Narcissus. "I'm talking to one of the guys."

"Hey, it's Grace. Did you forget it is Wednesday and our date night? I am at Porshun's Restaurant waiting for you. I'd tell him about the porch when he got there."

"No, I didn't forget your little date night. I'm on my way. I'll be there when I get there. I have to stop by the house first."

My heart began to race I had to think of something quick. Narcissus, I cleaned the oven and we need to stay out the house for at least another hour." Whew! that was good.

"Okay," he said and then hung up.

"Forgive me God." I said as I looked toward the sky.

I don't know why I have continued to meet him. While he agreed to the weekly dates, he had never wanted to be there.He'd always behaved as though it was an inconvenience he barely tolerated.

About 20 minutes later, Narcissus arrived at Porshun's and entered the restaurant. I stood with a forced smile and motioned him to our table with bandages on my hand and elbows.

He approached the table with his cell phone pressed to his ear.

"Yeah, man. That's right. No. Not right now."

He took a seat at the table and continued his conversation while looking over the menu. Narcissus snapped his fingers at me to get my attention and threw the menu across the table. He stabbed the entrée he wanted with his finger to let me know which one he wanted me to order.

"Grace, can you move over so I can see the TV? I think it's the Florida Marlins playing." And then without a beat he kept speaking to his friend. "Yeah, man, they beat those New York Yankees last night, didn't they? I wish I could hang out with everybody, but I am on a date with my fun wifey," he said, glaring at me.

The server came to take our order. I was so embarrassed my husband showed so little respect for me.

"He'd like . . . " I said.

Narcissus paused his phone conversation to interrupt me as if I was incapable of placing the order.

"Give us both the same—two of the Baked Chicken dinners. I never like what she suggests for dinner. If she were a better cook, we would be eating at home," Narcissus said, smiling at the waiter.

I glared at him and was silent. Narcissus had no idea this was his last chance to treat me right.

"Young man, you'd better think twice before getting married," he laughed.

The waiter walked away, shaking his head. Narcissus finally ended the call after about twenty minutes. Then he turned his attention to the baseball game. The server brought the meal and I ate my dinner in silence as Narcissus fixed his eyes on the flat-screen TV in the corner of the restaurant. He chomped on his food and talked to the TV rather than to me.

"Go Marlins, go!" he shouted.

I glared at him, feeling the weariness of our intimate-less, lifeless, conversation-less dates. I was glad it would be the last.

"Narcissus, do you realize you didn't even greet me or ask about my day? Or question these bandages. You've been on your cell phone the whole date. You do this every week. Don't you care about me or have anything to say to me?"

"So, what did you do, hit yourself and plan to call it spousal abuse? No, I don't have anything to say to you. If you don't like it, don't let the door hit you where the good Lord split you," he said as he laughed and continued to watch sports.

Anger welled in my heart. He was insane.

"Narcissus, I know you're just joking. But I've been thinking. You are really busy with your computer work, so I will find something else to do on date night," I said.

"First, who told you to think? Ha-ha! And second, I'm glad you finally figured it out. I'm tired of these dates," he said brutally smiling, "You can see I give a flipping catfish."

I dropped my head as the man in the adjacent booth stared at me. I wished Emma could see this performance and I could disappear.

Narcissus finished his meal and put cash on the table for the ticket and tip. Then he finally looked at me.

"Keep the change and buy some more band-aids," he said. Speaking to me as if I were his servant.

" I have another customer. See you later. Be careful driving home."

Narcissus walked away from the table.

I'm leaving you. I'm not telling you anything. You'll find out.

Without looking up, I waved goodbye. I didn't believe a word he had spoken anyway. The change was three dollars. For a short moment I tried to convince myself he still cared. I knew, however, my wellbeing and safety was of no concern to him. He only cared about his insurance rate.

I could die for all he cared. And maybe that's just what he had planned—my death. Did he hate the weekly date that much? This meeting marked our last date and the end of my miserable marriage.

For a moment, I looked at the three one-dollar bills and imagined myself in rags. I'd cleaned, cooked and worshipped Narcissus. I looked old and was grateful for any crumb he threw my way as a thank you. Then I imagined myself in a coffin. He and his friends laughing, standing over my body.

I drove away and knew I had to survive.

Maybe, though, he'd fall through the porch. Stop it Grace! You must face the fact your life is in danger. The porch incident was no coincidence.

I wasn't sure so I left him a message on his cell to be careful at the front porch. Why did I care what happened to him? Because I could not help myself.

Leaving Narcissus Bentley Little was the hardest thing I had ever done. Facing reality was the second hardest. I took a hit, but my sanity meant more than anything. I sat in my car behind the restaurant eating a hot fudge sundae cake. I desperately needed comfort food.

I found myself like a vagabond moving about after I walked out the door. Anxiety filled every waking moment. I didn't realize how trauma bonded I was to him. I communicated with him at times due to our unfinished married business.

Before I left, I remembered the times Narcissus had sat and stared at me from across the room when we were alone in the house together or as we watched TV. I'd thought he was admiring me with my stupid self. Wrong! He did not even like me.
He'd just been looking for reasons to end the relationship—every wrinkle, and every extra inch and pound.

He had flaws, too. However, I covered them with love and never spoke of a potbelly, a sagging butt, or a double chin—sexy things like that. I chuckled out loud—natural aging upon which most people don't base their love for another person.

What happened to us? He never said what happened.
I felt increasing numbness with each bite of the chocolate sundae.

"What had I done for him to treat me the way he had? Why was he so delusional as to think he still has his schoolboy good looks?

I wasn't sleeping. I had no appetite for healthy food. I did not want to go to work. Old friends and family members avoided me. Likewise, I avoided them. The rumor mill was running amok. Rumors spread that I was in trouble with the IRS, had committed a crime and was crazy. People were being advised to stay away from me.

I had told only a few people about the separation. Where was all this coming from? So, who was talking? I knew it was all Narcissus' doing. It could only be him. He was wicked.

Worse, his smear campaign was successful. I believe it began when he walked into the house that night and realized I had gone.

Narcissus had laid out a red carpet when we first met. He was now pulling it out from under me inch by inch and day by day. I was reeling. I thought I might even die.

No, you will not die! Don't make Narcissus happy. You did exactly what he wanted you to do. He pushed you out of his life.

I was distraught but I almost finished my fudge cake. I left the restaurant parking lot and later that day, I ran into Emma at the college. This time, Emma seemed more sympathetic and encouraged me to schedule an appointment for counseling at a Jewish women's center north of Greenville.

"It is a free service, and no one will ever know," she said.
I agreed because Narcissus' smear campaign was killing me. I felt I was dying slowly. I was a fish out of the water and didn't know how to get back into the pond. I was sliding on a bar of soap and a banana peel into a bottomless abyss. People had never talked so badly about me before. Last bite of that cake. Yummy.

A few days later, I decided to schedule an appointment with the counselor. It was time. I had huge circles around my eyes, and clothes hung on my body. Octavius advised it, too, after he walked into the office and touched me on my shoulder to get my attention and scared the bejeesus out of me. His eyes flashed a concerned stare.

"Grace, did Narcissus put his hands on you? Hit you, I mean?" he asked choosing his words carefully.

"No, he didn't." Yet I stood visibly shaken.

"Well, you're acting like a woman who has been beaten. You're showing a symptom of post-traumatic stress."

"If he beat me, it wasn't with his fists. It may have been his words, actions and the despicable look he often flashed. Now, those hits left my heart black and blue," I said as I leaned against the wall in the break room.

"I warned him once that if he ever hit me, like Sophia in the *Color Purple*, I'd kill him dead then gouge his eyes out and step on them," I said, laughing out loud. Seriously, I told Narcissus he would only beat me once. I would leave and never come back. I told him Papa was the last man ever to whip me. No other man would lay a hand on me and live to describe it."

Octavius seemed proud of me.

THIRTY-SEVEN

I arose early the next morning. I just couldn't comprehend why things had changed with Narcissus and me. Why had he changed toward me? What had I done to make him so unforgiving and angry? I must have done something. At least that's what an unsupportive family member had said.

I planned to rest and watch old movies. I put on my most comfortable sleepwear and climbed in bed.

I was drawn to The Biography of Freda Hall and Alvaro Perez. It was next in my queue. As a child, I had loved The I Love Freda Show. What a handsome couple they were. He was good-looking, suave, and talented, and she was gorgeous, likewise talented, and had red hair and crystal blue eyes.

By the way, Freda was not a natural redhead. I would be willing to bet she changed her hair color for Fred. He must have loved redheads. That's what women did.

Every young girl in America dreamt of having a relationship like Fred's and Freda's, including me. I was captivated. They were the perfect power couple. They'd worked together seamlessly on set. Their children were born and became part of the show. Then in 1960, Freda suddenly got a divorce.

No, no! That was not supposed to happen.

America was both shocked and brokenhearted. Later, the world would learn the truth they hid. The lies they portrayed on stage were the antithesis to what was going on backstage and at the Perez home. The fact was, according to the biography, Freda turned down several movie opportunities to create projects so she and Fred could work together. A lot of it was propaganda. Freda knew he needed a supervisor.

I guess she hadn't heard the song by Millie Jackson, where Millie sang about not wanting a man in her life she had to supervise. Freda must have felt she had no choice.

When Fred was on the road without her, he did not seem to have any self-control. He had numerous affairs. He drank too much. His life followed the blueprint of his father, who had been a womanizer. He'd tried to convince Freda his affairs meant nothing. It was just what men of his generation did as their wives looked the other way. My heart ached for Freda.

Today, we would tag him as an alcoholic and a sex addict and encourage counseling and rehabilitation.

The movie included numerous fights in the Perez home and many lonely nights for Freda. She, however, loved going to work. It became her therapy. Her fantasy life on the set was the marriage she'd wanted with Fred and where she found happiness. Her experience at home was the reality show. Even her children said the woman at home was different than the woman on the stage. The children's friends were shocked.

She was a controlling wife who just wanted her husband to be faithful, adore her and value her. Her husband, on the other hand, had wandering eyes and had medicated himself with alcohol and women.

It appeared she'd loved too much from some lack of love in her childhood, perhaps. The movie revealed Freda was three years old when her father died of typhoid fever. She never knew the love of a doting father, so she appeared to be looking for the love she hadn't received and never would. Fred, on the other hand, medicated himself with extramarital affairs and alcohol. It seems he, too, may not have received the needed love. He'd searched for it in the arms of strange women.

I remember the scene in the movie when Freda cried. Through gut-wrenching sobs, she'd questioned Fred about his infidelity.

"What do they have that I don't? Why am I not enough?" she'd said as tears flooded her cheeks.

I cried with Freda that night. The scene still makes my eyes burn with tears.

What woman didn't have those thoughts when she discovered her man was unfaithful? While she eventually divorced him, and they both went on to marry other individuals, they always had a great love for each other. I think I know why.

When they first met, they were looking for a fantasy, fairytale love—something that did not exist. They found it on the set of the show. However, when the cameras went off, they were left with a cheating husband, a controlling wife, alcoholism and a community that had believed in their world of make-believe .Well, Freda had eventually discovered that the fantasy wasn't possible. That was two of us.

I'd found myself comparing my marriage to Freda's and Fred's, and I saw some similarities. My stage, however, was in front of friends, family and strangers. People saw us together and wanted to believe a perfect relationship was achievable for themselves. They saw the riches, the expensive automobiles, the four thousand square foot home. However, no one dared to ask what happened privately between us. They did not see Narcissus' real side. They didn't see my silent pain as I smiled and went along with him, hoping he would change.

Few people knew Narcissus talked about me behind my back and shared private information about me. Some of them did because they'd joined in it. No one saw all the nights I'd spent alone, thinking someday the police would bang on my door and ask me to go with them to identify Narcissus' dead body. Like

Freda, I never knew where he was or who he was with. I'd finally learned to stop worrying and put Narcissus and his whereabouts in God's hands. I would close my eyes on those nights he didn't come home. I learned to release him. Oh, what relief I obtained.

Narcissus and I had a fantasy life. As I look back now, I can see it was not real. When the doors shut at our house, I went to my room and he turned on the TV or left the house. There were short conversations, a few meals eaten together, lies, manipulations, criticism and the silent treatment.

Narcissus and I were characters of our situational comedy. However, I found little about which to laugh. I could do nothing to please him—not the meals, not the cleaning, not my inspiring projects. *Nothing*.

Nothing was perfect enough for him. The difference between Freda's situation and mine was Narcissus wanted out. Fred had begged Freda not to leave him.

The only time Narcissus appeared pleased with me was when I did something for him. I was being depreciated and I didn't even know it. When we first met, he'd treated me like the ten-million-dollar woman. Now, he treated me like maybe I was worth $10K for a burial.

At first, I'd thought it was just a passing marital crisis. To my surprise, he secretly wanted out.

When our show came to an end, many were saddened. They thought we'd be different and prove a perfect relationship was indeed possible.

It isn't. That's fantasy. There is no such animal as a perfect anything.

I laid on the bed stared into the ceiling as tears rolled down the side of my face. I, too, had succumbed to the Hollywood rose-tinted stuff.

I woke an hour later and could hear Fred singing, "I love Freda, and Freda loves me."

I switched off the TV, grabbed my phone and scheduled a counseling session.

THIRTY-EIGHT

I was running late and was thirty minutes away from my next counseling session and further awakening about my life. I rushed in the door and Dr. Sherry was already waiting with pen and pad in hand.

"Sorry I'm late," I said, catching my breath.

"That's okay. You're only a few minutes late," she said. "Besides, you're my last client today." She'd planned it that way.

"I have learned so much about myself, I didn't want to miss this session," I said.

"All is well. Let's get started and talk more about how you and Narcissus addressed conflict. When you and he would communicate about an issue, how did it go?" Dr. Sherry asked, pushing her glasses up on her face.

"'Narcissus, we have a problem. Let's talk about this,'" I'd say.

"'If you don't like what is going on around here, then leave,'" he'd retort. It was like he was channeling what one of his parents might have said to the other.

"So, that's exactly what I did after hearing those words for six years. He refused to discuss any issues. Telling me to leave him was the best advice he ever gave me. I was heartbroken and could not see it at the time.

"I remember the first day I moved into his house, and he warned me his attorney friend lived close by and was prepared to give him a divorce if he needed one. I was shocked to hear him drop the D-bomb less than two weeks after the wedding. We hadn't even had our first disagreement. Now he's talking divorce. Why?

"That day he got rid of my things without consulting me when I first moved to his house. That should have been our first fight. I sucked it up as I continued to do numerous times to keep the peace. I cannot number the times he said divorce throughout our marriage. Little did I know he just couldn't help himself.

"I finally said, 'This is the last time you are going to ever tell me to leave this house. You never want to resolve any issues.

"'What issues do we have? I don't have any issues,'" he'd say.

"This was his usual line whenever I would express my concerns that we needed to talk.

"'I have to go to work,' he'd respond and I'd I hear the door slam and the garage door." I scoffed and shook my head, frustration coursing through me.

"Did you talk to a friend or relative about what was going on or that you needed support?" asked Dr. Sherry.

"Yes. And the person I called . . . there was no doubt in my mind she would help me. When Narcissus left for work one day, I moved to the guest room and I called my sister Sylvia.

"Hey Sylvia, how's it going?" I'd asked.

"It's going okay," she'd said, speaking in her usual short phrases when she didn't want to be bothered.

"My marriage isn't working out, and I need a favor. Can I stay with you for a while, until I can find a place to live?"

There was an extended pause and sigh.

"Are you still there?" I'd asked, as steam started to form on my brow.

"Yes, I'm still here. My answer is no. It won't work for you. And it won't work for me." Her voice had been void of expression. "Grace, Narcissus told me you're disturbed," she continued. "He's been telling people you are crazy and in all kinds of IRS and criminal trouble."

"Do you believe Narcissus instead of your sister?" I'd asked in shock.

"You have been acting strange over the past few months. I appreciate you were there for me in the past. However, it just won't work. I can't help you."

'How could you be so selfish?' I'd asked."

"I'm not. I just have to think about myself right now," she'd said.

I looked up and met Dr. Sherry's gaze, tears burning my eyes. "There are no words to express the hurt and disappointment I felt. I was thinking to myself she had no empathy for me or my situation. She didn't even bother to ask how I was doing or what had happened. I was shocked. She showed no interest in my life. We had always been close before that moment. My mistaken belief.

"Just a few years before Narcissus and I got married, she and her husband separated. She called and asked whether she could move in my spare bedroom. I didn't ask any questions. I didn't pause. I didn't sigh. I didn't ask for collateral or her firstborn child. I didn't have to pray about it. I just said, yes. I wanted to show her support because we are family, and I love her."

"So, Grace, what did you learn?"

"Two things: 1) Sylvia may be like Narcissus with no empathy, and 2) just because you help someone else or are related, don't expect them to help you in return. I also found out who was there for me, who was not, who never was, and never would be there for me. Sylvia never called again to see whether I was dead or alive."

"An unknown author wrote, don't cross oceans for people who wouldn't even jump a puddle for you." I quoted.

"Yeah, I made a huge sacrifice for her. I will consider more carefully future crossings of oceans for people I have rarely or never seen jumping a puddle for anybody. I found out family does not mean friend. Family are simply people with the same DNA. Some help each other and some will not.

"Thank you, Sylvia. I am now stripped of the illusion my family owes me anything. This situation reinforced my faith in God and how I must depend on Him first because very few people will do the right thing or reciprocate when you need it the most," I said as I stared at the scars on my hand.

"After that, I called Octavius. He knew I didn't have any place to go. He offered me a room in the lower level of his house. He came with a truck and moved me just like Leesa, the tarot card reader had said. A dream she'd told Octavius about had come true. I knew mine eventually would, too."

I paused and took a moment just to breathe. "I told him I would only be at his house until I could get an apartment. He said I could stay if I needed to, and I could pay what I could afford.

"In the following weeks, I attended a family gathering. I overheard a family member say, 'If people were spying on me and following me around, I'd get my gun out.'

"Another one looked at me and said, 'You know Narcissus is not your friend? Right?'

"I did not know for sure what they were talking about. No one ever really talked with me. They didn't seem to know how or want to. I will never allow family members or anyone to treat me this way again. I will walk."

She shook her head. "Forgive me for jumping around a bit. Octavius was so supportive. I loved him as a friend. Unknown to him I'd had a dream one night he would become more."

"'Grace, if you left me, I would be breaking in the door, trying to get you back,' Octavius once said.'"

"At no time did Narcissus ever ask me to come back,' I'd told him sadly.'"

"'I am sorry this is happening to you, Grace,' Octavius had said."

"It was quiet and peaceful at Octavius' house. He allowed me the freedom to decorate my downstairs area anyway I wanted to. He said to decorate the entire house. He thought it would be therapeutic for me. We painted the room a fresh new color. The space was a small studio with a private bath. Narcissus had been controlling and this felt like freedom. I loved it. However, I was struggling financially being separated from Narcissus. My pastor encouraged me to file for a divorce to get needed finances. So, I contacted legal counsel and started the process right away. I was shocked when I visited my attorney."

I rubbed my hands together nervously. "'Ms. Little, we believe your husband has been secretly planning a divorce for some time,' the attorney had said. However, Narcissus had pressured me to initiate it."

"I did. I was tired of him telling me to leave. I was tired of not being able to please him. I was tired of being criticized. I was tired of being the last one on his list. I was tired of being gaslighted. When I went to San Francisco for the conference and returned home and could not find my wedding rings, I knew he had taken them.

"One of Narcissus' friends called me to ask why we were getting a divorce. I thought he had been drinking. It confirmed what the attorney said. He'd been planning to divorce this do-do bird. While he accused me of cheating, he was planning the breakup long before I even knew Octavius.

"Dr. Sherry, one night when I couldn't sleep, I was watching one of those forensic shows. A woman was murdered in her apartment. The old school detective assigned to the case decided to contact a psychic to solve the crime. The psychic told him it was the neighbor upstairs. It was true. He did it and confessed. Bullyah! After I saw the episode, I contacted the police department to get her contact information and I called a psychic.

"'Hey Ms. Johns, the other night I saw the crime show where you helped a detective solve a murder. I wondered whether you could help me with something. What's your price?'

"She ignored my question and asked, 'How can I help you?' She seemed to know I did not have much money. So, I told her how my rings had disappeared.

"She paused, then said, 'His last name is Little. and he gave the rings to a young girl who pawned them. Your husband did this. It's amazing how we think we know people, isn't it?'

I agreed and we ended the conversation."

"Wow! Do you believe Narcissus did it?" asked Dr. Sherry, looking surprised.

"I don't want to, but I think while I was at the conference, he took my rings back as he had taken or destroyed every other gift he ever gave to me. Nothing he gave me was ever really mine.

"Yes, I found out I was a work-for-hire wife, and he terminated the contract without giving me advanced notice," I said.

"You haven't said much about your family giving you support during those hard times. How does this make you feel?" she asked.

"Sad. Narcissus had once told me I loved them more than they loved me. He may have been projecting his feelings about his own family, but maybe he was right. My dad was the only family member who consistently supported me and came to check on me."

"In counseling, we have observed two types of family boundaries," she said as she walked to the whiteboard she kept in her office. She wrote the words: Disengagement and Enmeshment on the board.

"Let's discuss them," she suggested. "In a disengaged family boundary, family members do their own thing when and how they want and show very little family loyalty. Family members may not request support from others when needed.

Communication is also lacking, strained or guarded. They are not close. When a family member is under stress, the disengaged family hardly looks up."

"Sounds somewhat like the Smith family," I chimed in.

"Now let's move to the enmeshed family members. They are overly concerned and overly involved in each other's lives. They place a high value on family bonds or closeness. They show love differently. When someone is under distress, enmeshed families respond quickly and intensely. Which one do you feel represents your family?"

"Well, as I said, it sounds a like our family boundary style is disengagement. It appears a healthy family boundary would fall somewhere in the middle of these two types. When in distress, the disengaged system might not come to your aid. On the other hand, dealing with an enmeshed family every day might feel too smothering. I think my ex-husband's family was more enmeshed. This helped me understand the family dynamics better. I like the way you explained this to me. Thank you," I said, feeling lighter.

"Okay, Grace, good session today. See you in a couple of weeks. I will be on vacation next week. When I get back, let's talk more about malignant narcissism. There are things you need to know. Also, see what you can learn on your own."

I gave her a thumbs up and walked out the door.

THIRTY-NINE

I never saw those wedding rings again except in a dream. A dark setting that appeared to be underneath a house or an attic. However, I felt certain about who had taken them. I stayed at Octavius' house for a couple of months. We ate together. Prayed together. We laughed together. He protected me and encouraged me. We were already best friends. Our feelings deepened over time, and we realized we cared about each other. We knew we were more than friends. We had each other's back.

One day we sat across the table from each other and could not make eye contact. Something had changed. I knew then our emotions had crossed the friend line. I made the first move.

"Octavius, I had a dream about you some time ago. I believe we are supposed to be together," I said one morning at breakfast, shaking a little.

"I know. I feel the same. I heard the best romances begin with friendship," he said as I relaxed.

I smiled, blushed, and cried at the same time.

I was right.

I supported him, and he continued to have my back. Many days Octavius held me in his arms. Sometimes I emitted gut-wrenching sobs. I had not wanted a divorce. I believed marriage was for a lifetime. It was my second, and it was not supposed to end. However, there was no stopping it now. I deeply felt the loss of the marriage I'd thought would last forever.

While Narcissus blamed me, he had been planning an escape strategy for months. He was finally getting what he wanted, with me as his sacrificial lamb. I didn't understand what was happening in my life. However, the divorce was quick and unbeknownst to me at the time . . . dirty.

I reluctantly moved to an apartment. I exhaled and thought I'd finally found peace. That peace would only be temporary, as things went vastly awry. Every day I'd leave my apartment, someone would go in. They'd eat my food, steal my clothes, and remove small valuables. They'd even riffled through my files and lingerie bureau. Anything with lace was destroyed and left for me to see. I had read many detective magazines and watched crime shows. I just knew a serial killer was stalking me. Everywhere I went it seemed I was being followed.

Then, a hacker sent viruses to my computer. Obscene emails with viruses were sent to people in my contact list. Everyone was blocking me. I couldn't receive calls or make any. Someone would lie in my bed when I was away from the apartment. I'd smell their cologne or sweat. Sometimes, I'd smell the scent of a dog on the carpet and bedding. It was both scary and disgusting. Octavius became concerned and encouraged me to contact the police department after about two weeks.

I called 911 after dinner one evening, and an officer was dispatched to my place.

"Ms. Little, we don't see any evidence of forced entry," the police officer said as he scanned my apartment. "We recommend you purchase a nanny cam and hide it in your apartment. Who do you think is doing this? Do you have any enemies?" the officer asked, as he wrote his notes.

"It could be my ex-husband. However, we had an amicable separation. He no longer wanted to be married," I said.

"He just wants you back," the officer said with a grin as he slid his hands over the handle of his pistol.

"Stalking me is not the way to do it. And besides, I don't believe what you are saying. It can't be true," I said sternly.

"He wanted this separation and was planning to divorce me. But what does add up for me is he could be furious with me because I filed for divorce before he could."

"Well ma'am . . . there is not much we can do here without any evidence. You might want to hire a private detective."

"Thanks for your help. Good night officer," I said as I shut the door and vowed to never contact the police again. At the time I was unaware the chief of police was Narcissus' friend.

I showered and got ready for bed. I slid between the covers for another sleepless night. I hated living alone. Every night I'd fall into a deep sleep, and someone would knock on the wall outside my bedroom or drop something on the floor in the unit above mine. It sounded as if someone was rolling a bowling ball across the floor. I'd awake suddenly, my heart pounding, and wouldn't be able to go back to sleep. Or I'd poke the ceiling with a broom.

"Go to sleep," the neighbor would say.

Really. I thought.

One night someone was outside the unit weeping. I could hear guttural sobs . . . I couldn't distinguish whether a man or a woman made them. I thought it was Narcissus. I prayed and prayed. I went underneath the covers like a child and cried. I was so afraid. The still small, familiar voice inside my head said, your heart is broken, too. You gave it to someone you trusted. It's okay to be sad. He took a dagger and pierced you at center mass.

I often went to sleep with both anger and pain in my heart. I felt hatred for everyone who had ever hurt me. I felt unforgiveness and a desire to take revenge. However, an attack was never in my nature. While I had a good imagination of what could be done, I believed God gave the better revenge.

The next day, after all the sobbing, I went to the dentist for routine cleaning. I knew when I got in her chair, I could relax from

all the chaos. The dentist said something strange. When she came in to check my teeth after the dental hygienist finished, she said, "You don't seem crazy to me."
I stopped mid-chuckle when I realized what she'd said.

"I don't seem crazy to me, either. I studied crazy in college. I think I know what it looks like and know it when I see it," I said.

I left the dentist office feeling fearful and violated. How had this information gotten to my dentist about me? This was insanity in the making.

When events like this occurred, I would get in my car to go anywhere, continually looking in the rearview mirror. I glanced in every passing car. I didn't even know what I was trying to find. I felt people were following me. I was under siege.

I became paranoid. I imagined I recognized a few of their faces behind their tinted car windows. I fought off the paranoia daily. One day, a truck was parked outside my apartment. The word S U I C I D E was painted in gigantic letters on the window shield. I could have gone crazy, but there was no way I would allow that to happen. I knew Narcissus was behind it all. I just could not prove it. Darn he was good!

After all, he was a retired FBI special agent. He had skills. I was determined not to give him what he wanted—my insanity or suicide.

"Lord, help keep me to keep my sanity day by day," I'd pray each night.

And He did.

Prince, Cedric's large white male Ragdoll cat, puffed his white fur, humped his back, and ran sideways when he was showing aggression. Now, that was a crazy and hilarious sight.

He'd sit in a loaf in the doorway of my bedroom at night as if waiting for someone to come in or he was a good boy trying to protect his cat mom. His behavior proved it was not my imagination—someone was coming into my apartment. Someone played with Prince. Or his cat instincts sensed something wasn't right.

"Prince, you aren't crazy, and neither am I!" Cat Mom whispered.

My stalker even switched on the light on the back patio. How nice.

Whoever this individual or individuals were, they loved to eat fruit jam. I was continually replacing it. The feeling was short of disgust. I'd throw it out and open a new jar each week.

After a couple of weeks, I finally decided to contact a private investigator. I found one on the internet. I called him up and explained my situation.

"Ms. Little, this sounds like something husbands, governments or organizations commission people to do to ex-wives, ex-employees or whistleblowers," he said. I was shocked.

"What can I do about it? I can't catch these devils. Theresa ordered me security cameras and had Amazon ship them to my apartment.

I installed them and I checked them every day. I only saw my cat, Prince, running sideways," I chuckled.

"Well . . . they could have some type of camera blocking device," he said.

"He also has some undercover investigative skills, equipment and lots of friends," I added.

"The least expensive service I can provide is to do a sweep at your apartment to check for hidden surveillance cameras for six hundred dollars," he said.

"Let me think about it, and I will call you back," I said. When I hung up the phone, I already knew I would not call him back. I had no budget for a private investigator. I was broke.

Narcissus was doing all these things because he knew I had no financial ammunition to fight back. When I went to bed each night, I knew I had to trust God more than ever.

I had also made a couple of trips to the hospital emergency. I'd call Octavius, old faithful, and he'd drive me to the ER and stay with me for hours. My heart raced and would not stop without medication. I had developed a heart condition from all the stress

I had endured since the "amicable" divorce. The tactics being used were intended to destroy my life.

Yes, I believed ol' Narcissus wanted me dead. My ever-increasing faith and God's grace, however, was my sustaining power. All his cruel actions were making me stronger.

Narcissus once told me he kept his enemies close. Well, he was always a phone call away and pretended to come to my aid at times.

I finally realized I was his public enemy number one that he kept close. He thought he was so much smarter than everyone else. But I had his number. After all the cruel things he'd done, I finally came to terms with the fact he hated me. He couldn't help his actions. However, at the time, I couldn't understand what I'd done to incur the wrath of Khan.

I was also probably showing symptoms of the Stockholm Syndrome, where abuse victims form an attachment to and show concern for their abusers after experiencing a terrifying or life-threatening ordeal. Yeah, me, Grace.

FORTY

It was a warm, sunny day in Greenville. Theresa and I met for lunch. She always seemed to bring me joy, although, I hadn't heard from her in several weeks. I was a little miffed.

"How are you, Grace?" she asked as she greeted me with a hug.

"Just trying to get myself together. I've been seeing a counselor and living from pillar to post. I've now moved a few times since leaving Narcissus. I am beginning to feel like the city bag lady. It'll certainly feel good to have a stable environment again. I haven't heard from you in a while. It's been a while since the last time we got together. How are things going with you?" I asked trying not to show my disappointment.

"I've been busy, too," Theresa slowly replied, looking down.

"I thought so. I've been thinking about whether I should go back with Narcissus. Sometimes I feel strongly about it. Then other times, I think he's behind the stalking and other strange things that happened to me. It would be difficult ever to trust him again. I feel so confused," I said, my voice cracking.

"Grace, Listen. I think you should stop talking about what he did. He's become such a resource to everybody around you. Even if he did it, they'd continue to look the other way. Your family members and friends seek him out for advice and use his resources regularly. They don't want to believe you, and it makes you seem unstable.

"I think Narcissus planned it this way to make himself look good and you look bad. It worked. Has he asked you to come back, honey? He had a chance when you sat at the table with the attorneys to sign the divorce papers, but he said nothing, right?" Theresa asked.

"You're right. He never asked me to come back. But the things I've told you are real. I didn't make up any of it," I said.

"Well, honey, I believed you and gave you the surveillance cameras to prove it. I've never known you to be a liar. The truth is he doesn't want you. Just face it. If he wanted you, why would he do these things you say happened? Why hasn't he attempted to reconcile? It doesn't seem logical unless he's just evil. And I never got the impression he was the type," she said with little feeling.

I stared at Theresa and wondered why she, too, had betrayed me and could say something so hurtful. And why was she so confident Narcissus didn't want me? What did she know I didn't? Did he want her? What a heartless thing to say to anybody.

Everybody seemed to know more about my situation than I did.

However, Theresa was right. It was over now. Narcissus had never approached me about getting back together. *He'd only tried to drive me crazy. Fool! That's not love.*

"Theresa, it's been good to catch up. I've got to run," I said as I got up from the table.

"Okay, Girl, call me if you want to talk. I 'll pay the tab. You can pay me later."

Don't hold your breath, Sistah! And I could care less about a tab. Subtract it from our friendship! And wipe the smudged lipstick stain off your face. Smile.

I was angry. I didn't look back and continued walking in the other direction. I decided I wouldn't tell Theresa I was job hunting. For now, I just wanted to get as far away from her as possible. Theresa and her comments sickened me. I'd share the good news of a job when it happened.
Maybe.

What a disappointing best friend Theresa had turned out to be. Why would she of all people side with Narcissus?

FORTY-ONE
Twelve Months Later

I hadn't yet returned to work full-time. Octavius ran the business practically on his own with a temporary employee. I had moved back to his basement from the apartment. I was still being stalked and now had health issues. I learned those came with the narcissistic experience. I was also depressed most of the time. I hid out in the basement and didn't come out for days at a time. I didn't want to talk to Dr. Sherry—or anybody else for that matter. I'd go back to see her later.

Working the business kept Octavius busy. I, on the other hand, recalled a forgotten dream job. Octavius encouraged me to go for it, so I scoured the job sites, sending out resumes and scheduling interviews. I was hoping something good might finally happen.

I had been called back by one employer for a second interview. It was a position as a talk show host. I had told Emma about the first interview when we were chatting by phone.

"With your background in retail, you'll never get it," Emma said bluntly. "You don't have the right experience."

However, I believed in the God of miracles, and I felt in my bones, something good was about to happen. I ignored Emma and encouraged myself daily by reading my two favorite stanzas from Maya Angelou's famous poem, Still, I Rise.

You may write me down in history
With your bitter, twisted lies,
You may trod me in the very dirt
But still, like dust, I rise.
Did you want to see me broken?
Bowed head and lowered eyes
Shoulders falling down like teardrops
Weakened by my soulful cries.

Still, I began to rise. No bowed head or lowered eyes. And I, too, began to feel I walked like I had diamonds between my thighs and oil pumping in Octavius' living room. I didn't yet have my own.

Maya Angelou, what a phenomenal woman! I, too, was determined to allow nothing or no one to keep me down. In Proverbs, it says: A wise man falls seven times and rises again. I kept that Scripture close to my heart, too. After all, I was at fall number two or three.

I loved the verse. I felt it was written just for me.

Bump negative voices! It was a new day. It was Friday and I had only cried twice that week. I was thinking high so I could rise. I knew I would rise, even though Narcissus or somebody wanted me done, dead, destroyed.

The phone rang.

"Hello. This is Grace."

"Hi, Grace. This is Neville Jones at FBN TV. I'm calling to let you know we have made a decision."

"Should I sit down?" I asked as I began to shake.

"If you want to, but we have good news." Mr. Jones said. His voice smiled. "We selected you as our top candidate for the new talk show host opening. We reviewed your application, your digital interview, profile pictures, professional references and your mock show video. The team was impressed with the group interview. You're just what we're looking for to fill this mid-morning slot."

I made a fist and pumped it in victory.

"Your show title recommendation was also acceptable. Still I Rise will change lives. It will address current life issues of people who are overcomers of their situations. After we heard your story and saw your background in psychology, we knew you were the woman for the job. If you need to think about it, talk with your family and call me back . . . " he said.

"Mr. Jones, I don't need to discuss this with anyone. Your offer is an answer to prayer and a dream come true," I replied as I sat stunned in my chair.

"Okay. We believe in prayer and providence over here, too. Welcome aboard! Meet me downtown at the station tomorrow at 10am. We'll get the paperwork done, discuss the compensation and the contract, you can meet the show producer, and then we can start to work and get this program on the air. There will be a short orientation and training program. Your life will never be the same, Grace Little. We believe the audience will love you. The first show is next month."

"Okay. See you tomorrow. Goodbye."

I hung up the phone. Then I hit the floor prostrate and said,

"Thank you, Jesus! Thank you, Jesus. You never left me!"

My next thought was to call Octavius. My mind raced. I tried to take in all that happened. I picked up my cell and Facetimed him.

"Hey, Octavius! You won't believe in a million years what just happened," I said enthusiastically with tears streaming down my face.

"Hey!" Octavius said. "What's going on, Babe? Are you okay? Just slow down and breathe, Grace."

"Yes. I'm okay. I'm better than okay. I got the job! I got the talk show host job at FBN TV! I believe this is what God called me to do. This is the reason I was born."

"I'm so happy for you. I'll take you out to celebrate soon. Just let me know when you're free. Did you call Cedric and Theresa? Your dad?"

"Not yet. First, I had to thank you for being there for me. Through the tears. The darkest days. You brought me food and kept the business going when I was too depressed to even get out of bed—you prayed for me when I could not pray for myself. You've been my best friend. I'm grateful for all you've done and continue to do. You're a good man, Charlie Brown."

"Ahh! It was nothing. I was supposed to support you. Now call your son. We'll talk later when I get home," he said.

I picked up my iPad to Facetime with Cedric.

"Hey, my favorite son!"

"Hey, Mom, what's going on?" he asked with my favorite smile.

"I got some good news, Cedric. You're talking to the new talk show host at FBN TV in Greenville."

"No way. Get out of here, Mom!"

"Way! The show starts next month!"

"I'm so proud of you. I'm so glad things worked out for you. We're going to be rich," he said and laughed heartily.

"No . . . Mom's going to be rich. You just get better gifts," I said, laughing with him. "I have to call Peepaw. Talk soon. I love you." I then dialed Papa.

"Hey, Grace. What's going on?" he asked.

"Papa, you won't believe what happened for me. I got a job at the TV station. I am a talk show host," I screamed into the phone, with tears in my eyes.

"Wonderful, Grace. I'm so proud of you. What channel will you be on? You know I like to watch Rifleman," he said.

"I'm on after him. I made sure I wouldn't be on at that time." I laughed as I happily paced the room.

"Good. Bye now. Thanks for letting me know," he said. He was never one to be longwinded on the telephone.

Grace imagined her dad looked toward the sky and said, "Mama, you said she'd do great things. You said she was a fighter. I know you're proud, too. I wish you could be here to see it. Our daughter . . . a celebrity."

After so much suffering, I was finally ready, and I felt I deserved a fresh start.

Fortuitously, the divorce became final the same day Mr. Neville offered me the talk-show host job. I'd have to let them know my new last name would change to Smith.

"Thank you, Narcissus, for getting behind me and pushing me into my destiny," I said to myself. I sat down and wept for joy.

Narcissus had said he knew I'd be famous someday and he wanted to be a part of it.

What powerful words he spoke that day. I couldn't imagine that my tragedy would end in triumph! God is awesome! I made one final call that went to voice mail.

"Emma. Guess what? Two hours ago, I answered the phone and heard unbelievable words, "FBN-TV is offering me the talk show host job." I will start next week. I guess I had the right experience after all." I said and hung up the line.

I danced over to my desk and made a note in my planner to make by first guest on *Still I Rise* the woman whose boyfriend had taken the life of her son in Georgia.

It is true. Weeping lasts only for a night, and joy comes with the morning light.

FORTY-TWO

"Lights, cameras, action! It's the Grace Smith Show. And here's your host, Grace," shouted the announcer when she gave the action cue.

I came out of the side stage energetic, dressed in a beige sweater dress and ankle boots trimmed in mink with a big smile on my face. I greeted people at the end of rows of the studio audience, just like Oprah. I took my seat center stage in a queen's chair. My aura illuminated that stage. I was finally home.

Thank you, Jesus.

I walked across the stage as the audience applauded me. I stood tall and attractive if I don't say so myself.

"Hello everybody, and welcome to today's show!" I said using the line I'd practiced a hundred times. The audience shouted, "Hello, Grace."

"Thank you all for such a warm welcome. You guys are awesome! This is the first episode of *Still I Rise*. These shows will always be about real people experiencing and overcoming real situations. Our maiden voyage begins today with our first guest, Madison Bellini from Ludowici, Georgia. Madison wants to share her story with us. Madison, come on out."

"How are you doing these days, sweetheart?"

"Much better, Grace. Thank you for inviting me to the show," she said strongly as she took a seat on the platform.

"Madison, thank you for being brave enough to come today. I understand you survived the horrific loss of your two-year-old son Josiah a few years ago. Can you tell us what happened?" I asked, then waited for Madison to speak.

"I left my two-year-old son with my boyfriend, Eric. Eric and I had been dating for about three months. He had moved in with me and my son Josiah. (The audience cringed with ahhs.) I had to go to work, and Josiah's sitter was sick. Eric offered to babysit for me because he had quit his job. I wasn't sure about leaving my baby with Eric.

"Eric drank and smoked marijuana and had been angry and depressed for several weeks. However, it was too late to find another babysitter, and I couldn't take the day off because I had used all my leave. Josiah had been sick often that year. My boss told me if I took another day off, she would have to terminate me. I couldn't afford to lose my job and Josiah's medical insurance. So, I kissed Josiah, gave Eric instructions and left for work.

"Later in the morning, two police officers came to my workplace and asked for me. When I reached the reception area, I was out of breath, wondering what had happened. The officer asked, 'Are you, Madison Bellini?' My pulse started to race. I knew I was about to hear some bad news." Madison paused, wringing her hands.

"'Come with us, Ms. Bellini. We think something has happened to your son Josiah,' they said.

They escorted me to the waiting police car and said I had to go with them. My heart sank into my stomach. Once I slid inside the back seat of the police car, one of the officers told me we were on our way to the city morgue. I had to identify the body of a small child who fell from the thirteen-story apartment building I lived in. It was possibly my sweet Josiah. They said they had my boyfriend Eric in custody. When they told me they had apprehended Eric, I started to cry.

"Eric had killed my Josiah. I'd trusted him!

"That monster had picked up my sweet, beautiful only child and hurled him out of the window because he would not stop crying.

"When we reached the medical examiner's office, I remember moving in slow motion, when they pulled back a bloody sheet and showed me the child. I saw the little blue sneakers with Mama's Boy monogrammed in blue and little blue lights still blinking on the side. I screamed, 'That's my baby!' and then I dropped to the floor and cried as I had never cried before. I didn't think I would ever stop crying. They also said there was evidence of sexual assault." Madison's jaw tightened.

"I wanted to kill Eric. I fainted and later was so hysterical, I had to be sedated. He should thank his lucky stars he was already in jail."

"Yeah, I'll bet you wanted to break his feet, torture him and toss him alive in an alligator pond," I said, trying to get control of myself.

"Ouch," said a man in the audience. "He deserved it."

"I know," she said. I'm grateful, however, for my family, who supported me through the investigation and funeral. I couldn't have gotten through the whole ordeal without them."

By this time, several audience members were wiping their eyes. One woman openly sobbed.

"I know this must have been hard. I can't imagine if it had been my Cedric. What have you done since the death of your son?" I said.

"Counseling, of course. I hated myself and have so much guilt because I did not protect my son. I have also started an organization so single mothers can network together. It's called Keep Your Child Safe. It provides sitters for single mothers and encourages them to only leave their children with professional, reputable and vetted sitters."

"Why did you come on the show to tell your story?"

"Hopefully, so no other child or woman will go through what I experienced," she said as she wiped her tears.

"What happened to Eric?"

"Eric was charged with child abuse, child molestation and second-degree murder. The judge called him a monster. He was sentenced to twenty-five years in prison without the possibility of parole. I have refused all calls and mail from him. I heard his inmates had taken good care of him," Madison said. "What they did to him was better than the death penalty." The audience applauded.

"Do you think you will ever be able to forgive Eric?" I inquired.

"Eventually. It'll take time. I'm still working on forgiving myself," she said.

"Madison, thanks for being my special guest today. I wish you every happiness."

I embraced Madison, wiped tears from my own eyes, as we both waved goodbye to the studio audience.

Then the announcer said, "If you know of someone who should be a guest on *Still I Rise* or you want to be a part of the studio audience, please call the station at 614-400-Rise."

"Goodbye, everybody! You're magnificent. We can't do this without you," I said as I exited the stage.

"Cut! You can go home, it's a wrap," said Nancy, the producer, speaking to the studio audience.

"Call time is Thursday at 9am. Great first show, Grace." She high fived me. "The recording was excellent—the show will air next week. Welcome again to the team."

"Thanks, Nancy," I said.

It was a tough topic. I was still drying my eyes.

I hoped people benefit from the content.

This is what I was born to do. Thank you, God.

FORTY-THREE

I was shopping on a chilly Friday morning. Lately, I was always looking over my shoulder for anything that reeked of Narcissus. I had one of those royal breakfasts of champions—fried steak smothered in gravy and hot biscuits.

I was feeling happy about my new job and my new condominium downtown. My job was a dream come true. My eighth-floor condo had a spectacular view of the city. I could see the studio sign from the window and traffic streaming and in and out of downtown.

"Oh!" I exhaled and hugged myself, feeling so blessed.
The first show had recently aired and had gotten excellent ratings. Nancy said I was on my way to stardom. I had so many powerful topic ideas for upcoming shows to help women. I was also getting invitations by women's groups to give talks.

And right then I was thinking of so many things I wanted to buy for my new digs. I was grateful . . . I'd gone from rags to riches, insane to sane, and then rags and riches again. I laughed.

"Won't he do it?" I sang. All I had to do was pick it out, and it was shipped and set up the same day. Since I'd moved out of Octavius' basement, I missed seeing him every day. The grapevine was smoking about me since the divorce, with the help of Narcissus and all his flying monkeys who had spread all sort of rumors about me. I didn't care. I knew the truth.

"Okay, girl, let it go. You've won," I said to myself. "The past is behind you. You made it out, and everything you lost, God is restoring to you," I said to myself, "and I will never forget what I learned. I have a much brighter future and a good counselor and close friend to help me work through all the pain."

Octavius had called that morning and suggested I focus on my bright future. And . . . bright it was. I had a good job and was making more money than I ever thought possible. Also, Octavius and I were in love.

"I have completed the happiness formula—something to believe in, something to do and someone to love." I thought.

I drove to the mall, and I proudly gave the valet attendant the keys for my Mercedes Benz so she could park my car.

"Nice car, Ms. Smith, I want to be like you when I grow up," she said, beaming.

"Know it's reachable. Keep your eye on the prize," I said as I patted her on the shoulder.

Then I walked inside the mall and I took the escalator to the second level. I ran into Theresa.

"Hey, Theresa," I said, averting my eyes.

"Hey, Girl. Long-time no hear. But I did hear from your sister Sylvia about your new job. She said she was proud of you. She said no-one ever hears from you."

"I wonder why?" I said sarcastically.

"I was thrilled to hear about your new TV job. I thought you would have told me yourself, but I probably deserved it. It's good to see you've regained your stability. Narcissus did a number on us, didn't he?" Theresa continued.

Yes, he did, and I hope you can forgive yourself for introducing him to me.

We sat together on a nearby bench.

"Well, Theresa, you, too, have been distant since the breakup. I must admit it feels so good to have made a full comeback—especially when so many people turned their backs on me. I thought you, too, had joined the team to persecute me—those who don't deserve the right to hear an update on my life."

"No, Grace. You and I will always be friends. However, I don't deserve it. I'm just in the valley right now. Since you and Narcissus broke up, Winston started to become distant. He'd say he was coming over and then stand me up. He no longer takes my phone calls. He says church business keeps him busy. He just wants to be friends. He also says our relationship isn't exclusive. He says I'm too much of a clinging vine. He's encouraged me to go out with my friends like I did when we first met."

"I already know the answer to my next question. You dropped all your friends because he was taking so much of your time," I said, leaning toward Theresa.

"Why do women do this? The man wants all our time and we drop everybody and stop doing all the things he liked about us. You did the same with Narcissus, didn't you?" she said.

"Yes, I did," I said, looking away.

"And you're right. It seems those were the very things they like about us, our independence and confidence. We throw it all away to be with them. Then when the chase is over, they quickly become bored. Girl let's not ever do this again. In the future, let's continue our predating activities and schedule in a man where we can. That's what men do." I laughed alone

Theresa wasn't laughing. Her hair was disheveled, and she looked tired, bloated and seemed distant. *However, her complexion was radiant.*

"Theresa, it'll be okay. You are an intelligent, educated and attractive woman and still have your schoolgirl figure. Someone is going to come along who will love you and accept you. Your fifty-fifty love is just around the corner." For a moment I forgot she had hurt me and tried to reassure her.

"I'm tired of kissing toads, Grace. How many more years before I meet my Prince Charming? I'm not getting any younger, you know. Remember, you even told me Narcissus was saying things about you getting older."

"Yeah, the jerk . . . all the while, he was magically getting younger. He had the nerve, didn't he?" I said sarcastically, then laughed.

"I know what you mean, though. You and me . . . we've been in the same boat." I smiled, trying to get Theresa to laugh.

"Things changed between Narcissus and me about six months after we married. When did things change between you and Winston?"

"Seriously. In six months? You never said a word," she said, astounded.

"Because I was ashamed I couldn't keep my marriage together," I said.

"Okay. When Winston and I first met, he called me every day. And every night to tuck me in. It was a whirlwind romance. He said he had never met a woman like me. He gave me greeting cards for every occasion and bought me gifts. Winston even sent roses to the school every month. I was the envy of all the teachers at work."

Well, this story certainly sounds familiar. He and Narcissus had read the same play book.

"Shortly after we introduced you to Narcissus, things started to cool a bit. I just thought we were getting closer, not coming apart."

"Was he still nice to you?" I asked.

"You know he wasn't. He would give me breath mints as if I had bad breath when we were talking and then would laugh about it." *I resisted laughing myself*.

"Then he started suggesting I should go back to school to become a principal. I was a licensed school psychologist. He also started complaining about the way I dressed or the meals I cooked for him. He would fall asleep while we talked on the phone or constantly clicked to call waiting. I couldn't do anything to please him. He's not interested in sex anymore, either. I think he's seeing someone else. I wish he'd tell me it's over. This limbo love is killing me. I don't enjoy anything anymore. It's getting harder to get out of bed each morning. It's hard to find a reason to live. So, I had a few one-night stands," she said, sounding fatigued.

There is no way I could tell Theresa I had seen Winston with a beautiful, redheaded younger woman just the day before. Since he was one of the assistant pastors at his church, I thought maybe the woman with him was a church member or relative.

"Theresa, when I was going through the tough times of my separation and divorce, I didn't tell anyone, but I was so depressed, Emma recommended I go to see a counselor."

"Emma! You trusted her?"

"Yes, she called to check on me. Like real friends do." Theresa looked at the mall floor.

"The counselor is helping me to work through everything. She also told me I was clinically depressed and prescribed an antidepressant and sleeping pill to help me rest. I called them my happy pills. I don't need them now as I did at first. I couldn't have made it, if not for the meds, the counselors and Octavius. Ever thought about dating someone else?"

"No. I had a particular one-night stand for which I haven't been able to forgive myself. I wanted to get back at Winston. I hate myself for being so weak and stupid."

"Well, forgive yourself. The Bible says we all sin and fall short of the glory of God."

"Grace, just between you and me, I think Winston is dating the pastor's wife," said Theresa, ignoring what I said.

"Really . . . be careful with such accusation. Describe the woman," I said curiously.

"She's a beautiful young redhead about my height," said Theresa pursing her lips and squinting her eyes, trying to remember.

A shot of adrenaline went through me. My heart went out to Theresa. I made no comment. We ended our conversation and walked off in different directions at the mall. I hoped she was wrong about Winston. However, Theresa had described to the letter the woman I had seen with Winston. I didn't want her anger misdirected at me, so I wasn't about to tell her anything. When we walked away from each other, I didn't know I might never see her again.

Later in the evening, I could still see the fake smile and "far away" look in Theresa's eyes. My Call Waiting activated while I was on the phone with Cedric. I didn't click over. I was helping Cedric with an issue.

When I finished the call with my son, Siri notified me of a voice mail message. I had planned to call Theresa back later when I'd settled in so we could have a nice, long overdue catch-up girl's chat. It was always easy for me to forgive.

After my evening chores, I finally listened to Theresa's message.

"It was so good to see you today. I'm going to bed early, Grace. Thank you for always being such a good friend. Please forgive me for not being there when you needed my support. You looked extremely happy today. I love you and will talk to you in the morning."

I was glad Theresa had gone home to rest. She'd looked so tired earlier.

"We'll plan a girl's trip, now that I have more money," I said on the voice message recorder. Then I got ready for bed.

The sun was breaking through the blinds as I rolled over and saw the name Hazel Thornton stream across my Caller ID as the phone rang. I knew it couldn't be good news. Hazel Thornton was Theresa's cousin.

"Good morning, Grace," she said.

"Good morning Hazel. What's the matter?" I quickly asked.

"The school was concerned because Theresa didn't report to work today. They asked me to go to her house and check on her,"

Hazel said in a sad voice. My heart began to race. I tried to take deep breaths.

"The principal said it wasn't like her to miss school and not call. When I got to her house, the garage door was open. Her kitchen door was unlocked. At first, I thought there'd been a robbery. I noticed candles were burning. A very soft fragrance was in the air. I took a butcher's knife from the block as I walked through the kitchen and across the family room. Then I walked up the stairs to the master bedroom. The house was quiet and cool with an eerie stillness.

"There was Theresa in bed with the covers pulled over her head. I called to her. She didn't answer. I pulled back the sheet and screamed. Her eyes were opened with a frightened look on her face. I touched her skin. It was moist and felt cold. There was a pool of blood around her neck. It appeared to have been slit. I began to shake. I called 911," she cried.

"Oh my God. We were going to chat this morning," I said as my heart sank. I tried to hold it together.

"I explained to the 911 operator my cousin hadn't reported to work, and I was at her house. She was in bed, bleeding, and didn't appear to be breathing.

"'Hurry!' I screamed to the operator, bursting into tears. I knew she was already dead. They dispatched the EMT and arrived within five minutes, followed by the police.

"The EMT couldn't get any respiration. The medical examiner arrived a few minutes later and pronounced her dead at the scene. They said it appeared the attack happened while she was her bed. They slashed her throat. There didn't appear to be a struggle. They think she had let her attacker into the house. It was someone she knew."

Hazel whimpered. "Grace, she's gone. They said she probably died sometime around midnight. CSI and the police said the attacker took the weapon. They also told me when killers cover the bodies of their victims, that's an indication to law enforcement he or she knew the victim. They felt some degree of shame for their actions."

I tried to console Hazel and managed to hold back my tears until I hung up the phone. Then I broke down and sobbed, too. I could not imagine who could have done this to Theresa.

Theresa had been my rock. My sister. My best friend.

FORTY-FOUR

Theresa's small funeral was held a week later. I drove to the church alone, mourning the loss of my friend. Winston wasn't there. I suspected he was feeling too guilty, because he had done her wrong before she died, or he had murdered her. He also knew he might run into me and wonder whether I knew about his relationship with the pastor's wife.

Theresa was the only child of a family from one of the New England states. Both her parents were deceased. She rarely spoke of her relatives. The service was attended mostly by her cousin Hazel, coworkers and neighbors.

Theresa's death made me think about my recent marriage, Narcissus's behavior, and how it had all ended. I also now wondered with whom she'd had a one-night stand that made her feel so guilty? Could Narcissus be her murderer? Was it Winston? Who else would have a motive to kill her and that she would let in? I was sure the police would get to the bottom of this. I left the Interment crying.

I took three days off work. I knew I could use a counseling session because of the triggers I was experiencing. Instead, I decided to plan a session for the show and include my counselor as a guest professional. I determined if I planned a show and included Dr. Sherry, I could also obtain more information.

I needed to focus on my work and heal at the same time. I was grieving both my marriage and Theresa.
Yeah, imagine that.

I planned to bring a man and a woman to the show who'd dated or married someone with a personality disorder. Yes, I asked the producer to send out a query asking for show guests who had been in a relationship with someone who'd love-bombed them then abandoned them.

"Lights! Cameras! Action! And . . . here's Grace," said the announcer loudly.

I entered the stage feeling sadness, but I put on my best face. The show must go on! I was dressed in a beige pantsuit with matching high heels.

"Welcome back to another exciting *Still I Rise* show," I said. "Today's guests are Emily Brown and Brad Silverman. Also, back on the show is Dr. Willow Sherry, a professional psychotherapist. Please welcome everyone." The sound of applause filled the studio.

"Emily and Brad are here because they were both involved in relationships with someone who proclaimed undying love, but the relationship ended, leaving them confused, traumatized and devastated. Both exes attempted to ruin their lives—literally. Dr. Sherry is an expert counselor who may be able to help us understand why these scenarios took place."

"Brad, I'll start with you." I waited for the audience to applaud. It's brave of you to come on a public show and talk about this and possibly break some man rule. When Brad isn't blogging with victims of relationship abuse, he's a mechanical engineer."

"I don't care about any man's rule. I was married to a woman who was so in love with me when we first met, I thought I'd died and gone to heaven." He grinned as the audience laughed. "She cooked. She bought me gifts. She said I was the best thing to ever happen to her. I wanted to squeeze her to death. Now, I wished I had." His grin turned wry as the audience continued laughing. "She said I was the man of her dreams."

"Sounds like things changed," I inserted. "Or the honeymoon phase ended."

"Yep. Man did it end! She turned from the Good Witch Glenda to the Wicked Witch of the West. She became controlling. Talking about me behind my back. Stealing money out of my wallet and bank account. She stopped being intimate. She would continually threaten divorce. And I was continually having stomach aches and headaches. I think she was putting something in my food.

"One day, I asked her to cook me a hamburger. She stomped into the kitchen. I followed her a few minutes later to tell her I liked my food cooked with love, so she didn't have to do it. I'd rather go out and buy a hamburger than watch her sling things around in the kitchen. Well, I walked toward the kitchen and stood in the doorway, waiting to get her attention. You won't believe what I saw. Evileen sprayed insecticide on the hamburger patty, threw it on the floor, stepped on it, and then put it in the frying pan, all the while smiling and humming the song, "It's a "Thin Line Between Love and Hate."

"No, she didn't!" said an audience member.

"Aahhhh!" The audience cried.

"The important question is, when did you decide to leave her?" I asked.

"I confronted her about what I saw her do. True story. She exploded and said she had not done it. And then asked, 'Why were you spying on me anyway and always lying to me?' She totally gaslighted me."

"How long before it was officially over?"

"She turned on me like a Black Mamba because I wanted a divorce. She quickly started trying to turn all my friends against me and tried to ruin my credit by making large purchases on our joint credit cards. She didn't want me to be able to buy anything. I ultimately had to declare bankruptcy. Today I am free of her.

Thankfully, we had no children. I went to talk to my pastor. He said with this type, he recommended no contact. So, I changed my phone number, hung a sale sign and moved." He laughed out loud. "I'm a real man. I cried many nights, though. I couldn't believe this woman who was the love of my life could start out to be so loving and turn so evil. My counselor thinks she has some type of mental illness. That's why I came to the show to share my experience."

"Thank you, Brad. What a story! Do you still want to be with her?"

"Do you want to kiss a King Cobra? Heck no! I still think about how beautiful it was in the beginning. She was the most attractive woman I'd ever dated. She had lavender-colored eyes like Liz Taylor. Her eye color was fake, too. She was so hard to cope with and she was high maintenance. I now realize she never loved me, and she was a liar. All I was to her was a paycheck and benefits. "He sighed.

"No, I don't want Bridezilla. Not now! Not ever! My counselor said she would never change. He said she'd only love-bomb me and eventually leave me again. That was the pattern. He said going back could lead to homicide or suicide. I knew it was not going to be suicide, so I used my wisdom."

I moved on to Emily.

"Folks, this is Emily." Emily had blue eyes, long blond hair and was soft spoken. "She's a nurse. She was married for 18 years and is divorced now with two children. What happened to you, Emily?"

"My ex-husband was handsome, intelligent, and wealthy but acted like a six-year-old. When we first met, we were in college together studying the same major. We had the same classes and homework assignments, so I always did our homework and wrote all our research papers."

I waited for the audience to react before continuing. The camera captured two women shaking their heads in disbelief.

"His parents had money and he had a substantial monthly allowance on which we lived. He spent a lot of money on me, so I didn't mind doing everything for him.

"A few weeks after we graduated from college, we got married and decided to have our children right away. He got a good job working long hours. He seldom came home early, he never had dinner with the family or helped with the children. He was also mean to the kids. After a couple of years, he started telling me I was fat. I had changed. I thought he was joking. I believe he started running around, too. When I'd confront him, he would become outraged and deny it.

"He had become a heavy drinker. He also wanted to do all kinds of kinky sex stuff. I refused. One day he said he was going to the package store. He never came back.

"He'd never wanted me to work so I didn't have a job. The house went into foreclosure and the kids and I moved to a homeless shelter. He went around spreading lies, saying I'd left him. The judge gave me alimony and child support and him visitation rights. However, whenever he comes to pick up the kids, he's always angry. He speaks ill of me to our children. When the kids are back home after weekends with him, they stay in their rooms and are not loving to me as they had been.

"One day my daughter screamed at me and asked, 'Why did you hurt Daddy?'"

"I can't believe the lies he told the kids about me. I had planned to ask him for a divorce before he left me. However, I was so afraid. It was like preparing to jump from a plane into the ocean or off a cliff. I was so scared of him. I couldn't find the courage. He did it for me. Although it was bittersweet, I'm happy it's over," Emily said and exhaled.

"Where is he now?" I asked.

"He still lives about a mile away. He took everything he could take from me. He even took gifts he had given me and the kids. He said he'd punish me for what I had done. But I had a female judge! After the judge's decision, someone broke into our house and took a lot of things belonging to the kids and me. I knew it was my ex."

"Did you file a police report?" I asked.

Emily nodded her head.

"Why do we women put up with this?" I said.

"Well, I was afraid he would continue to rub my name in the dirt or God only knows what else." I reached for a tissue and handed it to Emily.

"Dr. Sherry, why is it these two people never met each other until in the green room before the show and yet their stories are so similar?"

"While I cannot make a diagnosis without meeting someone, based on their stories, I would say both Emily and Brad were married to people with some type of personality disorder," Dr. Sherry said, looking at Brad and Emily.

"Why do all of them seem to hurt the very people they claim to love?" I asked.

"When they were dealt painful blows in childhood, they split and developed a false self to deal with trauma. They now look to their significant other to be the perfect person they will never become."

"Tell us in layman's language what the false self is, please," I requested.

"One theory is this is the façade or shield they wear daily to prevent more hurt and to be whatever the object of their desire is. It's also a shield used to deny feelings. They're empty vessels who fill their tanks from other people. Emily and Brad more than likely filled some need their spouses had. It looks as if they got out before they were severely wounded emotionally or physically. Emily helped with college work and it seems Brad was an ATM," she said as both nodded in agreement.

"What about the shield? Can it be removed?" I asked.

"With psychological work, it can be removed so the real self can shine through. A therapist can help them identify the behaviors that create stress, conflict and disappointment. Once the problem is acknowledged, an essential step to recovery has occurred. Then they can come face to face with what caused the problem, develop empathy and enjoy better relationships. Recovery is rare for personality disorders like narcissism since narcissists believe they're superior to everyone else and rarely seek help."

"Dr. Sherry, is it true they love-bomb you to get what they need from you? And when you no longer give it to them, they reject you or try to destroy your life? They're good manipulators, too. They've practiced manipulation all their lives."

"Yes, the next step is you are discarded or dumped. Once the narcissist starts criticizing you, abusing you or finding something wrong with you, they have probably already found a new source. They're usually finished with you. Some older narcissists will continue to stay with you, disrespect you and punish you for the rest of your life for not living up to the unrealistic expectations they had for you."

"Dr. Sherry, how can we avoid getting involved with a narcissist or recognize one?" I asked.

"Beware of someone anxious to get serious right away. They've probably just lost their supply. Someone who is always talking about themselves, fantasizing about perfect people and having the best of everything. Believe they are superior and need constant praise. Take advantage of others. Jealous. Want to be the center of attention. Can't show empathy. Associate only with high-status people. Put others down. Charming. Unforgiving. Can't accept correction. Are not there for you when you need help. A little scared child does not know how to help. If you see these traits, my advice is—run, run, and run fast!" she said.

"Okay, and we're running out of time. I am laughing, but of course, this isn't a laughing matter. Dr. Sherry, any final advice for Brad and Emily?" I asked.

"Maintain no contact with your exes, if possible. If you are not in counseling and you're feeling depressed, find a good counselor to get some much-needed inner healing. If kids are involved, get a trained child psychologist to help your children. Narcissists don't have a conscience about using their children. Also, if you are having startle reactions, you're probably hurt more than you realize. Some narcissists don't strike with their fists—they hit you with their words".

"Dr. Sherry, quickly . . . why no contact?" I asked with my hands in the air.

"He or she will never be able to forgive you. If you go back, be prepared for payback or torture. The cycle will begin again of love bombing you, devaluing you and wanting to leave. Only counseling intervention will help heal this. Conversations will be argumentative, blaming and fruitless. It's not a good situation. It's like alcoholism—no help is possible until you hear them say, 'I want to change my life.'"

"Dr. Sherry, one last question. What pushes them to get treatment?" I asked.

"Failed relationships will most likely push someone with this disorder to seek help," she said.

"That's what I heard, too. Thank you, Emily, Brad and Dr. Sherry. Thank you, my audience family. I couldn't do this without you. Goodbye, everybody!" I stood and waved as the audience applauded.

"Cut, you can go home. It's another wrap!" said the announcer, removing her headset.

"Call time is Friday instead of Thursday. Tell your friends about the show. See you then."

The lights were turned down and the audience had gone, but I remained on stage with Emily and Brad.

"Dr. Sherry, thank you for being here today," I said. "I'll be in touch with you soon." We embraced and she left the studio.

"Emily and Brad, you were terrific. I want to come back in the future after you've had more time to heal. You will heal. Just one question—did either of you ever see your ex hurt any animals?"

"Mine didn't like cats," Emily said.

"Mine was mean to the kid's dog. Bozo bit her and she gave him to the neighbor," said Brad. "The kids cried about Bozo for months. She told 'em to grow up."

"Okay. Thanks," I responded. I hugged them both, and the security guard escorted them to the parking lot.

Why do some sociopaths and psychopath hurt animals? Hmmm.

"How did it go?" I inquired of Nancy.

"Well done," she said as she turned off the camera and monitors. "But I would love to hear you interview a malignant narcissist. An interview with a diagnosed narcissist would make a great future show. Let's talk more about it," she said, walking away.

"Great minds think alike," I said with a smile. I grabbed my purse and headed for the door.

Mission accomplished. Maybe.

FORTY-FIVE

According to Sakina, my guests were still sitting on the edge of their seats while Emma continued to read my manuscript.

"Hey, let's take a bathroom or stretch break," as she looked up.

A lady stood up. "This is some juicy stuff! Let's finish it. Grace may be back soon," she said. As she looked around then lowered her eyes. No one agreed. Emma found the place where she left off and assured them she would finish soon. Most of the guests leaned closer as she continued . . .

"I hope today is not going to be another one of those days," I said to myself as the phone rang.

"Hello?"

"Hey, Grace. This is Winston."

"Yeah, Hey, Winston. What's up?" I said, trying not to sound hostile.

"Just wanted to tell you congratulations on your new job. I'm proud of you. I've been watching your show. I like it! Great format and lots of useful topics. *Still I Rise*! I love the title, too. Very informative! Narcissus told me the other day he watches it also."

"Good. He needs it," I responded, tightening my lips.

"Narcissus has been different since your break-up. You were good for him, Grace. Prophet Kahlil Gibran once wrote, Love knows not its own depth until the hour of separation. In other words, you don't miss your water until your glass is empty. I called to let you know how sorry I was about Theresa."

"Yes. I miss my best friend. It is shocking what happened to her. Who could do such a cruel thing?"

"Well, Grace, I'm going to cut to the chase. I didn't know whether you knew about Theresa and Narcissus' affair. I didn't attend the funeral because her family didn't know me, and we no longer saw each other because of what happened."

My mind raced back to my last conversation with Theresa.

So that's the reason she was always defending him when we had our girl talks. She also said she had had a one-night stand she regretted. Was it with Narcissus? Did he hurt her?

"She always flirted with him," Winston confirmed. "And she often talked about how good looking he is. One night she came to my house. Narcissus was here. He had a key. He used my house from time to time for his man cave. We often watched sports and hung out together."

"Man cave? Narcissus has a key to your house? Well, this certainly explains a lot."

"Now, don't be mad at me. He never gave me the key back after you two got married."

"He said one evening Theresa had knocked at the door. Narcissus said when he answered the door, she pushed away into my place. She had been drinking and was sad. She was lonely. He was lonely. It just happened. He's a man, Grace. And you two were having problems. After I found out, I wanted to knock Narcissus out," Winston said.

"However, I think, for Theresa it was about revenge, because she kept accusing me of dating a lady at the church, and I think Narcissus was just a lonely man.

"Yeah, Theresa told me it was not just a lady, but the First Lady".

"She was lying. Not true. Afterward, I told her we could only be friends. I think she continued to see Narcissus, trying to make me jealous. The relationship was over with her. Especially when she told me she was pregnant with Narcissus' child. I know I should have told you sooner, but Narcissus is my buddy."

"Okay, Winston. It's none of my business. But you weren't done with Narcissus, too?" I said almost swooning.

"Narcissus is my buddy. Man rule is you don't kick a buddy when he's down. After all, you were treating him mean. Theresa told him you had stopped calling her when you became a celebrity."

"Winston, thanks for your call. I have a meeting in about half an hour. I have to go."

"Well, good luck with your show. It's nice to hear from you again. The relationship with Theresa wasn't working out, but I didn't want her dead. Call me if you need anything."

"Yeah, Winston, I sure will."

I double-checked my cell phone to make sure I had hung it up. Then, I stood up.

"Narcissus' what?" My blood pressure was going up. I could feel steam rising from my collar. "That lying, busybody Winston and that lowdown, sniveling two-faced snake, may her anguished soul burn in the lake of fire! This explains the radiant complexion and her bloated look. She was pregnant! And Narcissus—I have no words for him. I knew he wasn't doing computer work all those odd hours. I also was awake early mornings when he came home after a fresh shower. He'd probably been with Theresa.

I didn't know what to think or how to feel. Theresa was my best friend, whom I loved, and now she was dead. Narcissus was my husband, and did he kill her because she was pregnant and he did not love her? He did n't even like her, he'd said. God, are there any good people left in this crazy world?

I sat in my leather, hand-shaped red chair by the window and sobbed uncontrollably for a few minutes. I was grieving the loss of Theresa, my past life with Narcissus, and friends I'd never had. I heard Papa say once if you found one real friend in life, you had done well. I had not done well and was still looking. God would have to send him or her because I didn't seem to have any skill or discernment for picking them.

I got up, went into the bathroom, and washed my face. I stared at myself in the mirror.

"Thank you, Theresa and Narcissus," I said.

FORTY-SIX

It was my birthday. I was looking forward to the celebration with Octavius. I missed Mama's 5:30am call. I missed Theresa and I don't know why. However, the good news was the show that week had gone well, and I left the studio to go home, soak, and go out to celebrate my birthday with my real friend Octavius. I smiled as I picked up my cell phone, because Cedric had left me a text message at 5:30am. He missed Mimi, and he knew how much I missed his grandmother, too.

My red-soled, high heels were killing my feet. I couldn't wait to get to my car to kick them off. It had rained, and the weather was comfortable. The parking lot was quiet and wet. I could hear the faint sound of traffic and water splashing on the main road.

Before I reached my car, a car with darkly tinted windows suddenly stopped in front of me in the parking lot. The front passenger door opened and my ex-husband stepped out with a wide smile. He was handsome as ever, but he couldn't charm me anymore. I knew what was behind that sexy smile and those enticing green eyes. The driver sped away, leaving us alone. A lump suddenly formed in my throat. I had not seen Narcissus up close since the attorney's meeting.

"Hey, little lady," he said as he blocked my way.

"Hello Narcissus, what are you doing here? What's up?" I said, showing calmness but keeping my hand tucked inside my purse.

"Is this the way to greet your loving ex-husband? You don't even have the decency to ask me how I'm doing. I need your help," he growled and leaned against the driver's door.

"So, Narcissus, how are you doing? And again, what are you doing here? Do I need to call security?" I asked sarcastically.

"Well, it certainly sounds like you could care less! Anyway, I see your little show is all over TV and the internet. I hope you haven't forgotten who helped you get there," he stated as if it was the truth.

"Yeah, Narcissus, you got behind me like Satan and pushed me into my destiny."

"Well, you were the one who divorced me," he answered like a kid had just taken his ball.

"Narcissus, please let's not do this," I said. "It's over and I did exactly what you wanted. And you know it. You didn't know it would hurt so badly because you didn't get to do it first. You pushed me out. You know it, and I know it. Now cut the shenanigans. Think about this—we were like formula for water. You were Hydrogen, and I was double Oxygen. We filled a lot of bottles. So, now you don't have any Oxygen, how's that going for you? It's hard to breathe. Isn't it? What exactly do you want Malevolent, I mean Narcissus? Now step aside," I said sternly. Narcissus looked confused, moved slowly away from the door.

"I'm stranded down the road, and I need someone to take me to my truck. I hate Uber so I hitchhiked to your job. You told me you would do anything for me at the divorce table. I wanted to see if it was true," he said, still playing mind games.

"All right, I'll take you," I said. "Unlike you, I'm a woman of my word," I said.

"You've got a little spice. You should have been more like this when we were married. It's quite sexy. You wouldn't even stand up to me back then. Why were you such a doormat?" he asked .I refused to respond.

"Where there is no wood, the fire will go out," I said loudly, smiling and thinking how I would run him over with my car when he got out.

Narcissus got in the car with me, a puzzled look on his face. He didn't try to hold any small talk. He only gave directions to where he said he left his truck. At times, I could feel his stare stinging the side of my face and wondered what was on his little pea brain.

"Where is your truck? How much farther?" I asked.

"The truck may not be there, but someone else is bringing it back to meet us," he said.

I drove on a narrow road about five miles into a wooded area. Narcissus's story changed, and I had begun to feel a little anxious.

He pointed to the spot where I pulled off the road and parked to wait for his truck. I was looking at my cell phone when a man suddenly appeared out of nowhere and was tapping on my car window. I about fainted.

He looked like an actor from the *Walking Dead*. He was expressionless, staring at me. What had I just gotten myself into? The driver also looked like the person who had just dropped Narcissus off at my job.

"What are you so jumpy about? This is just Bennie, my mechanic. What? You think I'm going to slit your throat or something because you're a big-time talk show host and driving an orange Mercedes Benz? Are you better than me now? And why orange?" he asked and laughed insanely.

"Narcissus, I gave you a ride. Now please get out of my car and go to your truck with Bennie. I have to go. The color of my car is none of your business. Why are you still playing games?" I asked.

Narcissus gave me a furious and despicable look, reached in his pocket, took out a pocketknife and raised it in the air. As I reached for my purse, he stabbed my car seat and then reached for the door handle to get out of the car. I remained motionless and didn't move a muscle. He stared at me with a look I'd seen before.

"I bet you told my secret, too, didn't you, Grace? You'd love to see me go to jail," he railed.

Then I reached into my handbag and pulled out my pink .380 semi-automatic handgun. I placed the barrel at Narcissus' temple.

"Get out of my car or I will blow your brains out," I calmly said.

Lord, if you allow me to survive this, I promise you I'll never do stupid again. Narcissus' eyes bulged. I had never seen him so frightened.

"You used to love me," he gingerly said like a child, pulling the door handle and pushing open the door while keeping his eyes glued to the pistol.

I continued to remain calm and squinted my eyes. However, I was scared as all get out. "Remember what I said I'd do if anybody hurt Cedric? Don't tempt me. I have nothing else to say!" *One way to shut up a narcissist*.

Trembling, Narcissus carefully placed one leg outside the door. I threw the car into drive and pressed the pedal to the metal. The car knocked Narcissus to the ground. He was still holding onto the door handle. The doors auto locked. I sped away, laughing hysterically, dragging him a few feet.

Looking through the rearview mirror, I saw him lying in the middle of the road, spouting words, while Bela Lugosi stood there pointing at me. I careened onto the narrow road, laying rubber. I roared away.

"You're not any better than me. I made you. I gave you everything you have," Narcissus shouted.

"No, but what you did was pee on my seat you coward! What made me think I could trust you?" my dumb self said as I took tissue to wipe my forehead and cover the yellow puddle.

I then drove to Octavius' house. By the time I arrived, my sanity had returned.

I got out of the car and knocked frantically at his door until he opened it. I rushed in, fell into his arms and cried. I told him what had happened. Octavius stared at me for a moment. Then he held me tight.

"I'm so sorry you had to go through that," he said. "You're going to have to stay away from Narcissus. It sounds to me as if he's escalating. Stabbing the seat could be what he wanted to do to you. He's going to make me show my Marine survival skills."

"Well . . . that's not the first time he cut something of mine. When we were married, he cut one of my wedding shoes," I explained as I sat down. "When I confronted him, he denied it. I still don't understand. I must have made him angry about something. I knew he had done it, or someone had broken into our house. But why would they leave other valuable items and cut a shoe? Didn't make sense then or now. He became enraged, denied he had done it and then told me where to take it for repair. He never mentioned it again. Something was happening back then. I think someone must have done it to his favorite shoes when he was a child."

"And his car seat when he was a teen," said Octavius with a serious look. "Well, it's your birthday. I know where we can get the seat repaired and sanitized," Octavius said and laughed.

"Grace, It's your birthday. Let's not allow the devil to ruin the evening we had planned. I've reserved a table for two at your special French restaurant, La Mignon's, with the river view for 7pm."

"I'm a little shaken by what happened," I admitted. "I have to put this behind me. And I learned my lesson. Can I park my car in your garage?" I asked.

"Yes. That was my next suggestion," he said as he walked into the kitchen and came back with a glass of pink Moscato. "This will help you relax. Did you hear from Cedric today?" Octavius asked as he was putting the glass in my hand.

"I didn't remember to tell you Cedric mailed a gift to the studio yesterday. He sent a box of chocolate-covered strawberries and a text message today?" I said, "Happy birthday to my favorite mother. Ha-ha!"

"I better be your only mother. Ha-ha!" I messaged back.

"He got you back, didn't he?" He asked as we left the house.

Octavius opened the door and helped me into his car.

"Be at peace, Babe. I've got you."

When we reached the restaurant, Octavius handed me a small box. I was so excited!

"Happy birthday. Open it now. I hope you like it," he said.

I opened the box. I tried not to show my disappointment. It contained a beautiful garnet bracelet. I thought it would be a ring.

"Oh, it's beautiful. Help me put it on. I want to wear it now," I said.

"These garnet beads have healing power," Octavius said as he focused on fastening the clasp around my wrist. "What do you think about us becoming an item?"

"I thought we already were," I said with a wink. Octavius smiled from ear to ear as he got out and walked around to open the passenger door. We held hands as we walked into La Mignon's and he ordered my favorite entree, Medallions of Veal.

It felt as if happiness was finally just around the bend. I could see the light from a sapphire engagement ring at the end of the tunnel. I hoped it wasn't the light of an oncoming police vehicle driven by Narcissus. Ha!

FORTY-SEVEN

After I threw Narcissus out of my car, I knew he'd run to his buddy Winston. However, something strange happened. My phone rang and when I picked it up, I was in a three-way with Winston and Narcissus. I pushed the mute button and remained quiet.

"Yo, Player. What's up?" Winston yawned and Narcissus could hear him pushing back the bed covers.

"Hey, Winston. Man, what's been going on?" Narcissus said.

"What you doing up so early? It's Saturday morning. You should be sleeping in," Winston said.

"Got a lot on my mind. Need to do some man talk," Narcissus muttered. "I ran into Grace a while back. I knew it was her birthday, and I just wanted to see her. I met her outside the station. Man, she was looking good, too!"

"So, you've been stalking Grace again?" Winston asked

"I have never stalked her and never will." Narcissus scoffed. "I just happened to be near her side of town, and I asked her to drive me to get my truck. I just wanted to harass her a little. It didn't work this time. She's not the same. She practically threw me out of her car and left me lying on the road after I stabbed her car seat with my pocketknife."

"Stabbed her seat? You're saying that as if it was nothing. I would have thrown you out and run you over. Man, are you crazy?" Winston squawked loudly.

"I don't know what's wrong with me. I wanted to control her I guess. I couldn't. I was so angry, I could cut her. So, I cut the car seat instead." He smiled.

"Well . . . I think you were lucky. Women are packing these days," he said. "She could have shot you or at least covered your face in pepper spray."

"She's different. She could very well be carrying a little handgun in her Michael Kors or Gucci purse." (Narcissus felt ashamed because he knew for a fact I packed, but he was not about to tell Winston how it had scared him.)

"Narcissus, did you watch Grace's last talk show?" Winston asked.

"Yes. I try not to miss them. I watch it mainly to see how she is doing without me."

"Looks like she is doing quite well," Winston mused. "Anyway, she had two guests on who were married to people who had been in relationships with people who loved them to death then dumped them for reasons that didn't make sense."

"Yeah. Why are you telling me this, man?" Narcissus asked.

"Because they sounded like you and me."

"Man, don't you ever let me hear you say something like this outside of this telephone line."

"Narcissus, you and me, we go way back. Let's get real. What women have we had long-term success with?"

"Winston, maybe we haven't met the right women."

"Maybe we have just not been the right men. I watched one of her talk shows. I saw myself in most of what they were saying. I started to shake Narcissus. I think I'm a narcissist. No—I really think I'm one," he said slowly.

"The girl had a nervous breakdown. I know we joked about it, Winston, but it wasn't your fault. And Theresa was murdered. You didn't kill her, did you?" He ranted.

"No, Narcissus. But I see myself. I get these girls. I treat them extra special in the beginning to win them over. I'm not just nice. I'm trying to win them. I hook them, I become bored quickly, and soon afterward I can't stand them and will start to reject them. Then when they start chasing me and begging for my attention, I leave them. And man, I can't stop. I can't help myself. I think I'm a hopeless sociopath, I think. If I don't change, there's no way I can continue my associate pastor role. I will be a damaged leader and end up hurting people. My reputation is beginning to precede me Narcissus."

"Well, I've been engaged a couple of times, and then I married Grace. What's abnormal about that? I'm no sociopath and neither are you. What does it even really means?" said Narcissus scratching his head.

"You know when I was nine years old, I killed the neighbor's puppy after my stepfather locked me in the attic, and my dog died. He took me to a shrink, and they diagnosed me with something. I can't remember what it was. But I grew out of it. You're normal just like me. Stop talking crazy."

"What about all those girls? The main ones and the side pieces? Man, I think we hurt those women." Winston said.

"Speak for yourself. I was nice to my real dad, and I was nice to Theresa," Narcissus drifted for a moment. "I mean, I always said nice things when I ended relationships. I once dated this girl named Makenzie. I told her our relationship wasn't exclusive . . . right from the beginning. She knew right off the bat. I was never just hers. So, she can't blame me if she was heartbroken. I warned her. I also told her she could ask for anything. Of course, I was glad she never did. Then one day, I called her and told her I was marrying Grace. I told Makenzie Grace was the woman I truly loved."

"Man, where do you get these lines? Did she go along with the non-exclusive line?" he asked.

"Yes. I sent Makenzie a gift and went out with her one final time. I knew when I met her how it was going to an end. I liked her a lot, but then I met Grace, the girl I had dreamed my whole life about."

"How did Makenzie take it?"

"Man, she took it well. She was in love with me. She didn't even cry. At least not in my presence. She was so calm; I was looking over my shoulder for retaliation. You know it's a thin line between love and hate. Now I recall, I did have a flat tire every thirty days for a while. It was just a coincidence. I don't think she was the spiteful type like me, but I don't trust women period. I won't let them cook grits either," he laughed.

"Seriously, I can call every woman I've ever dated—at least those who are still alive. I just want to see whether they are doing bad without me. I get a kick out of that. Now the girl at the bank—once I finished our business transaction, it was Adios Senorita! She was country and loud. I like a lady!"

"Man, you're crazy," said Winston with a laugh.

Don't like them fugly either." Narcissus belly laughed.

"Man, you are sick." Winston laughed, too. "Beauty is skin deep."

"But fugly is to the ba–ba-bones." Narcissus raised his eyebrows and continued laughing.

"I have to go Winston. Thanks for the man talk. Meeting a new lady friend I'm meeting for breakfast. She's the Governor's niece. "

"Okay, Man. You're never going to change, are you?" he asked.

"I hope not," said Narcissus laughing.

"Hey Narcissus, I got a lady issue, too. You got another minute?"

"No, you'll work it out. See you later."

" Man, you are hardly ever here for me," Winston complained as Narcissus was hanging up. I hung up too. Whew!

FORTY-EIGHT

"Still I Rise, the best talk show since the *Oprah Show*, is on at 10am every Wednesday. Today's show is extra special you don't want to miss it. Our guest will be a woman who wants to confront her ex-lover, whom she invited. We don't want to spoil the reveal. Tune in at 10am today for *Still I Rise* with Grace," the advertisement proclaimed.

"I just feel today's show is going to produce a miracle for someone," Nancy said to me after running the short commercial. All the staff was in high spirits about this show.

My guest arrived and took her seat. They had set up her ex in the Green Room.

"Cameras! Lights! Action! We're live streaming from the FBN TV studios in downtown Greenville. Here's Grace!" I walked onto the stage in my red houndstooth kick butt celebration suit. "Today marks one year for the show," the announcer said.

"Hello, everybody! Today marks our one-year anniversary. It's all because of you. Give yourselves and our TV audience a round of applause," I said as I pointed both fingers at them.

"Thank you. Today's show is about a condition where a man or woman is so self-absorbed, they cause a miserable existence for other people. Some relationships have ended in suicide and murder. Some of their victims have also developed illnesses from the stress they cause. They can be parents, siblings, coworkers or even high-profile politicians. It's quite unbelievable unless you've been on the receiving end of this type abuse.

"Today, you're going to learn about a little known existential threat to relationships. It's one of life's little secrets. And what you can do if you believe someone you love suffers from it. The body becomes sick sometimes because of the way we treat it and, likewise, the mind. Today's guest wants to confront a man she dated who doesn't know he has the condition and is undiagnosed. He will remain backstage and unidentified throughout the show. We've changed his name and voice over to protect his identity." *I had no idea I was speaking prophetically*.

"Welcome, Caryll. Come on out! Who did you invite?"
Caryll sat and waited until the thunderous applause died down before speaking. "I invited Nicolas. I heard he wanted to apologize to me for causing me to have a nervous breakdown. I spent six months in a mental institution."

"Welcome, Nicolas," I said.

"Thank you," said Nicolas in a deep, distorted voice.

"I also invited Dr. Moses Acquah, a renowned psychotherapist who counsels people with personality disorders. He is known all over the world and was recently featured in *Time* magazine. Welcome, Dr. Acquah."

Dr. Acquah nodded and smiled at the clapping audience.

"Thank you," he said in a deep baritone voice with an African accent.

"Caryll, what do you want to say to Nicolas?"

"Nicolas, we were introduced because it was believed you were the kind of man every mother wants her daughter to date. After a short romance, you asked me to marry you. You said you were ready to settle down. I had imagined you and I sitting in rocking chairs together holding hands into old age. I quit my job, packed up my house and moved to this area. You made a lot of promises and said there was nobody for you but me. You said I was the girl you'd been looking for. I was so happy, I bought us a house.

"But after the engagement announcement and celebration, I didn't hear from you much," Caryll continued. "I knew you were busy with your computer side gig and would contact me soon. However, I was watching YouTube videos and saw one of you at a nightclub with another woman. I fainted. I'd believed everything you had said.

"After seeing the video, I couldn't sleep. I couldn't eat. I became depressed and barricaded myself in my house. You lied and said it wasn't you. One night I decided to take a razor and slit my wrist and end it all. Then, I could hear Sophia from The Color Purple saying to me, 'It ain't worth it! It ain't worth it!' I made a tourniquet and called 911. I almost did not make it."

"I was committed to Cabin by the Sea for Mental Health. I stayed there for six months. I received only one letter from you telling me our engagement was off."

She paused when the audience booed.

"You left me for dead, Nicolas. But I recovered, and here I am to set the record straight."

Now the audience was applauding.

"Nicolas, what do you want to say to Caryll?" I asked, trying not to show my disgust.

"After I didn't hear from you, Caryll," Nicolas began, "I thought the relationship was over. I tried to call you and you never returned my call. Then, I heard you were in Cabin by the Sea. I told people you were probably stressed about the engagement and were getting older, so you had a breakdown. You tried to kill yourself? Well, I don't think this had anything to do with me. You're crazy if you think I'm at fault for you going to a mental institution," Nicolas said without any remorse.

"I'll bet you tried hard to find an excuse, Nicolas," Caryll screamed. "My counselor warned me you would deny this. I'm prepared to confront you. She told me about your kind. I studied your personality style. The research says if a narcissist's lips are moving, he or she is lying. Why did you pretend to love me?"

"Nicolas, just a minute. You say you aren't at fault," I said. "Are willing to come out onto the stage with us, since you have nothing to hide?"

"Since I agreed to come here, I've been troubled. I don't want to live my life like this anymore. I want to be happy. I want to be loved. It just seems so unreachable since I'm never satisfied with what any woman offers. People hate me, and I've failed in most of my relationships. Maybe I can figure out what's wrong with them or me. So, yes I am willing."

"Right move, Nicolas." I interjected.

"Let's cut to a commercial break, and we'll be right back. Come on out, Nicolas."

Nicolas exited the green room. Everyone watched him on camera. He was in the short hallway walking toward the stage when I finally looked away from my cue cards. Nicolas sure looked familiar as he stopped to admire himself in the mirror. He was a tall, handsome and distinguished looking gentleman. I was sure the studio audience could hear my heart racing and could see the vein in my neck pulsating when Nicolas stepped through the door. I suddenly gasped, "Narcissus?"

I knew those wild, green eyes and the wide grin anywhere.

"Yes, it's me. Grace, I wanted to be on your show. So, when Caryll invited me, I thought it would be a good time for me to clear the air with both of you. Kill two birds with one stone, as they say." He smiled.

"You dated Grace Smith? You sabotaged your relationship with her, too. You fool. What were you thinking?" Caryll asked shaking her head.

"I don't know what to say, but . . . let the cameras roll," I said, literally trembling in my boots.

"Now, back to *Still I Rise* with Grace," said the announcer excitedly.

"Audience, we are back. Our surprise is bringing Caryll's ex onto the stage with us. At the commercial break, I discovered Nicolas's real name is Narcissus. Narcissus is not only Caryll's ex but my ex-husband too."

The audience roared at the surprising reveal.

"I'm okay, everybody. I believe this will be insightful for both of us," I said.

Narcissus, please tell the audience why you decided to reveal yourself."

"Well, I'm proud to say I'm the ex-husband of Grace. She used to love me. I'm not a sociopath. I met Caryll two years ago, and some of the things she said about me are true. I think I'm a jackass. I mean, a jerk at times," he said as he stared into the audience."

"Why did you deceive me, Narcissus?" Caryll asked.

"I don't know. I think I say something for so long I start to believe it's true. It keeps me in control. I did everything possible to avoid the shame of what I did to you. While I didn't want to be concerned about you, I was embarrassed. I knew your family would blame me, so I blamed it on you," Narcissus said with pride.

"Most people would feel some degree of remorse," I said. "Do you feel bad about how you treated Caryll, or me, your ex-wife? Do you feel you have any empathy for us at all?"

"I regret how I treated you and Caryll, but I don't feel bad about it. You brought it on yourselves, being weak women. What I miss is the good feeling I had when people talked about Caryll because she's a scientist. I knew we were going to look good together. And you, Grace, you would do anything for me regardless of how I treated you. I told my buddies about how smart you were and watched their jealous faces. I missed you. I know how to pretend I can feel other people's pain, but in all honesty, I don't. That's empathy, right?"

Dr. Acquah joined the dialogue.

"Right. Empathy makes you a more compassionate friend, lover or parent. Your ability to empathize or feel compassion develops when you are a child. If you don't have it, when you hurt people, you don't feel anything or have remorse," he said.

"Speaking of a missing barometer, Narcissus, I feel you tried to destroy my life when I left you," I added. "You were the one who wanted me to leave, but when I left, all kinds of crazy things started to happen. Stalking, property damage, break-ins, and more. Were you behind it? Negative things about me appeared on the internet. People were talking about me. Someone sent viruses to my phone and computer. My car tires were sliced. Did you know you were committing a criminal offense? I have to know."

"First, I didn't do it," he said angrily.

"You were the girl of my dreams. I studied you. I listened to how you talked about your family when we first met. I listened when you talked about all the gifts they gave you. I wanted to show you I could love you just as much as they did. You treated Cedric like he was a prince. On the one hand, I was so jealous of you, I could have scratched your eyes out. I just wanted to tear it all apart. But on the other hand, you were showing me how you would treat me. I knew you would be kind, respectful, loving and forgiving.

"I had finally found someone who would support me and be there for me. Do what I wanted. Go where I wanted to go. Wouldn't question me. If I said jump, you would ask how high? You were the one I could depend on to supply me. You were the one. I wanted you to have everything because you gave me everything. You were my oxygen. Because of you, I had learned to breathe. I didn't do all those things to you. How could one person do all of that? You obviously have other enemies."

"Help us, Dr. Acquah," I said. "If we were all of this, why did Narcissus let all the air out of our balloons and our tires? Why did he cut my tires and my shoes? Take my wedding rings?"

"If he did it, it was because you took away what you'd previously freely given, whether it was your beauty, confidence, finances or respect—whatever was the reason he chose you to be his companion in the first place. He saw you as a failure. Therefore, he had to punish you. TSo he could find another supply," Dr. Acquah said as though he knew.

"You took everything from me, Narcissus," I said. Either you physically removed it or destroyed it. The things you bought. The stuff I bought. Gifts from other people," I said.

"Grace. Again, it was not all me. I think you had many enemies. You weren't as perfect as you thought. But you were my property. I gave you things because you were giving a lot to me. The way I saw it, if I couldn't keep you, you couldn't keep the stuff. I thought you could see I needed you. I knew you saw my warts and scabs. I thought you would tell everybody about me and expose me," Narcissus said, glaring at me.

"Narcissus, why did you start to pull away after we got engaged?" Caryll asked. "You didn't give me a chance to see the warts. And did you steal the engagement ring when I got sick? My house was broken into when I was in recovery. My engagement ring and only the gifts you'd ever given me were missing," Caryll said as she sat on the edge of her seat.

"Of course not. You let your guard down and started whining about setting a date for the wedding. I hate a whiner. You were getting on my nerves and at the same time were letting yourself go. Also, you stopped exercising. I noticed you had thick thighs. I like legs shaped like Grace's. I needed someone strong who could take care of me," he said angrily and without an ounce of shame.

"So, you hated me because I wasn't Grace? Why didn't you tell me, you jerk!"

"Because deep inside, I didn't know how. I feel like a worthless piece of junk no one will ever love." Narcissus shouted and dropped his head into his hands. "My friends and the family joined me in making your lives miserable. Please don't press charges against me."

I motioned for Dr. Acquah to intervene.

"Okay. Narcissus, brace yourself. You feel bad about yourself because of the way people treated you when you were a child. It made you this way. Are you comfortable telling us what your childhood was really like? Who mistreated you? No more faking it, Narcissus. Your family wasn't perfect. You're not perfect. You must stop pretending they were flawless and allow your healing to take place.

Keeping his head down, Narcissus spoke slowly.

"My childhood was tough. My real dad left us when I was seven. He was a monster. Mom said she couldn't do anything to please him. I was the one who stopped him from hurting my sister one day. He died suddenly. That was the last time I saw him." Narcissus said as he stared into space. "Then my mom moved Bernie, my stepfather, into our house the next week. I thought he'd be better."

"Bernie would sometimes beat me with his fists and lock me in the attic for days. No food, no access to the bathroom and no baths. Afterward, he'd strip me naked and water-hose me in front of the neighbors. Can you imagine what it was like for a nine-year-old? I felt so ashamed and humiliated. Bernie would hug me afterward with a big eerie grin on his face and buck those wild grey eyes and say, 'Narcissus, this is how life is.'" Narcissus groaned in misery.

"Whenever my mother was angry with me, she and my sisters would give me the silent treatment. If my mother couldn't control me or make me do something, she would take the kitchen knife and cut my clothes and shoes. She said I was a loser, just like my real dad. She said I was evil like him, too. She hoped life would do to me what I had done to the neighbor's puppy. I cried myself to sleep almost every night."

"Narcissus, how do you feel about yourself right now?" Dr. Acquah asked.

"I'm angry, and I'm scared. I wish my mother had aborted me. Sometimes I feel like a monster. I treat other people the way my family treated me. It's like misplaced revenge. When you left me, Grace, I thought my world had come to an end. You were everything to me my family couldn't be. But I was bored and restless. I pushed you away and you left as they had predicted you would.

"I wanted to kill myself. I called you a failure and said no one liked you. I didn't care. I wanted to punish you and find someone new. But I couldn't. I was off my game. Every time I saw you happy, I would explode in anger. You knew too much about me!

"Then, I met Caryll. She was gorgeous, smart and just too nice. When she had her breakdown, I knew she'd say I was the reason. I didn't know how to escape the prison I'd found myself in. I knew I was going to hurt her. I couldn't help it. Every time a relationship ended, I wanted to jump off a bridge or throw someone else off. I can't stop this miserable merry go round."

Narcissus became enraged, jumped to his feet and turned over his chair. The security guard rushed to the stage and restrained him. I watched Narcissus, wondering whether he would tell all. I had kept my word. I'd promised him I would never tell his secret. I was taking it to my grave. I was a better friend to him than he had ever been to me.

"I know something is wrong with me. Who can help me?" Narcissus screamed.

Dr. Acquah spoke gently to him. "You've had a narcissistic injury. There is help for you, Narcissus," he reassured him. "I got help. I used to be like you. A lot of counselors say change for people like you and me is impossible.

"I always say where there's a will, there's a way, but it's not going to be easy. I, too, was a malignant narcissist. However, change is possible. You can learn new approaches to healthy relationships. You can learn empathy and how to love and receive love. You can be healed and no longer suffer in silent pain. If you have been watching these shows, you know what the first step is. Go ahead. Face the audience and be a man," Dr. Acquah said.

Facing the audience with his face glistening with tears, he slowly said, "My name is Narcissus Bentley Little, and I'm a malignant narcissist. I want to be a better man, neighbor, coworker or friend, and have a happier life. I want to be free from myself. I want to know I am loved. I want to learn to love others. So far, it hasn't been in the cards for me. I was diagnosed when I was nine years old. I've hidden it all my life."

"Help me, God!" he cried and crumbled from his chair to the floor.

Both Caryll and I sobbed.

The audience exploded. Three robust men ran on stage, and the group-hugged Narcissus as he openly sobbed. I'd never seen a man so broken. There wasn't a dry eye in the studio, including mine.

"I'm not going to a commercial break," I said motioning my staff for tissue.

"What you see is real. If you're watching and you, too, are tired of hurting, find help or contact the station and we'll refer you to someone who can professionally help you," I said as I wiped my eyes.

"Every night I have the same dream." Narcissus said as he cried shamelessly. "A dark hooded figure tells me, 'You're going to hell . . . you're going to hell.' I can smell the scent of a pig pen and pigs snorting and flesh burning. It's horrible. I don't want to go to hell."

"Narcissus, I can help you," Dr. Acquah assured him again. "I can recommend you to the best treatment center in Greenville. My association will pay for it. There's a limo outside waiting to take us there and get you registered. Your life will never be the same." Dr. Acquah waved goodbye to the audience, and he and Narcissus walked off stage together.

"Thank you, Dr. Acquah. And thank you, Caryll, for coming and inviting Narcissus," I said. "Today's show was unusual. We accomplished something psychologists say is hard and rare. We compelled someone who has a malignant narcissistic personality disorder to seek treatment. You saw it with your own eyes, folks," I said as I looked directly into the camera.

"Love conquered again. You were all awesome today, and I couldn't have done it without you. Remember, we're all God's children, brothers and sisters on this journey called life. Never kick a man when he is already down. Help be the lifter up of his head. Goodbye, everybody."

"Cut," said Nancy, looking at the studio audience with tears in her eyes. "It's a wrap. I'll send you an email about the upcoming call time," she said as the audience exited the studio.

I hugged Caryll when the audience left.

"Bullyah! We did it! The best revenge was compelling Narcissus to admit he needed help. Today was the perfect silver bullet. Nice to meet you, Caryll. I think you knew exactly what you were doing when you contacted us," I said.

Caryll smiled.

"I'm so glad you, too, agreed revenge was not the best solution. All I've ever wanted was for Narcissus to get help. Let's keep in touch. You probably don't remember me but, I used to live two doors from you before you became famous, but it was so long ago you probably don't remember me," Caryll said.

"Your face is familiar. But I was deep in my troubles at the time, I'm sure. Don't take it personally the memory escapes me."

"I don't. Thanks for bringing me to your show," Caryll said and left the studio.

"Well, Grace, what a reality show today!" said Nancy, grabbing me.

"Yes. It was. I believe it brought closure for me."

"And our ratings skyrocketed today. Grace, you are an awesome lady. Goodnight."

"Goodnight." I took Nancy by the hand and we both took a bow, then left the studio.

As soon as I started my car, I called Octavius. He was waiting for my call.

"Hey Babe, well . . . it's over. I saw the show. I was so proud of you. You have closure now. You helped Narcissus. I always knew you wouldn't be happy until you could. Now I can call off the hit," Octavius said with a laugh.

"What? Man, you're crazy!" I said, joining in his laughter.

"Just kidding. I was praying for the perfect ending, too."

It looked as if Narcissus got his wish, after all, he was playing a part in me becoming famous.

FORTY-NINE
Back To The Wedding

Emma slowly closed the manuscript and put it back in her bag. Some of my guests were still wiping their eyes.

"That's it everyone. This is the story Grace wrote about her life," she said. "I know you can clearly see why I was so concerned and tried to discourage her to wait a while before marrying Octavius."

Suddenly the Reception Hall doors swung open as though a trumpet had sounded. Emma looked up like a deer caught in lights, surprised to see Octavius and me walking through the doorway. She forced an awkward smile and hand clap.

The band played the wedding song as applause and a standing ovation rang from the wedding party and audience. Octavius and I held hands and smiled in front of the happy crowd. Octavius assured everyone he'd had a successful release from the hospital, and the doctor had approved he could proceed in the wedding ceremony.

"I hope everyone was able to find some enjoyment in this beautiful room today despite the work of the devil," I said.

"I received a text message on the way back to the wedding. I understand Emma, my good friend, had quite an intriguing story to share from my private manuscript. Things I'd only shared with her and planned to publish someday. Thank you, Emma. The one thing I know for sure is the truth can free you from your prison."

Emma looked awkward and took her seat. Everyone glared at her. I find it interesting Octavius got sick, and Emma just happened to have my manuscript with her at the wedding. There is definitely a fly in the ointment, as Papa would say.

"Well, there's still going to be a wedding! Thank you for all your prayers. So, wedding party, let's try it again," I said cheerfully, looking at Octavius and giving his hand a squeeze.

"Please give a resounding round of applause to my sweet groom Octavius. I told you he was a trooper."

The audience stood and applauded as the wedding party hugged us and reassembled themselves in front of the reception room as they had been in the little chapel.

When everyone was in their place, Reverend Crenshaw began again.

"Now, where was I? Oh yeah," he chuckled. "Who gives this woman?"

"I do," said a tenor voice from the back of the reception room.

Our guests turned to see my handsome son set down his luggage and run towards the altar.

He kissed me on the cheek to give me away and say he was sorry for being late and took his seat. I winked at him through mink eyelashes. He'd made it in time to do the honor. His kiss left a soft rosy glow on my face.

I noticed Emma sneak toward the back of the room.
Then Reverend Crenshaw finished the ceremony.

"What God puts together, let no man or woman put asunder. Now, you may kiss your beautiful bride," he said in his booming voice. Octavius pulled me close and planted a big kiss on my red lips.

"Something tells me you two have already been practicing, "the pastor said as the audience laughed.

"Friends and family, I present to you Mr. and Ms. Octavius Washington."

The sound of hands clapping and the flashes from cameras and cell phones filled the room.

The DJ began to play, "At last, my love…."
Everyone grabbed their partners and the room filled with dancing and merrymaking. Nadine escorted Octavius and me to the bride and groom's table as pink confetti fell from the ceiling. It had been a glorious yet tiresome day, and we were glad to be together and finally sit. Many of the guests visited our table to share well wishes. And to see the big burly attendant in the Egyptian costume Sakina had hired as our bodyguard and to serve the bride and groom's table. Oo lala!

"Well, well . . . look who's coming through the door," Octavius said rising from his chair and moving closer to me. "I can ask him to leave."

"No. I think it's okay, Octavius. Narcissus looks calmer than ever. He appears to be in a good place. Besides, my steel magnolia is right here," I said as I patted my purse.

Narcissus and a man who both looked as if they'd just left a photo shoot for the Gentlemen's Quarterly magazine walked quickly toward Octavius and me to greet us.

"I'm not here to crash your wedding," Narcissus said, smiling. "I wanted to bring a gift and say congratulations and wish you both well. Grace, thank you for everything you have ever done for me and for introducing me to Moses. I hope you will someday be able to forgive me."

"Narcissus, I forgave you a long ago. Let's put the past behind us and live our lives. I have no ill feelings toward you for anything you've done. I want the best for both of us."

I finally looked over at the man with Narcissus.

"Hey, Dr. Acquah. I didn't recognize you," I said, surprised.

"Call me Moses. What a beautiful bride . . . and groom!" Dr. Acquah exclaimed. He looked first at Octavius and then me.

"Thank you," I said, while Octavius smiled.

"We're going to Paris for a two-week vacation," Narcissus bragged.

"And we hate to run, but our plane leaves in a couple of hours. The French would say, Au revoir, Baby," they both said. Narcissus handed me a note. Then they raced out the door to go to the airport.

Octavius and I stared at each other for a moment before Octavius whispered, "New supply? Did you know he was a down-low brother?"

"No, he isn't a down-low brother. Those two sneaky ones are probably meeting women at the airport."

"Well, whatever! We're not going to let them be happier than us. No way. Let's get this party going because we're flying to Italy tonight by private jet! And like the Italians, we say, Ciao, Baby." We both laughed. Sakina brought us the bride and groom's plates and leaned over to whisper in my ear.

Emma stared nervously at me, and I glared back at her.

"Ciao to you too, Emma! And don't you come back no more, no more. Hit the road, Jackie! Don't let the door hit you, where the good Lord split you. We know you caused the allergic reaction. Get out!" I mouthed as Emma walked toward the exit. "Good riddance, my friend."

"What's wrong Grace? Are you okay? What did Sakina say?" Octavius asked.

"Emma is the Uber Eats Driver who brought the dip! Theresa always said she was a fake friend. And I always gave her the benefit of the doubt she obviously didn't deserve. God rest Theresa's soul. She was right all along," I responded.

"Unbelievable, Babe. She thought you were going to eat it. Didn't she? What a witch! Speaking of Paris, look at this. Forget Emma. Look at this." Octavius was holding a miniature replica of the Eiffel Tower.

"Where did you get the little tower?" I asked.

"It was on the table in the groom's dressing room. I thought you had left it. Wonder how it got there?" he asked suspiciously.

"It was probably Emma."

"I'm sure we told everyone the honeymoon would be in Italy," I said.

"I hear what you're thinking. Don't go there. It's just a coincidence. It's over," he said.

"Don't say anything about flying monkeys, stalking, or the names Emma or Narcissus anytime soon. By the way, what's in the note?"

I unfolded the note Narcissus had given to me and read it.

My buddy at the hospital told me the groom got sick at the wedding. Don't eat the dip in Italy, especially if Emma sends it. Also, your employer, Rich Avenues commissioned everything that happened to you. I tried to tell you that you had enemies. You made the wealthy owners angry when you left the company. I, too, was upset when you left me, so we teamed up. Joe Earley was in on it also. They paid all of us well to torture you. I had to confess this to get it off my chest. I don't plan to come back to the U.S. I may be facing jail time. Always, Narcissus

I did not know what to think. I didn't say anything to Octavius. Cedric was approaching us with a big smile, so I quickly folded the note and tucked it in my purse.

"Congratulations, guys! Mom, I'm so sorry I was late. The Uber driver Narcissus sent was given the wrong address. I got in the car and napped after my long flight and woke up on the other side of town," he said, rolling his eyes up to the ceiling. "I thought he had changed," said Cedric.

"Does a zebra change it's stripes?" we both asked and laughed simultaneously as Cedric hugged Octavius and me.

The wedding planner said it was time for the mother and son dance. Cedric and I did a line dance for two. The audience roared. He took me back to Octavius.

Octavius grabbed my hand.

"Ms. Washington, you sure look lovely tonight. Could I have this dance?" he asked.

"Why sure. I'd be honored Mr. Washington," I said in my best southern drawl.

I discretely tossed the note and mini Eiffel Tower in the trash bin. I knew no one would ever believe what Narcissus had said. I barely believed him. And as for Octavius, it would be only on a need-to-know basis. The siege was finally over!

We joined our guests on the dance floor. The wedding singer sang, "At last my love has come along." Octavius spun me around and dipped me and almost dropped me. Our guests laughed and applauded, as I blushed a light shade of blackberry.

I knew the truth. I was free.

However, I heard that small, still voice I knew well whisper:

"Vengeance is mine. I will repay."

God's grace under a siege is always all you have.

The End.

EPILOGUE

Grace Under Siege is a fictional story. However, it reflects the real behaviors of malignant narcissists, which are real conditions that hurt real people every day. If you are in an emotionally abusive relationship and you could relate to what you read, find a counselor today. Ask whether he or she studied narcissism or was in a relationship with a sociopath. Unless someone has lived with one, was raised by one, loved one, worked for one or was hurt by one, they may not fully understand what you've been through or be able to help you. Knowledge is key for you and the counselor. Learn all you can about personality disorders. Narcissistic behavior is a coping mechanism for abuse, so you must protect yourself.

Also, find a blog where you can vent and hear the stories of the many other people living a similar experience. You'll find you're not alone. See how they are educating themselves and protecting themselves.

You don't have to be afraid. You deserve to be happy. If anyone is encouraging you to remain or go back to a relationship with someone who is like Narcissus, the fictitious character in this story, the person likely doesn't understand the abuse that can follow this disorder.

So, take your power back from a narcissist. Love yourself and practice no contact if necessary. Get in a relationship with someone who can genuinely love you and is emotionally equipped to appreciate your efforts to love. Or learn how to disarm someone with a personality disorder and live with them with knowledge, so you can avoid being damaged or destroyed by a love masquerade.

If your relationship has become unhealthy and you are being emotionally or physically abused, contact the National Domestic Violence Hotline (800) 799-SAFE (7233). Remember domestic violence is more than hitting.

If you suffer from malignant narcissism and you want help, there are counselors who can help you, too.

Love and Peace, René Voland

Topics for Book Club Discussion

Was Grace love bombed by Narcissus? Explain.
Was she devaluated by Narcissus? When?
Was she discarded? If yes, how? If no, what happened?
What are some characteristics of Narcissus?
Do you think he could control his actions?
Is Narcissus selfish? Did he lack empathy? How do you know?
Can narcissists ever change? Will therapy help them?
Why did the "flying monkeys" support Narcissus?
Who were Narcissus' "flying monkeys"?
Why do you think Grace attracted Narcissus?
Why didn't her friends believe Grace when she shared her story about what happened between her and Narcissus?
Should Grace have reconciled with Narcissus? Why? Why not?
What is the difference between someone with narcissistic traits and a full-blown narcissistic personality disorder? How can you distinguish between the two?
Psychologists encourage No Contact after ending a relationship with someone who has this disorder. Why?
What type of personality does the narcissist target in his or her victims?
How can you help a friend who Is being abused by someone who might be showing the symptoms of this disorder?
Which of the other characters showed narcissistic tendencies?

ACKNOWLEDGEMENTS

This novel is possible because of many men and woman who survived and are currently in relationships like the fictitious one described in *Grace Under Siege*. I read many of your experiences online. This book is dedicated to you.

A very special note of gratitude and appreciation is owed to my editor, Debra Kastner and my friend and proofreader Susan Fitzgerald. I am also grateful to Donald Wiese who gave the first editorial review and my readers/reviewers who provided feedback: Patricia Forte, Clara King, and Lisa Susong. Thanks T. Haddish and B. Leavell for actions and words of encouragement.

ABOUT THE AUTHOR

René Voland is a penname for an author, playwright, poet, private coach, publisher/editor, mom to gifted adult sons and daughters and one spoiled Ragdoll cat named Coco Kimba Mufasa. *Grace Under Siege* is her debut novel. She and her spouse live in Georgia.

Made in the USA
Columbia, SC
07 May 2021